Tough Prospect

by

Laura Strickland

A Buffalo Steampunk Adventure

Tough Prospect

Cover Art by *Diana Carlile*

The Wild Rose Press, Inc.
PO Box 708
Adams Basin, NY 14410-0708
Visit us at www.thewildrosepress.com

Publishing History
First Fantasy Rose Edition, 2018
Print ISBN 978-1-5092-2381-7
Digital ISBN 978-1-5092-2382-4

A Buffalo Steampunk Adventure
Published in the United States of America

"No, Tessa." He sat up straight and clasped his hands together. "We're going to get to the bottom of this, have it out."

"Have what out?"

"Don't play dumb. You're not dumb. I'm talking about how you act toward me, how you feel toward me."

She gave a hard laugh. "I should think that would be obvious."

Yeah, it was. Real obvious. But it couldn't go on much longer before Mitch snapped.

He said, trying to sound patient, "We've been married two weeks. You're gonna have to reconcile yourself to it."

"Am I?"

"Well, yeah. We live in the same house. We should be sharing a bed. What's it going to take?"

Tessa bared her teeth in a grimace. Tears filled her eyes. "It will never happen."

"What?"

"The deal was I should marry you. Only that."

For an instant, Mitch felt totally helpless, a condition he didn't tolerate well. Indeed, he'd worked hard since his days back in the orphanage to guarantee he'd never feel that way again.

And now here came this woman with her hands on his heartstrings, hating him.

"But…" he began.

She leaned forward in her chair and lowered her voice even though no one else in the house could hear. "I know what you are, Mitch Carter. A tough. A brute, a lowlife. You may have blackmailed me into marriage. That doesn't mean I'm ever going to like it."

Praise for Laura Strickland

Laura Strickland's novella *FORGED BY LOVE* won first place in the short historical category of the International Digital Awards.

~*~

"The world building is phenomenal."

~Daysie W. at My Book Addiction and More

~*~

"Laura Strickland creates a world that not only draws you in, but she incorporates it…seamlessly.…the kind of book that keeps you awake well into the wee hours, and sighing with satisfaction when you've finished the very last page."

~Nicole McCaffrey, author

~*~

"As I read I became so involved with the story, I found it difficult to put down the book. …Definitely …an author to watch."

~Dandelion at Long & Short Reviews

Dedication

A tip of the flat cap
to the immensely-talented Richard Thompson,
with gratitude for much inspiration
provided by his song, "Cooksferry Queen"

Chapter One

Buffalo, the Niagara Frontier, November 1884

"Show me the first one again." Mitch Carter, lounging in the doorway of the small shop on Chippewa Street, made the request in a lazy drawl, belied by the intense expression in his narrowed hazel eyes. A tall man wearing a good-quality coat and a pair of workman's boots, Mitch rarely raised his voice; he rarely had to.

People tended to jump and fulfill his requests.

Like this shopkeeper whose establishment he now visited, a thin fellow with scarred and work-stained hands, who seemed overly nervous. Under Mitch's gaze he hurried to bring out the first mechanical dog and once more set it in motion.

The damn thing, as Mitch had to admit, had been cleverly fashioned to walk and part its mechanical jaws in a pretended pant. It sat on command and could even, presumably, learn its own name.

Would Tessa like one? If he brought it home now, this afternoon, would she be favorably impressed?

The shopkeeper, who claimed to be the only craftsman in the city of Buffalo manufacturing these dogs—clockwork, rather than steam-powered—had three models for sale, varying mostly in size and shape. For reasons unknown to him, Mitch favored the first and smallest one. It would potentially fit in his wife's lap. Lucky dog, permitted to touch her so intimately.

Unlike Mitch himself.

"Not very cuddly, is it?" he observed, more to himself than the shopkeeper.

But the man answered, "Maybe not, sir. I couldn't come up with a viable way to attach fur that wasn't…disturbing. The toys kept turning out looking like they'd been skinned by a taxidermist and reanimated. I actually had one lady pass out."

Mitch couldn't imagine his new wife passing out; she was much too angry.

The shopkeeper rattled on, "There are a lot of other advantages to this model, though, unlike a real dog, I mean. You never have to walk it or clean up after it. You can shut off the bark feature if it becomes annoying—can let the whole thing run down if you get tired of it. You don't need to worry about grooming or fur around the house. And since these are clockwork, there's no expenditure for coal."

The man met Mitch's gaze briefly and faltered, "Not that you need to worry about that, sir."

Mitch grunted, "You know who I am?"

"Sure. You're King Carter—the King of Prospect Avenue." The man swallowed. "Everyone knows."

Mitch smiled inwardly, though it didn't show. Everyone in the City of Buffalo had at least heard his name—and feared it. You couldn't beat a measure of healthy fear, in Mitch's opinion.

And, by God, he'd earned it.

"So"—Mitch made a gesture with one big hand—"I could buy all these dogs."

"Yes, sir. Sure you could, sir."

"On the other hand, me having one would be a good advertisement for you. So it would behoove you to give me one."

The shopkeeper's expression became interestingly conflicted. Caution flashed across his face along with honest dismay.

"You wish me to give you one of my models? But sir, they take a long time to make. I'm the only man in this city with the ability to build these clockwork ones."

"Right. And they work real good. You should be proud of that."

The shopkeeper licked his lips and said, greatly daring, "I feel I should be compensated."

"And you will be. Just think about it; if the wife of the King of Prospect has one of these, people will come flooding in to buy them. You won't be able to keep up with the orders."

"I suppose so."

"You'll be a wealthy man." Mitch Carter grinned. He'd learned through experience that receiving one of his grins seemed to both upset and persuade people to his point of view. The grin of a shark, so he'd heard it described, in whispers, of course. "You'll have as much money as me."

"Yes, sir."

"As well as my good will. I daresay some of my boys will even keep an eye on your shop for you—in passing, like. Make certain no one gives you any trouble."

"I've never had any trouble, sir." The man's expression screamed, *Till now when you darkened my doorway.*

"Well," Mitch purred, "we'd like to keep it that

way, wouldn't we?"

The shopkeeper stared into Mitch's eyes. Then he swallowed, scooped up the mechanical dog and held it out. "Yes, sir. Please accept this as my gift to your wife."

Mitch took the unit and tucked it under his arm. Unpropping himself from the doorway, he nodded. "Thank you. Have a pleasant day."

"You also, sir. I hope your wife enjoys the little dog."

So did Mitch, though he had his doubts.

He left the shop and turned to his steamcar, which stood at the curb. Long and sleek, it gleamed with a smooth black finish, in which Mitch could see his face if he cared to look—which he didn't. His chauffeur and man-of-all-work, Marty, leaped forward to open the door for Mitch and the mechanical dog. They climbed in.

"Home, Mitch?"

"Yeah, sure."

The journey of only a few blocks wouldn't take long to walk, but Mitch rode anyway. It impressed people. The car did, he did, and he was all about impressing people.

Too bad he couldn't make a favorable impression on his new wife.

Two weeks they'd been married—just two—and he'd yet to see her smile. This despite the fact that he'd given her gifts, like this one, nearly every day. He'd as yet to kiss her, other than the smack he'd bestowed at the end of the marriage ceremony. He'd as yet to spend a night in her bed.

Even though he ached to.

He'd thought about it, he reflected as the long black steamcar crept through the streets—longed for it. He'd even considered forcing himself on her, but that wasn't the beginning he wanted.

He wanted her to want him. And it would be a battle getting her to move all the way from hating to wanting.

As Mitch had learned long ago in the murky days of his youth, there was a price attached to everything. A boy—or indeed a man—had to be willing to pay that price in pain, coin, or moral turpitude.

His wife's affection absolutely must have a price. He just hadn't found it yet.

****

Tessa Verdun Carter, sitting in the parlor of the house on Prospect Avenue, heard the slam of the door and the footsteps she'd come, through dread, to recognize. He was home.

Damn it.

She immediately attempted to gird herself, as an Amazon Maiden might, for battle. She might not be Amazonian in size, being a petite woman, but at least she remained a maiden, by God—her new monster of a husband hadn't stolen that from her.

Yet.

She figured it was only a matter of time before he got impatient. The man had a reputation, and not for being particularly forbearing. The day—or more precisely night—would come when he'd make his demand.

And then she'd have to consider killing herself, which seemed the only viable option.

The parlor door swung open; Tessa met her

husband on her feet, as any good warrior might.

As always, loathing flooded her when she beheld him. Neither handsome nor ugly, Mitch Carter had what she considered a brutal face, narrow and dangerous, and far too clever for anyone's good. Though he always presented himself well-groomed and expensively clad, the rough edges still showed.

What had her father said about him, while presenting his ridiculous proposition—that Tessa buy his way out of severe debt by marrying the brute? Mitch Carter had begun his career as an orphan at the Carter Home for Boys—he didn't even own his last name, in truth. That beginning, so Father said, had brought him up hard, a tough willing to do anything to survive. He'd apparently done more than survive, however—he'd thrived through a combination of cunning and ruthlessness.

Only take this house—the finest on the street. And he owned nearly all of Prospect Avenue.

He hadn't stopped bragging about the house since he brought her home. Pre-Civil War he called it, with architectural importance. Tessa admitted it was a fine house, built of red brick and well-appointed. To her it felt like a prison.

She narrowed her eyes at Mitch as he crossed the parlor floor. Black hair well cut like everything else he wore. A firm jaw and a hard expression. Hazel eyes bright with danger.

She nearly always found it impossible to read Mitch Carter's expression. He wore that strong face of his like a mask.

He couldn't be less like Richard Trask, with his fair hair, laughing eyes, and ready smile. Richard,

Tessa's best friend.

Richard, the man she loved.

Chapter Two

"What do you think?" Mitch made the query with deceptive laziness while he lounged in the big chair, studying his wife's face.

He might make a lifetime's occupation of that, just looking at her. A lifetime's pleasure. It never failed to gratify him.

She was, hands down, without dispute, the most beautiful woman he'd ever seen. And he'd seen a lot of women round this city. He could afford the best of them, and had.

He'd even tried one of those mechanical whores back before the Crystal Palace burned down. Now, of course, the automatons had revolted and demanded their rights. All those hybrid whores had scattered, and got married if you could believe what you heard.

These days he had to pay the steam units in his employ a wage. He didn't mind—he could afford it. At least the little mechanical dog came free.

Did Tessa like it?

She turned her exquisite head and looked at him. Today she wore her glossy, auburn hair—warm with a hint of red—piled on top of her head, just a few curly tendrils trailing down to kiss her cheek. She had a delicate chin, round dimpled cheeks, and guarded green eyes fringed by lashes so long they should be illegal.

What did he see in those eyes when she looked at

him? Wariness. Caution. Worse, dislike, and worst of all, disdain.

The damn dog didn't seem to have changed a thing. Though he didn't reveal it outwardly, despair touched his heart.

What was it going to take?

Tessa hastily averted her gaze from his and looked at the dog. "It's...charming."

"The fellow who made it said it will adapt to you, your likes and dislikes. Just like a regular dog but none of the work. All you need to do is keep it wound. Here, see?"

He leaned forward to show her the key. She nodded. She also shied, as if afraid his fingers might touch her instead of the toy. Like he'd try, given the way she looked at him.

"You want to keep it then?" he asked.

"I guess so." She shrugged one graceful shoulder. "But you don't have to keep bringing me presents."

"Yeah, I do. That's what a husband does for his wife." In truth, Mitch had no idea how a proper husband and wife treated each other, never having experienced the environment provided by such an association. But he could imagine. And since the first time he saw Tessa Verdun at one of her father's gambling dos, he'd wanted nothing so much as to be her husband.

"What you going to call it, then? It can learn its name."

"Well, certainly not 'Fluffy' since it has no hair."

"Yeah, pity, that. Would you rather have a real dog?"

The little toy chose that moment to sit down at

Tessa's feet and stare up into her face. Its glass eyes gazed directly into her eyes for a moment.

"Well, but," Tessa said, "then what would you do with this one?"

Mitch made a dismissive gesture, and Tessa switched her gaze to him.

"Pack it away somewhere, I suppose," he said. With the rest of the things he'd given her, beautiful dresses, jewelry she never wore. Damn it, he should just have bought her a real dog, or cat. Truth was he had no idea which she preferred.

Emotion kindled in her eyes. "You mean you'd just treat it like it's nothing?" she asked bitterly. "I should have known."

Mitch stirred in his chair, losing a bit of his casual air. "What's that supposed to mean?"

"Never mind."

"No, Tessa." He sat up straight and clasped his hands together. "We're going to get to the bottom of this, have it out."

"Have what out?"

"Don't play dumb. You're not dumb. I'm talking about how you act toward me, how you feel toward me."

She gave a hard laugh. "I should think that would be obvious."

Yeah, it was. Real obvious. But it couldn't go on much longer before Mitch snapped.

He said, trying to sound patient, "We've been married two weeks. You're gonna have to reconcile yourself to it."

"Am I?"

"Well, yeah. We live in the same house. We should

be sharing a bed. What's it going to take?"

Tessa bared her teeth in a grimace. Tears filled her eyes. "It will never happen."

"What?"

"The deal was I should marry you. Only that."

For an instant, Mitch felt totally helpless, a condition he didn't tolerate well. Indeed, he'd worked hard since his days back in the orphanage to guarantee he'd never feel that way again.

And now here came this woman with her hands on his heartstrings, hating him.

"But..." he began.

She leaned forward in her chair and lowered her voice even though no one else in the house could hear. "I know what you are, Mitch Carter. A tough. A brute, a lowlife. You may have blackmailed me into marriage. That doesn't mean I'm ever going to like it."

Mitch's reaction hit him like a blow to the gut. For an instant, a voice inside him wailed: *Why not? Why can't you love me?* It sounded an awful lot like the voice that, back in the dark days, used to ask similar *why me* questions while he cried himself to sleep.

That had been long ago and far away. He'd vowed never to listen to that voice again. But he wanted this woman the way he'd never desired anything.

So he swallowed his pride. It went down in a lump because he had a great deal of it.

"Look, Tessa, you're my wife. That isn't going to change. We can make the best or the worst of it."

She said nothing.

Mitch leaned forward in his chair. "If you'll just make your mind up to it, we can have a real good life together. I think I've shown you you'll never want for anything. And in time, I believe you'll come to care for me."

"You're wrong."

This time it felt like a slap to the face. "What?"

Tessa surged to her feet. The little mechanical dog, still staring into her face, raised a paw to her knee. She caught the unit up in her arms.

In a hard voice she said, "If you think I'm ever going to reconcile myself to this sham of a marriage— ever going to love you—then you couldn't be more mistaken."

"Why?" The word crept out of him this time.

"Because"—she raised her head high—"I'm in love with another man." A pained smile twisted her lips. "No, you didn't think of that, did you? Never considered it when you hatched your nasty scheme— when you trapped me. All your money, your gifts— your fine house—won't make one bit of difference. I'll never give you my heart because it already belongs to someone else."

Mitch sat where he was, stunned, while she gathered up her skirts and prepared to sweep from the room. He could feel his face turn into the well-practiced mask he so often wore. It did not protect him when she loosed her final barb.

"So now you know the truth," she seethed, "you can stop giving me presents and keep away from me. Just keep away."

Chapter Three

Tessa hurtled from the parlor and ran up the stairs so quickly she nearly tripped, still clutching the mechanical dog in her arms. She made blindly for the one refuge she possessed, the grand bedroom that, so far, had remained hers alone. The detestable Mitch Carter had not bulled his way in here.

She feared what she'd be forced to do when that day came.

Though maybe he wouldn't bull his way in, now that she'd told him. Told him about Richard. Told him this sham of a marriage would always remain just that. Maybe he'd leave her alone and they could live separate lives. She could see Richard on the side.

She set the mechanical dog, which wiggled in her arms the way a real dog might, on the bed. It sat down in the middle of the green satin coverlet and continued watching her as she moved around the room.

She had no idea why Mitch Carter had wanted to marry her in the first place, or how he'd expected her to accept him—in her life or in her bed. Perhaps he was mad as well as ruthless.

One couldn't force affection; the heart went where it chose.

"That," she said aloud to the dog on the bed, "is a lesson the dreadful Mr. Carter needed to learn. Hopefully I've taught it to him."

The dog cocked its head at her, and its ears twitched as if it listened. Its burnished metal finish shone almost white.

Just like Mitch Carter to bring her such a thing. As if he supposed it might make a difference in how she felt about him. All it did was demonstrate what a cold, unfeeling bastard he was. Why not go out and get a real dog if he wanted one in the house? Rescue one off the streets or from the Buffalo Animal Refuge over on Niagara Street.

But no, he wouldn't think of that. Her husband never considered such trivialities as *feelings*.

The little dog on the bed whined as if it sensed Tessa's distress. She gave it a thoughtful look, her heartbeat—wild with distress—beginning to decelerate.

She wouldn't let that man make her cry. She wouldn't.

The bedroom door flew open.

Tessa spun about and the mechanical dog gave a short, sharp bark of alarm. Smart dog.

Mitch Carter stood in the doorway, his face—no longer expressionless—like thunder. Tessa's poor heart once more sped up, on a shot of panic.

"What do you want?" she demanded. He'd never done this before, intruded on her in her stronghold. And the look in his eyes terrified her.

"Who is he?"

"What?"

"Who is he, this other man? The one you say you love?"

Belatedly, Tessa realized what she'd done. Placed Richard in danger, that was what—oh, what a fool she'd been to expose him to this man's wrath! For she knew enough about Mitch Carter to understand he had resources. A great many people in this city feared him. He had means, when he set out to enforce his demands and settle scores. He'd made much of his money in property, yes—it was whispered he also engaged in the protection racket.

Carter could crush Richard like a bug—if she, Tessa, further endangered him by revealing his name.

Wildly, she shook her head.

"Tell me."

"No. There's nothing you can say or do that will make me."

Mitch entered the room and shut the door behind him. "No?"

Panic spiked, rendering Tessa breathless. But she managed to croak out, "No."

"I can find out, you know. He must be someone in your circle."

"No. Please. He has nothing to do with—with our marriage."

"Hasn't he?" Mitch smiled grimly, terrifyingly. "Seems he's right here in the middle of it."

Tessa shook her head still more wildly. "You're wrong."

Mitch advanced toward her; she retreated till the backs of her legs hit the bed. An unfortunate move.

Mitch reached out and seized her shoulders between his hands. Up till now, he'd barely touched her; his hands felt hot, and with the contact something searing and dangerous flared in his eyes.

"Have you given yourself to him?"

"What?"

"Have you made love with him?" The words

sounded like a growl; Tessa tried to shrink away and failed.

"No."

"I'm not sure I believe you. If you can accommodate him, you'll take me also. I have the right."

He pulled her into his arms, up against his body. Shock raced through her like the kiss of lightning.

"No, I—"

She wanted to tell him she'd never been with any man. Unfortunately, once her lips parted to speak he took advantage. His mouth covered her mouth, his arms enfolded her, and his tongue mounted an invasion. Horror suffused her from the point of entry outward.

She'd never dreamed of such violation. In the past, when they were alone, Richard had kissed her, soft chaste kisses that teased, warmed, and titillated. Nothing…nothing like this.

She stiffened, she resisted, she fought to free her arms, and when one hand escaped, she struck Mitch in the side of the face. It didn't make him stop kissing her, though—if a mere kiss this could be called. It smacked of something else—pure male domination and desire so hot it might burn her up.

She struck him again and wiggled; they fell together onto the bed.

Another unfortunate move surely, surely—for the rhythm of his assault and the movements of his tongue changed, became slow and languorous, a blatant caress.

Oh, God, oh, God, he was going to have his way with her right here. At last.

She made a sound in her throat, the closest she could manage to a scream. The mechanical dog, now right beside them, barked again.

Mitch Carter stopped kissing Tessa and raised his head. Not far—his lips hovered right above hers when he said, "You're so beautiful, Tessa. He can't want you as much as I do—whoever he is."

She could feel Mitch's heart pounding against her breast—proving he had one after all. She clenched her teeth together in case he tried to kiss her again and said, "Get off me."

Instead his intense hazel gaze inspected her face before he said, "Give yourself to me. Give yourself to me, and maybe I won't hunt him down."

"Hunt him down?" Tessa's heart thumped still harder. "You won't. Not if you want to keep my good opinion."

"You don't have a good opinion of me. That's pretty clear."

"You won't ever win it through coercion."

"Do I have a chance in hell of winning it?"

He kissed her again, this time a gentle contact of lips on lips, a single sweep of his tongue. "Seems I might just as well demand my rights."

"You do, and I'll hate you forever. Let me up."

"Not sure I can."

She attempted to heave him off, putting every bit of her strength into it, but he was all muscle, hard beneath his fine clothing. A brute in a suit, her bemused brain quipped madly. She knew then she lay at his mercy—he could truly take what he desired.

Disregarding her efforts, he said, "All this time we've been married, I've barely had a chance to touch you. I haven't even seen you naked."

"You won't."

"No? I could strip you now."

Tessa supposed he could.

"Bury myself in you."

Tessa had a pretty good idea what that meant. Her cheeks flamed.

"You're mine. My wife."

"That doesn't mean you can rape me."

"Wouldn't be rape. I'll make you want it."

"Never happen."

"Never say never."

He dove for her mouth again. From beside them on the bed came a flurry of movement; Mitch withdrew hastily and grabbed his wrist. "Ah! That damn thing bit me."

"Did it?" Good dog.

"Damn it! I should throw it against the wall."

"Don't you dare." His weight withdrawn from her, Tessa gathered the mechanical dog into her arms and retreated to the head of the bed.

Mitch glared at her. "I suppose you like that thing now?"

"Yes." She dropped her gaze to his arm, where a spot of blood showed. Good, good dog!

"Just so you know, if it gets possessive of you, it's going. And know this too, Tessa—there'll come a time when I'll walk back in through that door and you'll welcome me."

"I've a word of advice for you, Mitch Carter: don't hold your breath."

He went out, and Tessa sagged, her fragile defiance flown. She cuddled the mechanical dog in her arms and told it, "I suppose now I need to name you. No men welcome here, so that means you're a female. You need a strong name—the name of a warrior. I'll call you Valerie."

Chapter Four

Mitch went back downstairs and made straight for his office at the back of the house, where he rang for a servant. One of the mechanicals hurried in.

He employed two human servants—one of them the chauffeur and the other the cook—and three automatons. All the mechanicals were high-quality, silver models, none of the hybrids for him, though the hybrid automatons in the city, as it was now rumored, had started producing their own.

The one that rushed in had been created to act as a housemaid. It had blue glass eyes in a burnished, vaguely sculpted face.

"Bring me bandages and iodine," he told it.

"Yes, sir."

"I've cut my wrist."

"Yes, sir."

"Oh, and get me a scotch."

"Sir."

The automaton hurried out, and Mitch gazed around his office with distracted eyes. He'd situated it here at the rear of the ground floor where his men could come and go through a separate entrance, taking care of business without disturbing the workings of the household.

Now he suddenly realized the place looked like a tip. He wasn't much with paperwork—never had been.

Accounts were even worse. But he knew how to rake in a buck.

He always thought of this room as the heart of his kingdom. But at the moment, his kingdom looked a little tarnished.

What had he done? What, upstairs in his wife's room? Frightened her? Spoiled his chances? Lost her for good?

No, he hadn't lost her. You could only lose something you'd once had; he'd never had Tessa in the first place.

Now he knew why.

She loved somebody else. Another man. She'd come to him with her heart already engaged elsewhere.

He'd never had a chance.

"Damn it." He pounded his hand on the desk, behind which he sat. That only made the bite hurt more.

Somebody might have told him that before he married her. Her blasted father might have—if he knew. Or Tessa herself might have.

Would he have cared? Honestly, he doubted it. He'd wanted her from the first, and the fire had only built from there.

He shouldn't have kissed her like that, upstairs. But he'd seen red when she said she loved somebody else. He'd wanted to show her—

What? That he was the brute she already believed him? That he loved her more than anyone else ever could?

Now he had choices to make.

He could let her go. No, that would never happen.

He could continue waiting for her to come around and want him. Which might never happen either.

He could find out who this man was, the one she said she loved, and off him, thus eliminating the competition.

Yeah, he liked that option best. Of course if Tessa found out, it would make her hate him forever. Which just meant he couldn't let her find out.

The mechanical came back in with a basin and some bandaging. Mitch submitted himself to her cold touch, thinking all the while of his wife upstairs. How hot and sweet her mouth had tasted. How it felt when she flexed her body beneath his. The thrilling feel of her breasts touching his chest, even just through their clothes.

Only imagine when he had her naked and willing, crying his name in demand.

It would happen. He always got what he wanted, however impossible. He just had a few obstacles in the way this time.

On one thing he'd insist—when it happened he wanted her to want him.

After the maid left, he went and summoned one of the fellows from the yard. A few always hung around back there, runners and agents, in case he needed anything.

Tiny came into the office, his flat cap pushed to the back of his head, the stub of a cigar between his teeth. Tiny had a wizened look, a result of growing up in Carter House with the rest of them. A wonder how Mitch had grown so tall on the poor fare provided in that hell hole—except he'd got out first and started providing for himself before he could ransom the rest of them. And he'd perfected the art of stealing food long before that.

Tiny had little, pale blue eyes in a face like a monkey's and wore a perpetually worried look.

"Yeah, Boss?"

"I've got a job for you. Strictly on the Q.T."

"Fair enough." Tiny's standard response to most things. Roll an old man for a penny? Fair enough. Steal a carriage? Fair enough. Blackmail a policeman? Sure!

"Nobody can find out, mind. I'm trusting you."

"What is it, Boss?"

"My wife," Mitch began and got no farther before Tiny's expression set. None of the fellows had approved of him marrying Tessa, as he well knew. A few, including Tiny, had even said so.

You can do better, Boss. Those had been Tiny's words, as he recalled. *Find a real woman.*

Tessa was a real woman. Having just felt her body beneath his, he could testify to that.

"I want you to find out something about her, about an acquaintance of hers." He corrected himself carefully. "Former acquaintance. There'll be a man, one who has…engaged her affections."

Tiny's eyes bulged. "You don't say?"

Mitch silenced him with a glare. "I just want you to discover the man's name, nothing more. You understand?"

"She been two-timing you?"

Mitch didn't know, but he wouldn't admit that. He shook his head. "I just need his name. And where to find him. He and I may need a talk."

"Damn, Boss. I did warn—"

"You did, and that's in the past."

"I'll put our best men on it. I think we've got a contact—a ladies' maid—in her father's house."

23

"Good. I trust you, Tiny."

"You can trust me with your life, Boss. You're the one got me out of Carter's. I'd do anything for you."

"I know."

"Hey, Boss, you ever think about going back there?"

"To Carter's? Hell, no." Only in nightmares.

"I mean to, maybe, destroy the place. Burn it down."

"An interesting idea."

"I think about it a lot."

"What about all the little kiddies inside, eh, if you torched it?"

"They'd thank us."

"Not if they fried."

Tiny said with certainty, "Death would be better."

"Maybe. But they'll get out in due time and make men of themselves, right, Tiny? The way we did."

"God help 'em. Boss, do you remember—"

"I don't want to think about that place, Tiny."

"But do you—"

"I said I don't want to think about it."

"Right, Boss. I'll go start making these inquiries."

"Good man."

"Meanwhile, do you want someone to follow your wife? If she goes out, I mean."

"Might not be a bad idea. But be discreet, right?"

****

"I wanted to say," Mitch drawled the next morning at breakfast, "I think you should quit staying so close to the house. I wouldn't want you to feel like a prisoner here."

Tessa looked up and encountered his gaze—very

hazel in the clear light coming through the dining room windows, and dangerously watchful.

She'd barely been able to look at him since their encounter in her room yesterday—had barely been able to stop thinking about him, either. The way he'd kissed her, with such thoroughness and heat. The sensation of his body covering hers. The way he looked at her.

The way he watched her now.

What did it mean?

And his words—they must be a trap of some sort. Had to be.

"Uh…" She hesitated. "Where would I go?"

"Shopping, maybe. I can arrange accounts at any shops you like. Socializing. Visit your family or friends."

A trap, most definitely. He thought she'd lead him to Richard.

As if she'd be that foolish.

"Well, perhaps." She looked at her plate. The food on it suddenly sickened her.

The little dog, Valerie, sat on her lap. She ran a hand over its smooth back. "I'll give it some thought."

"Tessa…" Mitch spoke her name to regain her attention. "I feel we've begun badly. But I want our marriage to succeed. We need to strike a balance where we both get what we need."

Tessa's eyes narrowed. What did that mean? She had her suspicions, and they made her heart start to beat double time. After what had happened yesterday in her room, she couldn't doubt what he wanted. Would he bargain for it?

Of course. Men like him always bargained or threatened. Coarse men, toughs, hard—

She halted her thoughts there, when she remembered the way his body had felt against hers. Hard. She flushed involuntarily.

Breathless, she said, "Depends on what I say I need, doesn't it?"

He eyed her steadily. "I'll give you anything within reason, if we can have a regular husband-wife relationship."

By God! He still wanted her, even though she'd blurted out the truth about Richard.

But would he be willing to let her see Richard—have a relationship with him on the side—if she shared his bed?

For an instant her mind blanked on the thought. Alone in the bed with Mitch Carter, at his mercy, naked and utterly vulnerable.

She whispered, "You saying our marriage should be a bargain?"

"All marriages are bargains, at least the way I see it."

She tipped her chin up. "Ideally, there should be love."

Something flickered in his eyes. "Ideally. But you've confessed you're in love with another man."

"A person can't help her feelings."

"That's true."

"So—what are you saying?"

"I'm saying I want you to be…content. I want both of us to be."

"And…and what will make you content?"

"You. In my bed."

There it was, out in the open. Heat stained Tessa's face. The mechanical maid came in carrying a fresh pot of tea. Tessa looked down at the dog in her lap while the maid bustled around.

Not till she left did Tessa say, "I'm afraid I can't…"

"Not yet, maybe."

Silence fell, alive and vibrating.

Tessa broke it with sudden haste. "Perhaps I will go out today, visit my parents."

"Good I'm sure they'd like to see you. I have business all day anyway. Why don't you take the steamcar? I'll get a cab."

"I don't like the steamcar."

"Why?"

"It's too big, too ostentatious." Did he even know what that word meant?

"Then I'll use the car. You have the doorman call a cab." He flashed her a sudden, sharp-edged smile. "There now, we're already discussing things like a proper man and wife."

Chapter Five

"Tessa!" As soon as she came through the door of the house on Bidwell Parkway, Tessa's mother flew through the parlor door and enveloped her in a sea of lavender scent.

Mother always smelled of lavender, a fragrance as indivisible from her as her smile and her tendency to chatter.

Tessa relaxed for the first time in many days; tears started in her eyes. "Mother."

"My darling girl, I've been so worried about you." Elise Verdun backed off far enough to stare into her daughter's face. "Are you all right?"

"I—" Abruptly Tessa discovered she couldn't answer that question.

Elise's eyes, as green as Tessa's, flooded with dismay. "Has that brute hurt you? He hasn't…"

"No, Mother." *Not yet.*

"Thank God."

Tessa glanced around the hallway. Since the city's automatons revolted two months ago, most of the servants had fled. Father couldn't afford to pay them— only the ancient doorman had stayed out of loyalty, foregoing any demand for a wage.

Even though no one could hear, Tessa disliked discussing her personal situation where any servants could hear.

"Let's go into the parlor," Elise said, "where we can talk. Earl will bring us tea."

"Earl will?" The doorman.

"Yes. He's jack-of-all-trades now. But I'm worried about him. He creaks so when he moves, and sometimes a joint will seize up. What we shall do if he breaks down, I cannot say."

Make your own tea. The thought appeared in Tessa's mind, though she didn't voice it. Instead she asked, "Where's Father?"

"Up in our room." Elise's beautiful face clouded. "I'm so worried about him." She towed Tessa into the parlor and to the brocade sofa, where they sat next to one another.

Tessa sighed. Hugo Verdun's desperation over his financial plight and Elise's worry over his state of mind had, in large part, forced her into her present predicament. Hugo had brought his family to Buffalo from Montreal well before Tessa was born and started a very successful business as a clothier, outfitting the wealthiest men in the up-and-coming city. He and Elise had raised their family—of which Tess was the youngest—and acquired wealth enough to afford them this grand house.

Now the family lay scattered, Hugo's business virtually ruined, and the ownership of the house hung by a thread.

So, Tessa thought bitterly as her mother clasped her hands, her parents were still miserable, her mother still worried. Did her sacrifice to Mitch Carter mean nothing?

"I thought," she said carefully, "Mitch Carter bailed Father out. Wasn't that the point of all this?"

"Yes. Yes." Elise squeezed Tessa's fingers. "Though it seems there were a few more debts your father didn't tell us about, that have surfaced since. Just a few…creditors still come to the door."

That, Tessa remembered all too well—she, Mother, and Father hiding out at the rear of the house while creditors pounded on the front door.

"That's not what worries me," Elise confessed. "It's your father's state of mind. He's distraught. Distraught, I tell you."

"Why?"

"Why, over your marriage, of course. Over what he felt compelled to ask of you. Seeing you, his little princess, in the hands of that tough, that rough brute—I do not think he will be able to forgive himself."

Tessa wasn't sure she could forgive him either. She began, "Maybe he should have thought—"

"Oh, yes, he should, Tessa. But all that's water under the bridge now, isn't it? Anyway, he couldn't help getting us into this trouble. I'm convinced gambling is a sickness. And it's cost him everything."

Me as well.

"He's been so worried about you," Elise rushed on. "Will you speak to him while you're here? He doesn't want to see anyone, not even me, I swear. I despair for him. But I believe he'll see you."

"Mother, I don't know." Tessa had come here seeking refuge from her own despair and pain, not to play nursemaid to her father's wounded feelings. But so it had always been: no matter what Hugo did, Elise put him first in her attentions and in her heart.

Elise hurried on, "If he lays eyes on you, sees that you're all right, I'm sure it will go far toward providing him some comfort."

The parlor door opened; Earl came in with the tea. It reminded Tessa forcibly of the scene on Prospect Avenue that morning when the mechanical maid had performed the same task.

Except Earl truly did creak alarmingly. And his arms appeared to freeze when he lowered the tray half way to the table, regaining motion only with a jerk.

Poor old unit.

Elise said, in a perfectly audible aside, "I'm not sure how much longer we can keep him supplied with coal."

"Surely he doesn't take very much." And surely Mother needn't express such reservations in the unit's hearing.

"Never mind." Elise waited till the automaton had rumbled away before she said, "Now tell me everything. And then you can go up and see your father."

And what, Tessa wondered, should she tell? How alone she felt in the big house over on Prospect? How frightened, how conflicted and resentful toward her parents?

How she dreaded encountering her husband on a daily basis, how uncomfortable he made her feel?

How it had felt lying beneath him?

She could say none of that because Elise had started to cry. She did so beautifully and with great distress.

"Tess, I can't tell you how it feels knowing you've sacrificed yourself for us. And to a man like that. One who came up from the gutter, quite literally. Oh, please tell me he's not cruel to you."

"He's not cruel. But Mother, I can't quite trust him."

"Quite wise. You daren't trust a man like that. Ever since your marriage people have been coming to us, relating the terrible things he's done. Did you know he owns properties all over the city? And he's ruthless about collecting rents."

"Yes."

"Those men of his—a squad of toughs, that's all they are. Nothing more. They've beaten people up, people who owe Carter money. Why, I hate to think what he'd have done to your father if you hadn't…"

"Yes," Tessa said hastily.

"But when he asked for your hand in exchange for expunging your father's debts, he promised he would treat you well. Said you'd lack for nothing. Tell me at least he's kept his word."

"Yes. He gives me gifts."

Elise brightened. "Well, that's good."

"Presents I don't want." *Except for Valerie.* Tessa found she did like the little dog. "But Mother, I feel like I've been sentenced to a lifetime of punishment. It's only been two weeks. When I look ahead…" Tessa couldn't let herself look ahead. "And then there's Richard."

"Yes, I know. Most unfortunate. Such a suitable young man, and of good family. I'm sure you would have made a fine match with him."

"It's not just that, Mother. I'm afraid I've endangered him—Richard, I mean. In the heat of the moment, I told Mitch Carter my affections are otherwise engaged…now I'm afraid he'll retaliate."

"Oh, dear."

"Promise if Mitch comes here asking questions, you won't breathe a word about Richard's identity."

"Of course not. Now come upstairs and speak with your father. Perhaps you can alleviate some of the guilt that's dogging him."

****

The large bedroom lay thick with shadows, draperies drawn against the daylight. Elise, having scratched at the door, thrust Tessa inside and said, "Hugo, darling, only look who's come."

The man sitting hunched in the chair by the window turned his head.

A tall man, and usually most elegant in both clothing and demeanor, Hugo Verdun showed in full his Gallic heritage. Over the past months, Tessa had watched him sink into careless disregard for his appearance; his narrow shoulders slumped. Even his once-proud moustache sagged.

Now, though, she could barely see him for the gloom.

"Tessa?"

"Father, why are you sitting here in the dark?"

He ignored the question. "I am surprised you have come. I'm surprised you can stand to so much as look at me."

Indeed, the last time Tessa had seen her father had been at her wedding—a rushed and hasty affair that contained little sense of celebration. Then, he'd looked like a man beaten down, but she'd assumed he would recover.

He always did.

"I can't say I'm happy to see you," she admitted. "I can't say I'm happy at all."

He began to cry. Just like that, he crumbled into a heap from which big, ugly sobs issued.

Tessa heard the door close softly behind her. To her horror, she realized her mother had left her alone with the wreck in the chair.

She jerked forward, moving very like Earl. "Here, Father, let's get some light in the room."

"No, Tess. I don't want to see myself."

"But I want to see you." Was that true? Or did she want to flee, run from this house and never return again?

She crossed the room and lit the lamp. Then she sat on a chair opposite her father and looked at him.

A mess. His once well-trimmed hair lay plastered to his head, his eyes looked sunken. His clothes, creased and crumpled, hung from him.

"Father, when's the last time you washed yourself or changed your clothing? When have you slept?"

"I don't remember. I can't sleep. Tess, remorse is a merciless mistress. How I suffer beneath her weight!"

Not *How are you, Daughter?* Not *How is he treating you?* Not *What can I do for you in return for the tremendous sacrifice you have made?* It was all about him, him, *him.*

"Father, I suggest you pull yourself together and get on with life, to make sure you never come so close to losing this house, and Mother's security, again."

"Get on with life? How am I to get on with life?"

"We all must," said Tessa, thinking of the house on Prospect Avenue and the man with the dangerous hazel eyes. "I suggest you begin by opening the drapes, getting out of this room, going back to work, and making an income. And giving me a promise you'll never again get the family in such trouble."

He stared at her, his droopy moustache making him look like a sad, skinny walrus. "I have destroyed your life. Will you say you forgive me, Daughter?"

Tessa rose to her feet. She knew what he wanted to hear—she usually did. Anything that would comfort him. But she didn't know if she could forgive him this time. She had to return to the man on Prospect and life in a cage, and so couldn't bring herself to say the words.

"Pull yourself together, Father," she repeated instead, and swiftly departed the room, leaving him there, wallowing.

Chapter Six

"Boss, we've got a problem with the old couple over on Spring Street. They still haven't paid their rent."

Mitch placed the report he'd been reading on his desk and leveled a look at Tiny. He couldn't help but notice his man appeared troubled and unhappy. He sighed.

"How late are they?" he asked.

"Two weeks."

"And how many times have you been over there asking for the rent?"

Tiny shuffled the flat cap he held in his hands. "Three."

"Then toss 'em out."

"Right, Boss. But—"

"No *buts*, Tiny. We've been over this. It don't do to be soft. You can't make any money that way."

"But, Boss, the old man says his wife's been sick. It's just the two of them, see. Usually he goes out and does a few odd jobs to pick up some coins. He's had to stay in, though, and look after her."

"Not our problem. Toss 'em out."

"But, Boss, where will they go?"

"Family."

"Haven't got any." Tiny looked even more uncomfortable. "I asked."

Mitch hardened his expression. Though few would warrant it of the little monkey, he knew Tiny possessed a kind heart. Too bad for him.

He pushed the report away. "Tiny, I've told you and told you. You give people leeway, they take advantage. You wind up paying, in the end. There's always a price. Isn't that what they taught us at Carter's?"

Tiny straightened. "They taught us lots of things."

"That pity makes you weak."

Tiny wrinkled up his face. "Not sure I agree with that, Boss."

"More fool you. Now take care of it, or do I need to assign somebody else?"

"If I toss 'em out, the old lady might die."

"What do you want me to do about it?"

"Give 'em another two weeks. If she gets better, he'll be able to work again."

"And if she doesn't get better?"

"She might."

"Damn it all, Tiny, in two weeks they'll owe another month's rent. I'm not a charity."

Tiny stepped up to the desk, dug in his pocket and slapped down some coins. "There you go."

"What the hell's that?"

Tiny's chin jerked up. "Their rent."

Mitch bared his teeth. "You fool. Why would you do that?"

"The old feller reminds me of my granddad. You remember I told you about him."

Mitch nodded. Tiny—whose real name was Francis—had lived with his granddad before the old man died and Tiny got shuffled off to Carter's. Tiny was one of the lucky ones—he knew his last name, Haskins, and remembered someone who'd loved him. A luxury Mitch didn't have.

"It's your money," he said. "I won't tell you how to spend it."

"Thanks, Boss."

"Don't thank me." Mitch turned his eyes to the report once again. He hated reading these things. The opportunities at Carter's had been so poor, he still struggled to read or write. Further complicating matters, most of those he employed had come from Carter's also, and could barely scribble two words together on a page.

A sudden thought made him jerk his gaze back up. "Any news on that other job I gave you?"

"You mean your wife?"

Mitch scowled. He didn't like being so direct about it. Hadn't Tiny ever heard of discretion?

He gave a hard nod. During the last week, Tessa had left the house three times. He very much wanted to know where she'd been.

Tiny raised his chin and recited, "Mrs. Carter went to her parents' house on Bidwell Parkway once. Went shopping. Didn't buy anything. An unusual woman, Boss, who can go shopping and not buy anything."

Yeah, and it made Mitch suspicious. Maybe she hadn't been shopping so much as expecting to encounter someone.

"She meet anybody while she was out?"

"Out shopping, you mean?"

"Out shopping," Mitch confirmed, trying to hang on to his patience.

"No, Boss."

"And the other day?"

"What, Boss?"

"She went out of this house three days."

"Oh, right. She saw friends."

Mitch's spine stiffened. "What friends?"

"Well, I don't know 'em, do I?"

Mitch growled, "Male or female?"

"Oh, I see what you mean, Boss. Female—two other girls. All real pretty. They went out for tea."

Seemed innocent enough. "All right. Keep an eye on her when she goes out. Understand?"

"Right, Boss."

"And if she even looks at another man, I want to know about it."

"Got you, Boss."

Tiny went out. Mitch scowled at the coins he'd left on the desk before putting them carefully into the drawer. If Tiny insisted on having sympathies, he'd need to pay for them.

****

Tessa exited the door of the house on Prospect Avenue and froze. She'd expected the car to be waiting for her, and it was. But instead of the chauffeur, Marty, poised to open the rear door for her, she saw her husband.

"Oh," she said, refusing to go down the steps. "I'm sorry. I thought—"

She broke off, trying to sense his mood. She hadn't seen her husband in days. She'd been busy attempting to reorganize her life as best she could, and taking advantage of his permission to go out.

Though it galled her to require his permission.

"Are you planning to use the car?" she faltered.

"I am. I have a meeting with an agent. But Marty tells me you requested it too. So I'll drop you wherever you want to go, on my way."

"That's all right. I don't really like the car anyway. I'll call a cab."

"Don't be foolish. I have the time."

He swung open the door of the car and made a slight bow, leaving Tessa no choice but to descend the steps and climb in.

He got in directly after her. The back of the car, large and luxurious, immediately felt far too small.

"Where to?" Mitch asked.

"I—uh—have a meeting also."

"You do?" Curiosity looked at her from his eyes.

"Yes. I've decided that if we are to coexist, as you've requested, I need something to occupy me."

"I see. And what have you chosen to occupy you?"

"I haven't decided yet. Not specifically, that is. I'm going to speak with someone today about the possibilities. I thought"—she shot a look at him—"I'd concentrate on good works."

"Good works?" he repeated, as if stunned.

"Yes, you know. Philanthropy."

His expression turned blank.

"Charity."

For an instant she thought he'd choke. He tapped on the glass that separated the back of the car from the front and told Marty, "Once around the park, please."

The car pulled away from the curb.

Tessa pressed her hands together. "I take it you don't approve."

"Well, it's your choice what you want to do with your time."

"Is it?"

"Absolutely."

"I don't need your approval?"

He shook his head. "All I have to say is, be careful not to let these people take advantage of you."

" 'These people'?"

"They'll bleed you dry if you let them, time and money. They'll know you have money, see, through me."

"Will they?"

"No doubt. Me, I make it a point never to give to charity."

"Why?"

He stared away through the window so long she thought he wouldn't answer. At length he said, "I know what happens in them places. People give money and it never reaches the ones who need it. It ends up in the administrators' pockets."

"Not all the time, surely."

"More often than not." He gave her a bright look. "I grew up in one of them places. I've seen it first hand."

"Carter's Home for Boys, right? I've heard a lot about it, not much good."

His fingers tightened on the edge of the seat till they turned white.

She said lightly, "I'm meeting with a Mrs. Wright, who oversees a number of foundations in the city. Others will be there from animal sanctuaries, orphanages…charity hospitals. I thought I could get an idea where my interest might best be placed."

"I see."

"Today's meeting is at the Meadows Club." She

added on impulse, "Why don't you come with me?"

He stared. "Me?"

"It could only be good for your reputation which, quite frankly, isn't exactly sterling, around town."

"I have other business, as I say." He tipped his head, studying her. "But I suppose it wouldn't hurt for it to be seen that my new wife is engaged in charitable causes."

"Yes?"

"Just choose carefully, mind. I won't have my money wasted."

"Your money?" She raised a brow. "I intended all my contributions to come out of the allowance you so generously give me." She couldn't keep a sharp edge from her voice.

"Still…"

"What matter to you if I spend it on a new frock or a child's dinner?"

"The difference is you'd have the frock. The child might never get the dinner."

"You're very cynical."

"I'm very careful. Marty? To the Meadows Club, to drop off my wife."

The car promptly changed direction. Within minutes they pulled up in front of the Meadows Club on Delaware Avenue.

"Thank you," Tessa said. "I'll get a cab home."

"No, I'll have Marty waiting here for you."

He opened the door and exited the car in order to usher her out. When she would have pulled her fingers from his, he instead raised her hand to his lips and pressed a kiss on the soft flesh of her wrist, just above the short glove she wore.

Tessa's pulse leaped. She snatched her hand away from him and fled.

****

Good works, of all damn things, Mitch thought as the car pulled away from the Meadows Club. Couldn't his new wife find something better to occupy her?

He sat back against the seat, still relishing the sensation of his lips against her skin. He got to touch her so seldom. It felt like the hunger he'd known as a child.

What did women of a certain class use to occupy them? He wondered. He knew what poor women did— they labored from before sunup to after sundown, all the hours God sent and then some. The girls on the streets worked all night and slept most of the day.

But his wife, she had class. He had little experience of such women.

In his opinion, she should be concerning herself with *him*. Morning, noon, and night, stark naked.

But he hated bullies, even though in his professional life he often had to play that role. He'd sworn not to bully Tessa.

No matter how low his beginnings, he could do better than that.

Chapter Seven

The gathering at the Meadows Club proved far different than anything Tessa expected. She'd thought it would be a rather fashionable affair, a tea at which those engaged in philanthropy—mostly ladies—discussed their efforts and exchanged fundraising ideas.

Indeed, some such ladies did prove to be in attendance, matrons clad in expensive clothes who gathered in clutches like hens; younger women, pale and elegant, who put Tessa's attire to shame.

But another element attended also, a well-represented, rougher form of Buffalo's society—women in shabby shawls and men with scuffed work boots and keen eyes.

Tessa, who'd never before done anything like this on her own, felt intimidated even before the whispers started.

Well, she told herself as she stood awkwardly in the middle of the room, they probably all know one another and they're catching up on news. Normal enough, yet a certain furtive quality in the low-voiced discussions and the way all eyes turned to her told Tessa the truth.

They whispered about her.

It started among the hens on one side and spread quickly, catching the attention of Mrs. Wright, the hostess, who quickly headed over with her hands outstretched.

"Welcome! Welcome to The Meadows."

Tessa focused on her gratefully. Mrs. Wright had well-coifed white hair and kind eyes. The hue of her peach-colored gown picked up the color in her cheeks.

"You must be Mrs. Carter, yes?"

Ah, so that was it; they knew who she was: Mitch Carter's wife. Word had got around. He, and not she, was infamous.

Indeed, her ears—sharper at the moment than she liked—caught a whisper from the side, "King of Prospect Avenue."

And another, "Certainly no better than she should be."

She flushed in mortification. She wanted to flee, walk right back out of there away from all the staring eyes. But her hands lay trapped between Mrs. Wright's, and the last thing she wanted to do was make a scene.

"Yes," she admitted unhappily. "I'm Tessa Carter. I thought I'd attend the meeting today and…well, I've been thinking of taking up some good works and wasn't sure what will suit."

Compassion flooded Mrs. Wright's eyes. "This is an excellent place to start, and we're very glad to have you."

She tucked Tessa's arm beneath hers. "Let me introduce you to a few people." She began towing Tessa away from the center of the floor, adding in a whisper of her own, "And don't pay any attention, my dear, to those loose tongues. They think charity is a social event and exercise their small minds accordingly."

"It isn't? A social event, I mean."

"Oh, my goodness, no. It's hard work."

Tessa nodded. All too aware she—and Mrs. Wright—remained the center of all eyes, she let herself be led.

"In what sort of endeavor are you interested, Mrs. Carter?"

"That's just it. I don't know. It's why I came. I thought…"

"Very wise. There are so many worthy causes. Topaz Gideon—the woman there in the red gown—helps get girls of the night off the streets and into a better life."

Mrs. Gideon, who stood with a number of other people, took Tessa's breath away. Not a small woman by any means, she carried her height and extra weight with a bold confidence that declared her stature. Black hair, dangling earrings, and a pair of amber-colored eyes all added to her exotic air.

She stood next to a couple; the man—tall and strapping—wore the uniform of a Buffalo police officer; the woman, almost nondescript and with soft brown hair, clung to his side.

All three of them smiled when Mrs. Wright led Tessa up and made introductions.

"Glad to meet you," said Topaz Gideon, with a fierce stare.

The police officer held out his hand. "Patrick Kelly. And this is my wife, Rose."

Her fingers engulfed in his large ones, Tessa managed to murmur, "Pleased." Kelly had eyes as green as her own.

"Mr. and Mrs. Kelly are engaged in the fight for automaton rights."

"Oh? How—how interesting."

"We always welcome new members," said Mrs. Kelly, also kindly.

Mr. Kelly inclined his head. "And do not worry about the gossip. People always talk about us, do they not, my love?" He clasped his wife's hand. "You see," he confided to Tessa, "I am a hybrid automaton. My wife is human."

"Truly?" Tessa couldn't help but stare. "I'd never have been able to tell." Though now that he'd identified himself, she could hear something a bit odd about his voice.

"It's true," Kelly assured her. He thumped his barrel chest and emitted a soft, grinding sound. "Steam powered."

"Uh—"

"You must meet the Michaels," said Mrs. Kelly. "Lily Michaels is also a hybrid automaton—there, that's her in the aqua-colored dress."

Tessa, who'd just begun to relax marginally, turned her gaze where indicated and caught her breath. Mrs. Michaels stood speaking with a burly, brown-haired man; she looked exquisite and utterly human.

"My goodness," Tessa breathed.

Mrs. Gideon gave her another smile, this one rueful. "Not all the company here consists of chattering magpies. There's a lot of work to be done in this city, Mrs. Carter, and some of us don't care where you—or your husband—started life. We'll fight among ourselves for your time and your dollars, even though we're all friends."

"Well," Tessa said, "I'm not at all sure…that is, I only came to test the waters, so to speak. I understand there are a lot of worthy causes in which to invest."

"That is true," Kelly agreed. "My friend over there, James Kilter—you see him, with the tiny woman who's expecting a child—founded the Buffalo Animal Sanctuary and is affiliated with the Anti-Cruelty League."

Tessa once more looked where indicated, then tried not to stare; James Kilter had in essence only half a face, if a handsome half—the other side of his countenance, constructed of what looked like scar tissue, might well appear in a nightmare. The heavily pregnant woman on his arm didn't seem to notice.

"The Michaels," Kelly went on, "while understandably interested in automaton rights, are also concerned with the plight of the city's orphans. Or you might choose to help the elderly. Come, allow me to introduce you."

Tessa moved off, escorted by the automaton whose arm felt disconcertingly natural beneath her fingers.

She liked the Michaels immediately, felt reassured by Rey's level brown stare and utterly charmed by Lily's open guilelessness. She found herself thinking she could be friends with such a woman.

Only she wasn't a woman.

"Don't let yourself be thrown off stride by that lot," Rey advised, nodding at the gossipers on the other side of the room. "They'll talk about anyone. They talk about us, don't they, Lil?"

"Yes, Rey." Lily Michaels sent her husband an adoring glance. "I am assured it *goes with the territory*." She laid her hand on Tessa's arm and leaned closer. "Do you think I look human?"

"Very much so."

"Thank you, but I am not. Like my good friend Patrick, I run on coal and steam. Oh, Mrs. Carter, you must sit with us. The lectures are about to begin."

"Lectures?"

Rey Michaels made a face. "Folks get up and spout off about their latest projects, hoping to win supporters."

"I see. I would like very much to sit with you."

"Good. Rey, let us find seats together before they are all taken."

The afternoon went much as Rey Michaels predicted. First Mrs. Wright spoke, and one by one various others rose and outlined their programs.

The man with the scarred face spoke about getting cart horses off the streets, saying the city had lost no fewer than five in the heat last summer and many others suffered gross mistreatment. "No need for them anymore, given the rise in steamcabs," he concluded. "And no animal should be a slave."

Mrs. Gideon went next, describing with frank speech the plight of prostitutes, especially in the poorer districts. Tessa learned she ran a home called the Haven for Disadvantaged Women, where girls could go for help, leaving the life and instead training for other jobs.

Lily Michaels squeezed Tessa's hand and gave her a look from wide blue eyes.

"I stayed there once," she confided softly.

"Oh?"

"I was a prostitute back then. At the Crystal Palace."

"Of course." Pieces clicked into place in Tessa's mind. "You must have been one of the—"

"Mechanical whores. Now I am Rey's wife." She

stated it proudly, as if she could conceive of no higher place in life. Some wives, it seemed, were more fortunate than others.

The briefings went on.

At last, Lily rose and walked to the front. Rey leaned over and said, "She does all the speeches—I'm not good at public things. But she's very good."

So she was—direct, earnest, and sweet. As Tessa listened, her heart responded. Lily spoke of the children in the city, the orphans who, through no fault of their own, found themselves without a single relative to care for them.

"As many of you know, my husband Rey and I are in the process of trying to adopt. I believe anyone who can, should. But many of these children will never be adopted. There simply are not enough families. We must improve conditions at the orphanages and children's homes. No one should live the way these little ones do. I suggest we introduce legislation to improve the institutions. Meanwhile we must make our presences felt—let the administrators of these hell holes know we are watching them and that we see the atrocities."

Tessa glanced at Rey, who glowed with pride. "Are conditions in those places really so bad?" she whispered.

"Yes, Mrs. Carter. As part of my job, I've been inside. It would break your heart."

"And you're adopting?"

"If they'll let us." He hesitated. "You see, with my wife not being human…"

"Seems like she's more human than most people I've met."

His brown eyes warmed. "You should come on a tour with us sometime."

Tessa nodded. Lily returned, slipped into her seat, and put her hand into Rey's.

"Did I do well, husband?"

"You were wonderful." He raised her hand to his lips.

A gesture of love. Tessa started, remembering her husband performing the same gesture earlier.

Love, or possession?

Chapter Eight

"How was your afternoon?" Mitch asked his wife across the dinner table. One of the few places they met was here, for meals; as a consequence he went to great lengths to assure he could attend.

At least he got to look at her for the duration of the meal, watch the emotions flicker in her exquisite eyes, and follow the way the auburn curls caressed her cheeks.

He wanted so badly to touch those velvety cheeks himself, with gentle fingers. To touch her everywhere.

She looked different tonight, brighter, and more cheerful.

"It proved quite interesting. I was very glad I went. I met other people engaged in philanthropic undertakings."

Bunch of soft fools, Mitch thought, though he didn't say it. "Yes? And did you decide where you want to put your money?"

She lifted her eyes to his. "It isn't all about the money."

He tried not to snort and failed. "Most of it is."

"Well, I suppose people become involved for all sorts of reasons—because they want to be seen"—she thought of the gossipers—"or want to feel good about themselves. But not everyone there's the hoi polloi."

"No?" He scarcely dared breathe. His wife was

talking to him, really talking. And for the moment at least she seemed to have abandoned her anger. Her sadness.

"Not at all. Some are in great earnest. Have you ever heard of a man called James Kilter?"

"I have. Isn't he the fellow tends to go off kilter?"

"What's that?"

"Falls into rages, beats people up." Mitch's sort of man, when he thought about it.

"I don't know about rages. He's founded a refuge for animals."

"That's right." Mitch snapped his fingers. "The Buffalo Animal Refuge. No, he's not hoi polloi."

"And a woman called Topaz Gideon spoke about relief for prostitutes. And a man called Patrick Kelly, he's involved in rights for automatons."

"I've heard of him too. He's a member of the Irish Squad."

"He's very nice."

"Not human." At least he didn't have to worry Tessa might get interested in him.

"I know."

"Who else was there?" Had Tessa's lover attended? Was this how she intended to see him?

"A charming lady called Lily Michaels. She's not human either, but I liked her very much."

"Another one of those fighting for automaton rights?"

"No, for children. She and her husband want to reform the orphanages."

"What?" Mitch froze with his fork halfway to his mouth.

"They say some of the institutions for children are

53

just horrible. Children starve there, or are neglected, even beaten. Do you think it's true?"

Mitch's fork fell with a clatter, and he recovered it with great deliberation. "I know it is."

She stared at him. "That's right... You were in Carter's—you came from there, didn't you? Tell me what it's really like."

At last, he had her attention, and in the one way he didn't want it. He could tell her tales all right, ones that would straighten the curl right out of her hair. But he didn't want to. She knew from whence he'd come, everyone knew, but she hadn't made a connection, obviously, between him and those starving children. And he didn't want her pity.

He'd left off even pitying himself.

He said in a hard tone, "When it comes to them places, whatever they told you is true."

And what did he see in her eyes, those bottomless pools of emerald green? Not pity, no, but consideration. A hint of understanding.

God, but she had beautiful eyes.

"Well, then," she said softly, "maybe that's a good place for us to put our money."

Our. Had she said *our*? A veritable leap. And Mitch didn't want to rock that boat. No, he didn't. If it would bring her closer to him, he'd spend any amount of coin she named.

He said only, "Perhaps."

"Either way, I really did like Lily Michaels. I wouldn't mind having her for a friend."

"She's a machine."

"She doesn't seem like it, though. She's funny and very sweet. Anyway, Valerie's a machine." She reached down and stroked the little dog that sat at her feet. "And I love her."

Love. So she was capable of that emotion.

"Well, all right," he said slowly. "Just so long as you don't let anyone take advantage."

She made a face. "Like everywhere else, there are factions; I think if I stay clear of the nasty people I'll be fine."

"Nasty people?"

"There were these women—" She broke off and eyed him again, this time with speculation.

"Was someone rude to you? If so, I'll—"

"You'll what? Send some of your toughs to set them straight?"

Exactly what he'd been thinking.

"That would just reinforce what they already think of you."

"Me?"

"They whisper about you. They refuse to speak your name outright."

"That's a mark of respect, isn't it?"

"No, it's a sign of fear. Of loathing. What is it they call you? The King of..."

"The King of Prospect. What's wrong with that?"

"You're proud of it?"

In a backward, half-assed way, he was. King of anything sounded pretty good, considering where he'd started.

Before he could answer, she went on, "If you wish to be known for anything, I should think it would be something noteworthy and beneficial."

Cunningly he said, "Then perhaps I should go with you to one of these meetings sometime."

"Would you?"

If it brought him closer to her, he'd walk through fire. He'd go into her meeting naked, revealing all his scars.

He said, "Maybe."

The dining room door opened and the mechanical maid rolled in.

"A message, sir, for Mrs. Carter."

Tessa looked surprised. Mitch held out his hand. "Give it here."

"It's mine," Tessa protested.

The maid, ignoring Tessa, placed the envelope in Mitch's hand. He scrutinized the front—which, as she could see, had her name on it.

"That's my father's handwriting."

"Is it?" He handed the envelope across the table and watched while she opened it and read the writing inside.

She paled, thrust the letter back into the envelope, and laid it aside.

"What does it say?"

"He asks me to come and see him."

"You can have the car tomorrow."

"He wants me to come tonight, this evening. Says he must speak with me."

Mitch hesitated. As so often, he found it difficult to read her mood. "I'll ask Marty to bring the car around, shall I?"

"No."

"I'll go with you, if you like."

"I don't like."

Mitch huffed a breath. There went all the ground he thought he'd gained.

"Then go alone."

"I am not going."

"No?"

"No. He'll just snivel and whine and complain about how miserable he is. How miserable *he* is! Him." She glared at Mitch, all her frustration and unhappiness on display.

Oh, shit. Oh, shit, she still detested being his wife, detested *him* as much as ever.

Very carefully he said, "You must do as you like."

She nodded, all her earlier enthusiasm flown. She pushed away from the table, picked up her dog, and left the room without so much as another look for Mitch.

Curse it all, he thought. If the only way he could win Tessa's regard lay through good works, so it must be.

The last damn thing in which he'd ever choose to engage.

Chapter Nine

"Boss, Danny Dwyer's asked for a meeting. He says he wants to discuss terms."

"Before breakfast?" Mitch had just come down from his bedroom to the office and hadn't yet got his head on straight. His dreams last night had been about Tessa—deep, and so erotic they'd wrung him dry. The last thing he wanted to think about was the South Buffalo lowlife trying to muscle in on his territory.

"Well, he ain't here in person," Tiny said. "He sent word, like, through the usual channels."

"Tell him, through the usual channels, to keep to his own patch. I've let him have South Buffalo. Isn't that enough?"

"I think he's got ambitions, Boss. Eddie's here. He brought the message. Want to talk to him? Only, he's on his way to the hospital."

"Hospital?"

"The message had teeth, like."

"Bring him in."

Eddie Carter came, with his dirty blond head bare and bowed, blood and bruises all over his face and one arm braced against his chest.

Mitch gave him the once-over unhappily. "What the hell happened to you?"

Eddie gave Mitch a look out of squinted gray eyes. No softie, Eddie. They must have roughed him up bad.

"Got jumped, didn't I?"

"When?"

"Early this morning. Still dark."

"Where?"

"Swan Street."

"Who?"

"Danny Dwyer and his boys. There were four of them, and they caught me alone."

"He was there, with them?"

"He was, and did the talking. The others did the hitting. Held me down. I struggled. Think I broke my arm."

Indignation filled Mitch, hot and bright. He'd seen Eddie whipped, back at Carter's, and denied food for three days just for speaking out of turn. Eddie hadn't cried then. But as Mitch knew, there were triggers, moments that took you back. A haunted look now hovered in Eddie's eyes.

"Damn mick," he said. "He thinks I'm going to let him push in on my ground, he's got another think coming."

"He said to tell you he wants downtown."

"Neither of us has downtown—yet."

"Yeah, but he knows you've started negotiating for property there. He's warning you off, Boss, and he wants the message to stick."

"He'll pay for this, Eddie. Don't I always make them pay?"

"Yeah, Boss. Well"—Eddie considered on it— "except for old Master Fink."

"Don't call him that. He ain't our master no more. Besides, he's retired, isn't he? There's somebody new running Carter's."

"No better, from what I've heard."

"No. Anyway, old Fink's gonna pay. I'm working on it. You've got my promise."

Eddie brightened. "What you going to do to him?"

"You'll see."

"I heard," Tiny piped up, "he's real sick, lying in that house of his over on Michigan." Tiny's eyes moved to Mitch's face. Tiny could be surprisingly quick at times. "That's where you've been trying to buy property."

"Right."

"Oh." Eddie's eyes widened.

"Look," Mitch told Eddie, "you go get the quack to take a look at your arm. Tiny, you get me some of the boys—a small squad, like. We'll send a message back to Dwyer."

"All right, Boss."

Eddie went out, but Tiny hesitated before leaving. "Hey, Boss?"

"What?"

"You called Dwyer a damn mick."

"That's what he is."

"Well, but…" Tiny hesitated. "How do you know that's not what you are? I mean, you don't, do you? Your people could have been Irish."

"Do I look like a damn mick to you?"

"Don't know. Maybe. There's such a thing as black Irish."

"Go get the boys."

Tiny went, and Mitch started thinking about what he wanted to tell Dwyer. He figured his message should be as forceful as Dwyer's had been, which meant muscle. Of course, that could start a war. But he wasn't afraid of trouble.

You had to do what you had to do.

Oh, and yeah, he'd better accelerate things with that old bastard Fink, too.

****

Tessa, on her way down to breakfast in the dining room, stopped when the doorman hailed her.

"Mrs. Carter, ma'am, a message has arrived for you."

Another one? She'd just heard from her father last night. Surely he wouldn't ask her to call again so soon. Yet the doorman held out a hastily folded note, this one addressed in not her father's but her mother's handwriting.

Tessa opened and read it. The familiar writing blurred before her eyes as she distinctly felt all the blood drain from her head.

"Mrs. Carter? Ma'am, are you all right?"

The doorman's voice seemed to come from afar. "Doris," he called to the maid, "you'd better get Mr. Carter. She's—"

The note fluttered from Tessa's hand. Her knees gave way, and she sank down in a heap, still conscious, much as she might wish otherwise. Sound came and went in her ears as commotion erupted all around her. She heard the doorman's voice, the maid's exclaiming, and then her husband's.

She looked up and saw him approaching at a run, a small squad of other men behind him.

"What is it? What's happened? Tessa?"

"I don't know, sir. She received this message." The doorman thrust it into Mitch's hand. "She read it and came over all ill."

Mitch unfolded the note. Before he could read it, though, Tessa stared into his eyes and said, "It's my father. He's killed himself."

She must have fainted then. The next thing she knew, she lay on the settee in the parlor, with Mitch Carter's face swimming above her.

He repeated her name urgently. "Tessa? Tessa!"

She fought through the clouds of horror that enfolded her and grasped the nearest handhold, which turned out to be her husband's wrist. She stared once more into his face.

"He hanged himself, Mother said. In the note. Last night—last night…" She felt herself crumble. "When I didn't go to him."

Rarely enough did Mitch Carter's face reflect emotion. Now, though, Tessa caught a flash of horror and dismay before he pressed her back into the settee cushions and said, "Foolish woman—why didn't she send someone to break the news more softly? Here, now, Tessa, breathe. Just breathe."

She ignored the advice. Speaking more to herself than to him, she said, "She found him this morning—hanging there in his room. When she went in. That awful, gloomy room."

"Hush. You're in shock." Very gently he disengaged his wrist from her grasp. She felt him move away from her.

The parlor door opened, and a voice asked, "Boss, should we send for the doctor?"

"Yeah, that fellow on Franklin Street."

The parlor door closed gently. Mitch returned to the settee with a glass which he tipped to Tessa's lips. "Here, drink."

She did, and choked when the raw whiskey touched her tongue.

"Slowly, now."

"No." She pushed the glass away and tried to sit up. "I need to go to her. My mother—"

"All right." Mitch Carter's dark, narrow face looked grim. "You can do that if you like, but if you go rushing off now, you'll likely faint again. What good will that do, eh?"

"I can't worry about me. Don't you see?"

"I see."

"It's my fault."

"It isn't."

"I should have gone to him when he asked! Then he'd—he'd still be alive."

"You don't know that."

"He wanted my forgiveness. Last time we were together, he asked for it, but I denied him. And then last night—"

Again, emotion flashed in Mitch Carter's face like a spasm of pain. Did he realize the cause of the break with her father lay in her hatred of her marriage to him? Oh, he must.

But she couldn't worry about that now.

"I must go home. To my mother. I have to see him."

"You're not going to want to see him."

"But I—"

"Not if he hanged himself. They'll likely have taken him away by now anyway. If you want to go to your mother, that's fine. I'll take you."

"What?"

"But give it a minute. Here, take another sip."

She obeyed; the fiery sensation seemed less intense this time.

"Just lie here," Mitch said. "I'll go order the car 'round."

He left her again, and she lay staring up at the ceiling, her head buzzing. As she had learned, moments came in life when everything paused, changed direction, and started up again. Her marriage to Mitch Carter had been one; this was another.

Nothing would ever be the same.

Chapter Ten

Mitch Carter wanted to strangle someone, and he didn't much care who. He figured he could start with his mother-in-law, a vapid and utterly thoughtless woman who seemed to see nothing wrong with allowing the blame for her husband's death to rest on her daughter's shoulders.

Yeah, that would make a good start.

But Mitch didn't suppose watching him murder her mother would do Tessa any good, and anyway he had far too much self-discipline. A man had to have control; otherwise virtually nobody would be left alive.

But he hated this house with its fusty, ruined grandeur, the spaces on the walls where paintings had been, the empty tables in the parlor where trinkets had once sat. Hugo Verdun had sold them all to pay his debts.

Right before he sold his daughter to him, Mitch Carter, for the same reason.

He couldn't deny that, while sitting there watching her suffer. Seeing her curl up into a ball as her damned mother nattered on and on about what Hugo's state of mind had been, his remorse and grief.

All because of him, Mitch Carter—a disease in matrimonial form.

The worst part was he didn't know how to help, how to eliminate Tessa's pain. And all the while he couldn't keep from loving her so much it made him ache.

The doctor had been and gone, directed to the house on Bidwell Parkway by those back at Mitch's household. He'd prescribed bed rest for Tessa, but she refused to go home. He'd also prescribed a draught to calm her and had taken Mitch aside to say, "You will need to keep an eye on her. She may also try to harm herself. If I were you, I would not leave her alone."

Now, late in the afternoon, he didn't know how to move forward. Relatives and acquaintances had begun arriving, many of them friends of Tessa's—none of them male, not so far.

Yes, even at a time like this, he thought of that.

Mrs. Verdun wept, she wailed, she mourned and lamented. With every new arrival, she went over it all again—how her dear husband had sought forgiveness from his daughter for the dreadful position in which he'd placed her. How he had despaired and must have reached a point, during the night, of no return.

All the while Mitch, on his feet, paced and watched his wife shrink in upon herself.

At last he interrupted his mother-in-law, still in full spate. "Enough."

"What?" Elise Verdun turned surprised eyes on him, precisely as if she'd forgotten he was there; perhaps she had.

"Stop with your ranting. Look at your daughter. Can't you see what you're doing to her?"

"My husband—"

"Was a selfish bounder who cost you everything. I'll be damned if he'll take my wife's peace of mind too."

"How dare you? My sainted Hugo is barely cold."

"He can't take responsibility for his actions. That's convenient. But I won't let you blame her."

Everyone in the room now stared at him, their mouths agape.

One of the older gentlemen—an uncle, Mitch thought—stepped forward. "Now, look here. I won't let you speak to Elise this way."

"You think I'll stand here silent while she destroys my wife? Go ahead and hit me if you want."

The man withdrew fastidiously.

"Brute!" said one of the women. "Tess, you have my sympathies!"

Mitch looked at his wife. She stared at him with bruised, helpless eyes.

He went to her and hunkered down in front of her chair. "Come along, now. We're going home."

"I can't leave."

"You can, and you will."

Very gently he took her hand and urged her up. She sagged as if boneless, and she made eye contact with no one as he led her out. Before they reached the door, indignant whispers started up behind them.

The long steamcar still waited at the curb. Marty stood alongside, smoking a cheroot. He stubbed it out and came to attention when he saw them.

"Where to, Boss?"

"Home."

Mitch half lifted Tessa onto the seat. He couldn't tell if she felt ill or numb. Inside the car she held tight to herself, utterly silent.

Not sure what to do, Mitch sought desperately for words. He could think of none. Mere minutes brought them home to the house on Prospect. He climbed out ahead of her and held out his hand. Ignoring him, she attempted to climb out on her own and stumbled.

He caught her up in his arms. She weighed virtually nothing, this woman who now made up the center of his world.

The same woman who hated him.

Inside, he carried her right up to her room, where he deposited her on the bed. Immediately, she once more curled up into a ball.

It was then the miracle occurred.

"Don't leave me," she said.

****

"Would you like me to bring back the doctor? Or send for one of your friends?"

Mitch's voice again. It had become a kind of anchor in the midst of Tessa's pain. Something about his calm reassured her. She shook her head.

"Maybe another of those drinks," she suggested.

He rang the bell and, when the mechanical maid appeared, asked for scotch.

Tessa, still curled into a ball on her bed, didn't look at him. She didn't want to. For some curious reason, she just wanted him there.

If she didn't look at him, she could pretend he wasn't Mitch Carter, the husband who'd been forced on her, the man she was supposed to hate. Maybe she could pretend he was Richard instead. But he sounded nothing like Richard—felt nothing like him, either.

Mitch Carter had a surprisingly nice voice, soft and strong.

Maybe she didn't hate him. Maybe she hated her father—a terrible thing to say, with him dead—and herself.

The scotch arrived. The bed moved as Mitch sat down on the edge of the mattress.

"Here."

He helped her sit up and once more tipped the glass to her lips. She shuddered.

"Are you cold?"

"Yes, cold right through."

"Let me call the maid. She can get you into warmer clothes."

"No. Don't leave."

"All right, I won't." He shifted her on the bed and tucked her, fully dressed, beneath the covers. It felt comforting. Even more so when he brushed the hair back from her face and said, "Listen to me, Tessa. What your father did isn't your fault. He chose that act, and for selfish reasons. There isn't a more selfish thing a man can do than commit suicide. Do you understand?"

"If I'd just gone to him—"

"He would have found some other reason."

"Now I have to live with this. I don't know if I can."

"People can live with all kinds of things. You'd be surprised."

She took the glass in her hands and drank from it. She gazed into his eyes. "Stay with me."

"Eh?"

"Tonight. I don't think I can stand to be alone."

Chapter Eleven

They both lay fully clothed on the bed, Tessa beneath the covers and Mitch on top of them. Sometime during the night, the autumn chill touched him and he crawled beneath also. Still later, at some point, Tessa moved into his arms.

He woke from a fitful doze to find her cuddled into him, the scent of her beguiling his senses. Helpless against his feelings, he gathered her more closely in.

In slumber, she didn't push him away. He lay there miles from sleep and fought his impulses. Right now—for reasons he didn't completely understand—she needed him. Or perhaps she just needed someone who thought better of her than she did of herself.

The last thing he wanted to do was scare her away. Well, perhaps the second-last thing.

She breathed softly, exhausted, and her velvety cheek lay just beneath his lips. Through an act of sheer will he kept from brushing them against it, but he did run his fingers through her curls, tenderly.

Tenderness—an emotion foreign to him. He'd had no room for it in his life. No room for it amid the struggle for survival.

How? How did it find him now? Because, to his amazement, it seemed to come instinctively with this woman. He wanted to enfold her, protect her. He wanted to destroy anyone who might hurt her.

He'd happily kill her father all over again if he could bring him back from the dead for that purpose. He'd kill any man who touched her.

He wondered again about the fellow she loved. Who was he? How could he, Mitch, transfer her affections away from him?

Damned if he knew. But until he could figure it out, he'd live on this, *this*. He pulled her still nearer and closed his eyes.

****

Tessa woke to a sensation of deep warmth and complete safety. For several moments she failed to remember where she was. She opened her eyes and stared into darkness.

Someone held her in his arms. Richard? No; he didn't smell like Richard, but like…

Recognition flooded upon her, and memory burned into her senses. Mitch Carter lying on top of her, his body hard and his mouth questing.

In this very bed.

She stiffened and stirred.

He whispered immediately, "Hush. Hush, it's all right."

Was it? Finding herself lying in the arms of her husband, the man she detested?

How did he come to be here in her bed, holding her so tightly?

The balance of memory fell on her then, like a brick wall: her father's death, her failure to forgive him. Her fault.

She gasped and stiffened with pain, and began to weep.

"Here, here—no need for that." Very gently Mitch

swabbed the tears from her cheeks, using the edge of the sheet. She knew she should push him away. She wanted to. She did.

But it felt so damn comforting, having someone cradle her this way.

So instead of pushing him away, she lifted her face to his.

Could she blame him for what happened next? It began as the merest brush of lips on lips, tentative and inquiring. He asked a question; she did not refuse.

A sigh broke from her lips an instant before his mouth claimed hers. In the dark, she could not see him. And when he kissed her this way, she didn't need to think.

If ever kisses were designed to numb a woman's mind, these were. He blessed her lips with them, feathered them across her cheek and down her neck, setting her skin to quivering. When his mouth returned to hers, she opened to him, without conscious intention.

How long it went on so, she never knew. When at last he stopped kissing her and rested his forehead against hers, he sounded stunned.

"Tessa. I want you so much."

"You mean…" She froze there, unable to conceive of it. Or could she? He would remove her clothing, continue to kiss her, making her warmer and warmer.

She understood the mechanics of the act but could not imagine such intimacy. Not with this man.

"I don't want to ask anything of you that you're not ready to give."

That was good. She didn't know if she felt ready. Yet being with him this way in the dark felt so reassuring.

She was a terrible person, one who'd failed to save her father from suicide. But Mitch Carter, so it was rumored, had been found in a gutter. Perhaps that made him just as terrible as she.

"Touch me," she said.

"All right."

He kissed her again, ran his hands through her hair, along the slope of her neck and inside her bodice. He smelled so good, and tasted better. And, sweet heaven, what a sensation when his fingers ventured where no other man's had been.

He shifted his position so he lay on top of her, just like before, hard and heavy between her legs. When he spoke this time, he sounded drunk. "Touch me, too."

He wore trousers and a thin linen shirt. She could feel the heat of his body right through the fabric— shoulders, arms, chest. Her fingers found their way inside the front of the garment and met coarse, rough hair, a flat stomach that rippled beneath her touch, the waistband of his trousers, and—

No, no, no. She couldn't touch him there.

Panic reared its head. She gasped beneath his kiss and fought her way free.

He released her at once and rolled to one side. "Tessa?"

"I can't. My God, I can't!" She scrabbled away from him, sat on the edge of the mattress with her feet on the cold floor, and put her head in her hands. "My father's just died. What kind of person am I?"

His voice came slowly out of the dark. "It's comfort, Tessa. The sort a man gives a woman; the kind a husband gives his wife."

"Is it?"

"Sure. Let me give it to you. Let me take care of you."

Oh, what a seductive suggestion! At the moment, caught in self-loathing and need, Tessa could scarcely think of anything more tempting. Let him take care of her, protect her—and she had no doubt he could. She needed so badly to belong to someone.

Was it wrong that the someone should be him?

Yes. Yes, because he'd taken advantage of her father's misfortune, won her through coercion and demand, and contributed to her father's guilt, his ultimate downfall.

Not so much, though, as she.

That thought crept into her mind and set up the grief all over again. Maybe she deserved nothing better than to be Mitch Carter's whore.

He touched her shoulder softly, gently. For an instant she felt sure he would pull her back underneath him and take what he wanted. Surprising, really, he hadn't demanded it before now. It was part of marriage, so her friends said, and for men, a big part.

Yet Mitch Carter—feared throughout the city, the self-styled King of Prospect Avenue—did not drag her beneath him. He merely lay there with his hand warm on her skin.

At last he said, "Come back under the covers. You'll be chilled."

She was chilled. But in truth, she didn't trust herself to crawl back into that bed with him.

He sighed, a gusty sound in the dark. "I'll not do anything you don't want."

"No? You promise?"

"Tessa, I'll never do anything to hurt you."

Did she believe him? Believing—just like intimacy—would require trust. She wasn't sure she dared trust this man.

"Here, come beneath the blankets. I'll go to my own room."

She turned her head and attempted to see him; the room remained too dark. "Will you?"

"Yes."

She heard him get out of the bed. He moved immediately around the end of it, went to the door, and slipped out. The door closed with a soft thud.

Tessa drew her feet from the icy floor and crawled back beneath the covers, still warm.

But, she found, it didn't seem such a refuge with him gone—not the same at all. She wrapped her arms around herself and lay sleepless till dawn.

Chapter Twelve

Mitch turned to his wife, who sat in the steamcab beside him, and eyed her face—dead white and pinched, tense with strain.

He felt worried about her. He didn't think she would make it through today's obligations, toward which they even now sped.

Her father's funeral.

It would be a grand and public affair, despite the manner of Verdun's death. Hugo had been well known in this city, and to Mitch's certain knowledge his mother-in-law had commissioned a large service. Today would spare Tessa nothing.

If she made it through without collapsing, Mitch would be surprised. She'd taken nothing to eat since learning of her father's passing; water had barely passed her lips. Yet she insisted on coming. He'd virtually demanded she stay at home, had begged her to let him summon her doctor and send word to her mother she was indisposed. The next thing he knew she'd got herself all rigged out in black and came down the stairs clinging to the banister—the only thing, he figured, keeping her upright.

And that damned mother of hers, when they'd swung by to pick her up from the house on Bidwell Parkway, never stopped talking. The woman squawked like a magpie, anything that came into her foolish head.

Now she went on and on about her other children, all of whom were due to appear at the cathedral. Two of them there were—a son and a daughter, both older than Tessa and both married, living in their own households.

Mitch could barely wait to meet them.

"I tell you, Gerald wants a full investigation launched into your father's death. He's not convinced it was suicide."

What else could it have been? The man had been found alone in his room, hanging by the neck. Did they suppose someone else strung him up?

"Quite apart from the disgrace of it," Elise Verdun rattled on, "there's the question of the insurance policy your father had on himself. They won't pay out for suicide."

Tessa's fingers, clasped together in her lap, tightened till Mitch saw the white of the bone beneath the skin.

Shut up, he thought at her mother, but he did not say the words aloud.

His job, as he saw it, was to get Tessa through the day. Somehow.

The car pulled up in front of St. Joseph's Cathedral, finding a spot miraculously at the curb. Other cars and cabs were there ahead of them, and a small crowd stood gathered outside the building in the weak sunlight.

Mitch climbed from the car and assisted the women out after him. A chill wind came off the river, and he wanted to put his arm around his wife to shelter her but didn't suppose she'd appreciate such a display.

They'd barely reached the pavement before a man rushed up to them, wearing an intense look on his face.

"Oh, Gerald!" Elise threw herself into the fellow's arms. "How am I to bear it. How?"

"I don't know, Mother. But we all know who's to blame." Over Elise's head, Gerald Verdun glared at Mitch. He drew himself up. "Sir, I will have you know," he declared before all those gathered 'round, "this farce of a marriage you have forced upon my sister is over, with my father's death. It was the source of my father's great grief and the reason for his despair. I'll have you know I blame you."

Anger flushed through Mitch, though he held tight. "Your father's debts were the cause of his grief—and guilt."

"How dare you? You wanted my sister from the first time you saw her. Deny that!"

Mitch couldn't.

"And you pressed Father till he made the only deal he could with you."

"Gerald," Tessa said.

"Quiet, Tess. It's over. You're coming home with me."

Inside the church, an organ started up. Outside, the wind made the only sound.

Mitch could have spit. Instead he said carefully, "Tessa's future isn't yours to decide. She's still my wife."

"I'll see the marriage is annulled. You're not worthy of her. Everyone in this city knows what you are. Trash." Verdun smiled nastily. "Found in the gutter, weren't you? And you're nothing more than a trumped-up bully with your big car, your fancy suit, and your ill-gotten gains. Dorcas"—he turned to the woman beside him, dark-haired and petite—"lend my sister your arm and get her away from him. She's sitting with us."

"Sister-in-law, come."

Tessa didn't move. Neither did Mitch, his hand at her back. He wanted to leap at Gerald Verdun and tear him apart, but he didn't want to escalate this scene.

"Is there a problem, sir?"

A figure in blue edged up. Mitch had been dimly aware that several police officers oversaw the scene. Now one of them—big and strapping—loomed.

He spoke to Mitch and no one else. Looking into his face, Mitch saw he had a broad, Irish face and bright green eyes.

Before Mitch could answer, the copper switched his gaze to Tessa. "Mrs. Carter, I regret we meet again under such distressing circumstances."

"Officer Kelly," she said faintly.

The copper raised his voice. "Perhaps everyone should make his or her way inside, in an orderly fashion. I believe the service is about to begin."

Surprisingly, people obeyed. Mourners filed in through the doorway; Gerald Verdun backed down and led his mother away on his arm.

"Thanks," Mitch told the police officer—the first time, surely, he'd ever thanked a copper for anything.

The police officer nodded. Mitch and Tessa went inside, Tessa clutching his arm as if she needed its support.

"Who was he?" he whispered as they took a pew near the front. "How do you know him?"

"Remember, I told you we met at the Meadows Club? He's the automaton."

"Ah, yes, the hybrid—Kelly." The name did ring a

bell in Mitch's mind. Famous head of the Irish Squad.

"Would you prefer to sit with your family?" he asked Tessa. Gerald Verdun, with his wife and mother, had claimed the first pew, along with another couple who could only be Tessa's sister and her husband.

But Tessa shook her head.

"Sure? You might sit with them and not me."

She turned her head and looked straight into his eyes. In her pale face, stark under the little black hat she wore, her eyes looked impossibly green. He could see her emotions—remorse, guilt, and shame.

"I'll stay where I am."

He hoped she meant that in every sense—that she wouldn't decide to go home with her mother or brother when this was over. Throughout the service, he could focus on little else. He missed the words and speeches, but watched his wife's hands from the corner of his eye, gleaning her emotions through them.

He never went to church and knew little about how to deport himself. Their marriage had been a civil ceremony, performed in private by a justice. Now he got to his feet when the others around him did and sat accordingly also, assisting his wife each time.

His wife. But for how long? And what, precisely, was an annulment? He wasn't sure but thought it could only be declared so if the marriage had not been consummated.

Damn it all, he should have followed his instincts and taken her the other night. Now he might lose her.

The very thought made him go hot and cold in turns. Just showed what trying to be decent got you...the woman had become his weakness.

And he hated weakness.

He half expected Tessa to weep as she had in his arms, in bed. But she remained stoical, a white statue. Not until the service ended at last and they began to file from the cathedral did she falter, her legs failing her as she stood.

Mitch, ever attentive, caught her before she sank to the floor.

"Here, now. Do you want to go home?"

"Home?" Her lashes fluttered before she stared into his eyes.

Grimly, he elucidated, "My house."

"We're supposed to follow the casket to Forest Lawn."

"Supposed to, yes. That doesn't mean you have to, if you're feeling ill."

"Yes, it does. I have to show..." She broke off as her brother passed their pew. The other couple that had been seated with the Verduns paused, and the woman reached out.

She had to be Tessa's sister; the resemblance declared it. Same auburn hair, same lovely face without the green hue of Tessa's eyes. This woman's were brown.

She clutched Tessa's hand impulsively. "Come ride with us."

The man with her, tall and ascetic-looking, spoke, "I have my car just outside. You needn't remain with him." Pale gray eyes swept Mitch as they might a piece of trash on the street.

Would she go with them? Could he, Mitch hold her? No.

But she said, still faintly, "There won't be room."

"We'll make room," her sister assured her.

Tessa gently freed herself from her sister's grasp and seized Mitch's arm. "We'll follow along behind you. Right?"

Did she speak to him? He nodded, even as his heart swelled.

Yet the danger had not passed. When they turned to leave the cathedral, he saw how many people had attended. Friends of the family? Hugo's past clients? Or just curiosity-seekers?

As they started away in the wake of Tessa's sister, Mitch supporting his wife's weight almost completely, they became the focus of all eyes, passing person after person who stared.

At the rear of the church, they came face to face with one—a young man. Tessa checked, froze, and faltered again, staring as at a ghost.

Chapter Thirteen

Richard, here. And Tessa on her husband's arm.

She believed for an instant her traitorous legs—which refused to support her no matter how tight a rein she kept on her emotions—would fail her again.

She hadn't seen Richard since before her marriage, and hadn't expected to meet him now. She'd wanted to see him, had longed to, but this blow on top of all the others threatened to level her. And Mitch...

She felt him stiffen in every limb and felt the emotions flood him. Anger? Outrage? Jealousy? She couldn't tell, but she very much feared he'd guessed just who Richard was.

Mitch Carter might be a brute and a bully; he certainly wasn't stupid.

Indeed, he tried to brush right on past Richard with a curt, "Excuse us." Richard planted himself foursquare, refused to budge, and gazed into Tessa's face.

"Miss Verdun, are you all right?"

Tessa's heart, upon which her emotions had a stranglehold, failed in her breast. Oh, God, oh, God, did Richard care? The agony in his blue eyes argued so, as did the angry disdain that pinched his face when he glanced at Mitch Carter.

Mitch supported Tessa with his left arm while his right hand splayed across her back in a gesture of support. Now he drew her closer to him.

He said, in a voice like that of an automaton, "You're blocking the way."

Richard's jaw tightened, and his eyes cooled to twin shards of ice. "I just want a word with Miss Verdun."

"Her name is Mrs. Carter, to be correct. And who are you to her?" Mitch spoke in a growl.

"An acquaintance. Her friend."

Tessa's fingers, clamped to Mitch's arm, sharpened to claws. "Please." She looked into her husband's eyes. "Not here. Please."

He nodded and shouldered past Richard roughly; they left the cathedral.

Outside, mourners streamed to their steamcars and the cabs that stood by, some horse-drawn. Tessa wondered how many would follow to the cemetery. Glancing over her shoulder, she saw that Richard trailed them. She tried to send him a message. *Forgive me.*

The cold wind gave her the only reply. Mother had gone with Gerald; Mitch and Tessa barely filled the back of his huge car. Mitch, his face grim, rapped on the glass, signaling Marty, and they pulled from the curb.

"Was that him?" His voice sounded rough in the enclosed space.

"What?"

"Him. The man you say you love."

Tessa went breathless. Danger lay in Mitch's voice, not for her but for Richard. She'd wanted so badly to keep his identity hidden, to protect him. Now it all threatened to explode.

"No," she said.

"Don't lie to me. Whatever else does or doesn't exist between us, at least let there be honesty."

Amid the numbness that held her, Tessa found a spark. "You want honesty? I daren't say, for fear you'll hurt him."

"Hurt him?"

"Lay in wait for him. Beat him up. Break his legs." She added more precisely, "Have someone break his legs." He might not soil his hands—not anymore, him being the King of Prospect Avenue and all. She knew he had men for that.

"That's what you think of me?"

"Yes."

He took that like a blow; she saw him flinch. "Then why didn't you go with your brother?"

"I don't know." The truth again. "Maybe because he blames me for Father's death. You don't." Two tears slipped down her cheeks.

"He blames *me*, or so he announced. Ah, hell, Tessa, don't cry. Don't let them beat you down, understand? Never that."

"Is that your philosophy of life?"

"Damn close."

She dabbed at her cheeks and said nothing. They rode in silence for a score of heartbeats.

"I know you want to leave me, Tessa. You probably want that annulment your brother mentioned. But if you'll stay with me—"

She turned her head again to look at him. His narrow face looked tense and his eyes burned.

"If I stay with you, what?"

"I promise to protect you. From everything. It will

be me and you against the world."

"You think that's what I want?"

"No. You probably want him, with his gold-colored hair and his handsome face. But does he love you, Tessa? Will he do *anything* for you?"

Tessa had once believed so, that Richard was her destiny, her soul mate. Richard, the one man to whom she could give herself. But where had he been before her marriage? Why hadn't he fought for her?

She looked at her husband. "Will you? Do *anything* for me?"

"Yes."

Now, there lay a heady prospect. Tessa had never had a yen for power. A quiet, pleasant life, yes, warmth and laughter in the company of the man she loved. But the idea of commanding a man such as this with all his wealth and contacts—however dangerous—held a certain seduction.

And what did that say about her? She wondered even as the long car—one in a train of others—pulled off Delaware Avenue into Forest Lawn.

"I…" She faltered. "I need to get through this. We can talk about the future later."

"Will you be coming home with me?"

"We're supposed to go back to Mother's. There's a reception."

"You know what I mean. After that."

Again she stared into his eyes, bright and vital, terrifyingly intent. Abruptly, she experienced a flashback to that night in her bed, him with his weight on her and his hand at her breast, kissing, kissing, *kissing*.

She must be losing her mind.

The car halted; Marty came round and opened the door. Thank God. She needn't answer Mitch, not yet.

****

Three times, during Hugo Verdun's interment, did Mitch keep his wife from collapsing. They stood in the shelter of a little pavilion that had been erected over the grave, far too close to the other mourners for Mitch's comfort. The wind whipped the corners of the shelter, and the grave yawned at their feet like the mouth of death. The minister rambled on and on.

Tessa faltered once when her father's coffin was lowered into the dark pit and again when the dirt went on. When they turned into the face of the stiff wind, she sagged against him.

Not until then did Mitch realize he was there— Tessa's lover had followed from the cathedral. He stood at some distance, staring, and positioned so he could make sure Tessa saw him.

The man definitely looked like he might be a problem. Mitch would need to do something about him. He just couldn't let his wife find out.

Back at the house on Bidwell Parkway, he sat Tessa in a chair and got her a drink, ignoring all the ugly looks directed at him. A good number of mourners had come to pay their respects, though not the young man with the golden hair.

So, Mitch thought as he placed the drink in his wife's hand and stood guard over her chair like a mastiff, that's what attracts her. Now you know. He couldn't be less like you if he tried.

Still, he'd had a look at his opponent: an advantage.

One by one, the callers left. When only family

remained, they closed ranks. After a whispered conversation, Gerald approached Tessa's chair and said, "Carter, you can go. We have business to discuss with our sister, family business."

Mitch swept the others with a look. Elise Verdun, prostrate on the settee, looked beyond discussion of any sort, but the others glared at him in a united front.

He said, "Like it or not, I am family now."

Gerald gave him a grim smile. "Not for long. You'll get back the money you paid for my sister, don't worry."

Mitch narrowed his gaze on Gerald. "From where?"

"Let us worry about that."

Tessa's sister, Louisa, approached. "At the time of Tessa's marriage, we were unaware of the repugnant deal Father made with you, Mr. Carter. If we had known, we'd have intervened and raised the money elsewhere to bail him out."

"How?"

"We'd have found a way."

"I was under the impression your father had exhausted all avenues before I approached him."

Gerald's nostrils pinched. "I would have mortgaged my life, if I had to."

Mitch glanced at his wife; she sat as unmoving as an automaton on shutoff.

He said, "Too late. The deal is made, and a deal's a deal."

Rage flooded Gerald's eyes; he took a half step forward.

"Don't," Mitch warned him. "You won't come out of it very well." All the while his heart screamed, *She's mine, she's mine. Mine!*

Louisa's husband walked up behind her. Louisa said, "We will apply, on Tessa's behalf, for an annulment. I am certain it will be granted. If you've had your way with my sister, it can only have been rape."

Mrs. Verdun raised her head from the arm of the settee.

"So." Mitch's lips twisted. "You plan to make this as ugly as possible. Embarrass her as much as you can. If you mean to buy me out, then show me the money; I'll consider your offer when I believe it."

"It may take some time," Louisa said. "The sale of this house—"

"I happen to know this house is heavily mortgaged."

"Life insurance—"

"You can't collect for suicide."

"We'll prove it wasn't, in fact, suicide."

"You said that before, but I don't see how. The man was found hanging by the neck."

Mrs. Verdun began to sob.

"Then I'll mortgage my own house," Gerald retorted. "I'll—"

"Stop."

The word came from the woman sitting so motionless beside Mitch's knees. Tessa jerked suddenly to life and rose to her feet, swaying.

"Tess," her brother said, "don't worry. We're going to take care of you, get you away from him."

She looked Gerald in the eye. "Do you blame me for Father's death?"

Gerald paled. "Tess—"

"Answer me."

His jaw tensed. "No, of course not. But if you had only come to Father when he asked, given him the forgiveness he so desperately needed…"

Tessa turned abruptly to Mitch. "Take me home."

"What?" Even he thought he'd be leaving without her, that it would all end here and now.

Her eyes, full of pain and panic, sought his. "Take me home, please."

"Of course." He grasped her arm; she shrank against him.

The outcry from her brother, her sister, and their spouses erupted immediately. They all presented reasons she should stay with them, cast Mitch off, and follow legal channels to dissolve her association with him.

She withstood the storm like a woman unhearing, her face shuttered. She left the parlor on Mitch's arm, followed by threats and promises.

"We'll get you free of him, Tess," her sister called after her. "So I do assure you."

Chapter Fourteen

"Stay with me. I know I keep asking you that, but..."

Tessa spoke the words as soon as her husband closed the bedroom door behind them, and heard him draw a breath, precisely like a man in pain.

"What?" He sounded strangled.

"Stay, please."

"Here? With you?"

"Just like the other night. Please, I don't think I can bear to be alone."

Mitch hesitated. "Tell me something, Tessa. Why did you come home with me tonight? This...this was your chance. Why not go with your family?"

She searched through the feelings in her heart, a tangle of emotions so sharp and hurtful she could barely stand to confront them. She said, "How could I go with them? They despise me now. They despise you, too. So I guess we suit."

A wry smile touched his lips. "I asked for honesty, so I suppose I deserve that. Do you despise me, Tessa? 'Cause that's all I care about."

Did she?

She should. She had. Now her own feelings and her bruised self-esteem pained her so terribly she couldn't tell.

She said, "Does it matter? You said you wanted

me. Or has that changed too, now that you know what I am?"

"What are you, Tessa?"

"A terrible person, one who turned her back on her father and caused him to take his own life."

"I told you, Tessa, I don't think it works that way. I don't suppose we're responsible for making each other happy. Or for forgiving, when we can't find it in us."

"You haven't said. Have you changed your mind about me?"

"No."

"Ironic, isn't it?" she asked, speaking from the pain in her heart.

"What is?" For one of the few times since she'd met him, Mitch looked baffled.

"I refused to forgive my father because I hated being your wife so very much. Now—here we are."

"Where are we, Tessa?"

"What I mean is, I'm turning to you, of all people."

He drew another of those long breaths.

"I suppose," she went on out of the grief that possessed her, "that's not too flattering—that I'm only turning to you because everyone else in my life has turned against me."

"No."

"I'm sorry. You needn't stay if you don't want to."

"I want to."

"Then touch me. The way you did the other night. It's all right, isn't it? We are married."

"Yes. But Tessa, I think it would be better if you just get some sleep. You've had one hell of a day. If you're afraid to be alone, I'll sit here in this chair, and we'll leave the light on."

"That's a kind offer. A...decent one. By all accounts, you're not a kind or decent man."

"That's true. But it's different, with you."

"Why?"

"You know why. Tessa, you're exhausted. I'll call the maid to help you change and then come back to sit with you, as I say."

"Hold me. Please. I just need someone to hold me."

He stepped forward and took her gently into his arms. And what did she find there? Warmth, safety? A refuge? A place to anchor her pain?

When he spoke again, his voice rumbled through her. "Tessa, if you're offering yourself to me out of shame, because you think you deserve nothing better—you don't have to. I'll take care of you, no strings."

She laid her head on his shoulder and wrapped her arms around him. When she did, she could hear the beating of his heart. After this, just like the other night, she'd be able to declare the people who spoke of him were wrong—he did possess a heart, after all.

She tipped up her face so she could look into his eyes. Dangerous man, frightening man, but she seemed to have lost her fear of him, at least temporarily. "Does it matter why I want you to stay? Does it?"

Emotions moved deep in his hazel eyes: protest, acknowledgment. Maybe it did matter. Maybe he'd walk out the door.

Instead, after that one searing look, he swept her up in his arms and laid her on the bed.

****

"Put out the light." Tessa's voice came to Mitch in a whisper he obeyed immediately, snuffing the wick of the lamp between his thumb and forefinger, ignoring

93

the sting. He'd already removed his suit jacket and laid it on the chair. Other than that, both of them remained fully clad.

"Here." He put his weight on the bed, reached down, and removed her shoes one after the other. Very little light illuminated the room, just what came from outside; unlike the other night, the heavy draperies had not been drawn.

"Do you feel cold?"

"Yes."

Once again he maneuvered her beneath the blankets and this time crawled in beside her. Was this to be his wedding night, the one he'd half feared would never come?

If so, it had come to him for all the wrong reasons. That thought would not leave his mind. In fact, it insisted on shouting at him. But he couldn't walk away from her now if he tried.

He might well have the strength for many things— not that.

But she doesn't truly want you, the voice inside shouted at him. *She wants to feel better about herself for a few short moments. When morning comes, she'll hate herself even more.*

Shut up, shut up! I don't care.

How could he make himself care when Tessa moved into his arms there in the bed, and snuggled close? When she curled one arm around his neck in a gesture that unquestionably urged his mouth toward hers?

Their mouths met, and he found hers open, an invitation he couldn't resist. Hunger flared inside him, deep and insistent. Since the first time he saw her, he'd been living for this.

Lips meshed and tongues tangled. He dove for her the way a drowning man might reach for land. His mind blanked out—something that rarely happened to him— and he became pure emotion.

Pure need.

He kissed her as he had the other night, till he felt sure neither of them breathed. She made little sounds in her throat and melted against him, all the awful tension flowing away out of her body. Her fingers moved from his neck and splayed across his cheek before she traced his throat downward and burrowed inside his shirt.

He broke the kiss.

"Tessa. Do you want—?"

"I don't want to think."

Well, that was a hell of a reason for making love with him. For an instant, disappointment joined the desire crashing through him. It dissolved when her fingers mastered the last of the buttons on his shirt and tangled with the hair on his chest.

He could keep her from thinking. Till morning, no doubt.

At which time there'd undoubtedly be a price to pay. As for everything. She'd likely hate him all over again.

And herself, yes.

"Touch me."

Her voice banished all thought of tomorrow. He begged her, "Say my name." He might be willing to bargain over most things, but tonight he wanted to be sure she didn't think of *him*, the other man. Not now.

"Mitch."

Fingers suddenly nimble, he began working the

tiny buttons on the back of her dress. "Again."

"Mitch. Mitch, please."

Lost entirely, he stripped her of her lovely gown, his fingers screaming with delight. Soft, soft—she felt like silk and tasted like honey when he ran his tongue over her skin. He didn't want to frighten her with his hunger, but damn it, he'd very nearly lost his mind.

He removed his own clothing—somehow—while keeping his mouth on her. Now, now, he thought, she'll protest, realize what's happening, and call a halt.

How will I bear it?

But she touched him tentatively, fingers returning to the nest of hair on his chest before venturing a bit lower.

"Don't be afraid," he told her.

"I'm not, but I've never…"

"I know. Stop me if you want to." *Please God, no.*

By means of persuasion, he cupped one breast in his hand. She gasped, and the tension returned to her body, but in a new way. Heaven. Surely that was the only word to describe her softness and the way she tasted. Very gently he thumbed the bud at the tip of her breast until it hardened. The hunger pounded through him more fiercely.

Ah, such intimacy. Somehow it had never felt like this with other women. But if Tessa let him inside her now, he'd never ask for anything else.

"Tessa, let me show you. Let me show you how it can be, between us."

"Show me."

He laid his mouth to her breast.

Chapter Fifteen

At last, at last, Tessa didn't need to think. In fact, all thought flew away from her when Mitch Carter—her husband, as she reminded herself—laid his mouth to her breast. Then it became all heat and sensation, and a longing she couldn't begin to define.

Nothing existed beyond the two of them. Nothing could be amiss in a world that didn't exist. If she asked him to touch her, he did. He seemed able to understand the language of her body, mostly silent, better than she did. When she caressed his cheek, he suckled more strongly. When she sighed and arched her body, he played it with gentle hands. When she stretched her legs apart, he drew her beneath him and positioned himself there, hot and heavy.

Her whole body screamed for him now. When he took her face between his hands and said, "Tessa, are you sure?" She told him, "*Hush*," and kissed him. His tongue slid into her mouth at the very same instant—

Oh, she would never, ever, ever be the same.

Pain, a flash of light, and then a wave of possessiveness so strong it stabbed her through. She didn't understand it: did she possess him, or he her? No way to tell, no time to puzzle it out. He gasped into her mouth as he began moving inside her, and the light grew so bright it almost hurt, built and built until her world shattered.

She wanted to scream and laugh and weep. The tears won when he stopped moving and, when he eased down on top of her, they trickled down her cheeks.

"I've hurt you," he whispered, appalled.

"No, no, you haven't."

"I was too rough."

What was that she heard in his voice? No way to tell, yet it made her assure him, "No, you were...you were very gentle."

He withdrew that part of his body that fit so perfectly into her body, and tried to move away. Tessa clung to him.

"Wait."

"Tessa." That great, nameless emotion still lingered in his voice. "If I haven't hurt you, why are you crying?"

"I don't know. It was just..." She had no words that did not seem wholly inadequate for such an act, such depth of sharing. "It was fine."

"Fine." He repeated it like a man stunned. She felt his fingers smooth through her hair. "You're exhausted. Get some sleep."

Could she, possibly? Maybe. All her terrible thoughts had flown away when the light exploded through her body and mind. But she feared they'd return if he got up and left the bed.

"What now?" she whispered.

"Eh?"

"Are you going to leave me?"

"Leave you!"

"To sleep alone."

"Oh. No. No." He drew her back into his arms so her body fitted against his, her buttocks tucked against the hollow beneath his chest and his arms wrapped around her from behind. Back into the marvelous warmth he seemed to exude.

"Sleep," he told her.

"I'm not sure I can." His hand lay just beneath her breasts, tantalizingly close. She wouldn't mind if he touched her again with his rough thumb. It might be too bold of her, though, to ask.

Instead she said, "Is it true?"

"Is what true, darling?"

Darling. Never had she thought to hear such a word cross Mitch Carter's lips.

"Were you really found in a gutter? My mother said…"

Mitch moved restlessly. For an instant, Tessa feared he'd get up and leave after all. But after a moment he said, "It's true. I was found by a passerby, a newborn no doubt dropped by a whore."

"A whore?"

"Who else? Don't know who she was, and my father could have been anyone. Some john."

"Oh." Tessa tried to imagine it. Dropped by a prostitute. The lowest of the low. "What happened to you?"

"Foundling. Taken to Carter's. Spent my whole life there till the age of fourteen."

"That's why your last name's Carter. They didn't know…"

"All boys without a last name are given that one." Irony entered his voice. "There are a lot of 'Carters' hanging 'round the city."

"I see." She contemplated it. She'd always known where she came from, youngest child of Hugo and Elise

Verdun. Generations behind her, most of them French in origin.

"What was it like growing up there, at Carter's?"

He stiffened. His hand, on her belly, tensed and took a moment to relax again. "Hell on earth. I got out as soon as I could. Swore I'd never go back again."

"What was so terrible about it?"

"You name it. Hunger. Beatings. Remind me to show you my scars, some time."

"Scars! They beat little children?"

"Darling, you have no idea."

She shivered. He pulled her still closer, fitted his face into the crook of her neck. "Doesn't matter now."

"So you got out when you were fourteen?"

"Ran away."

"What did you do, though? No money, no people—"

"I survived. By stealing, mostly. Slept wherever I could. The one thing I knew was I couldn't let the coppers catch me, 'cause they'd return me to Carter's. I had two years left—you're supposed to stay till you're sixteen."

"How long ago was this?"

"Twelve years."

So when she'd been a girl of ten, living a comfortable life beneath Hugo's beneficence, Mitch had been fighting to stay alive. And fighting ever since.

"Well, how did you get from that to being—"

"The King of Prospect Avenue?" He laughed softly; it tickled Tessa's shoulder. "It's a long story, and you needn't worry about it. All you need to know is if I'm the King of Prospect Avenue, you're my Queen. All right?"

"I don't feel much like a queen."

"You will. I'll make sure you feel that way." He kissed her ear. "I promise."

She turned in his arms so his lips met her lips. She moaned with desire.

Very slowly and luxuriantly, he made love to her again.

****

When Tessa woke to bright sunlight flowing through the bedroom windows, her husband had already gone. She lay in the bed thinking about what had happened during the night—had any of it truly happened?—until the knob on the door rattled and the mechanical maid rolled in.

Tessa raised the sheet to cover her nakedness, though she couldn't say why. The maid certainly knew nothing about modesty.

Or shame. Or remorse.

At times, Tessa decided, it must be comforting, being an automaton.

"Good morning, Mrs. Carter," the maid said. "Mr. Carter asked me to bring your breakfast."

"Did he?" Sure enough, the maid bore a tray piled with more food than Tessa could eat in a week. "Where is Mr. Carter? Can you tell me?"

"Mr. Carter is in his office, working."

"I see." Tessa glanced at the window. "Is it late?"

The maid tilted her head to one side. "Late, as relative to what, Mrs. Carter?"

"What time is it?"

"Just after ten a.m."

"So late as that?" Well, she'd had little enough sleep during the night, though after the second time they made love she thought she'd more or less blacked out in Mitch's arms.

The second time... Oh, what had she done?

Guilt suffused her. She'd meant to save herself for Richard. The man she loved. Wasn't that how it was supposed to be?

But the need had been so overwhelming, last night. Not just the physical need, but that for a comfort she couldn't even begin to name.

Well, she resolved, it would never happen again. Even if she was no better than she should be, the Queen of Prospect. Oh, but she wanted to hear the rest of his story, how a baby pulled out of the gutter had grown into the king of anything.

And she had a strange, strong craving for one of his kisses.

Instead, now she had to face the day which, from where she lay, seemed impossible.

She looked at the tray the maid had laid across her lap, suddenly sure she'd be sick if she took a single bite. She waved a hand.

"Please take this away. And help me get dressed."

"Yes, Mrs. Carter."

She needed quite desperately to go downstairs and talk to her husband.

****

Mitch sat at the desk in his office, trying unsuccessfully to concentrate on the report his man, Dinty, was giving him. Important stuff. He was supposed to be listening to numbers concerning how Danny Dwyer had been expanding his territory.

Instead, he could think only about his wife—how she'd tasted last night. How she'd clung to him and trembled in his arms. How it had felt when he entered her for the first time.

Just like he'd come home.

Mitch Carter had never had a home. Oh, he'd bought a lot of houses, and had lived in this one for a while. Nice house. But it didn't feel like *home*.

"He's been liquidating some of his holdings," Dinty said. Dinty had a talent for numbers. "Must mean he's planning a big move. And there's a new consortium."

"What?"

"A new consortium. You all right, Boss?"

"Yeah, sure. Why wouldn't I be? Who's behind it?"

"Behind what?"

"The new consortium."

Dinty's muddy brown eyes lit up. Mitch had a sudden flashback to Dinty huddled in a corner back at Carter's, no more than six years old, with welts on his cheeks where the strap had caught him.

"That's what makes it interesting, Boss. No one seems to know. Whoever it is, they have money. And people are saying they're gonna make a big purchase."

"Downtown?"

"Downtown."

"Damn it. I—"

The office door inched open, and Tessa peered in. All other thoughts fled Mitch's mind.

"Morning," Tessa whispered.

"Good morning, Tessa. Come on in. Dinty, we're done here."

"But—" Dinty began.

Almost in the same breath, Tessa said, "I didn't

mean to interrupt."

"We're done here."

"We're not, actually," objected Dinty, who could be stubborn.

"Get back to me on this later," Mitch told him. "Meanwhile, find out all you can."

"All right." Dinty didn't look happy, but he left.

Mitch looked at his wife; she gazed back at him.

"Are you well this morning, Tessa?"

She nodded. God, how beautiful she looked with her auburn hair piled up on her head, a few curls trickling down, a blue ruffled blouse and straight, blue skirt covering the delectable curves he'd touched last night. He wanted to pull her into his arms and do it all over again.

But he didn't figure she had come into his office looking for that. Rather, following last night's events, he imagined she'd come to tell him she wanted to go home to her mother.

That she wanted out of the marriage after all.

Chapter Sixteen

And why, Tessa wondered, did her husband look at her that way, with such an intense yet guarded expression in his eyes? Difficult to say what Mitch Carter thought at any given moment. Impossible, now.

She cleared her throat, searching through all the inexpressible things she needed to tell him for the most important.

"I hope you did not get the wrong impression last night."

"What impression," he drawled, "would that be?"

He wore one of those white shirts—the thin ones—this morning, with the collar open. There, she could see some of the black hair through which she'd plowed her fingers last night. Oh, what had she been thinking? He wasn't even the type of man to whom she was usually attracted.

But he watched her the way a wolf might its prey as she shut the door carefully behind her. Like he wanted to eat her alive.

Darling. The memory of the word whispered through her mind.

Without answering his question, she said, "I must apologize. I'm afraid I misled you by asking you to stay with me last night. And what happened after…" His mouth at her breast. The heat of his hand sliding up her bare leg, his fingers caressing her most intimate place.

Oh, how could she have allowed it?

"I was…I was vulnerable. It should never have happened."

"I see." A muscle jumped in his cheek. The clever hazel eyes burned.

Tessa stumbled on. "I was in a terrible frame of mind. I despised myself almost—almost as much as—"

"As you despise me?"

"I was going to say, as my family does."

"So you slept with the lowlife from the gutter, is that it? Punishing yourself, maybe?"

"It wasn't like that." Only it was. He'd hit the truth right on the nose.

His lips curled in a hurtful smile. "You don't lie well, Mrs. Carter. I can see everything in your eyes."

"I'm sorry. Really, I am. I just wanted to make it clear…it can't happen again."

She turned to leave. Before she could turn the doorknob he was around the desk and had caught her arm. He swung her back to face him.

"Just a minute. There are a few things to be said."

"Are there?"

His gaze pinioned her, inescapable. "You didn't seem to hate what we did so much last night."

Color flared in Tessa's face and heat rushed through her. "I—"

"Don't try and deny it. You enjoyed what passed between us."

"No."

"Liar. What happened to the honesty you promised me?"

She bit her lip in agony.

"Don't want to admit it, right? Because I'm not

good enough for you."

"I didn't say that. But—things look a lot different this morning."

"Not to me."

"That's why I wanted to make sure and speak of this, first thing. I didn't want you to expect—well, think it would happen every night."

"No?"

"It can never happen again."

"So you said. But Tessa, why deny yourself the pleasure? We're married. If you enjoy it and I enjoy it, if," he added deliberately, "you need comfort—"

She yanked her arm from his grasp; his fingers slid over her skin and left a tingle. She lifted her chin. "Do I need to remind you I'm in love with someone else?"

"Ah, yes, how could I forget? The young man I saw at the funeral service. You must have forgotten him also, last night when you were writhing in my arms and parting your legs for me."

"How dare you speak to me that way?"

"How dare you toss your feelings for another man in my face?"

Tessa drew herself up. "Please do not come to my room again. You won't be welcome."

"Sure about that, are you?"

She swept through the door and let it swing shut behind her. With Valerie at her heels, she charged back up the stairs to her room. Haven? Or something else?

She paced; she raged and wept. She went over all Mitch Carter had just said to her and, once again, over all that had happened in the depths of the night. Touch by touch. Kiss by kiss. Why couldn't she get it out of her head?

She should leave the man, put as much physical distance between them as possible. But if she went home, she'd have to face the blame she saw in her family's eyes. Blaming herself for her father's death was one thing; living with their blame was something else again.

What of Richard? She wondered suddenly what would happen if she ran away to him. Would it matter to Richard that she was now, in essence, damaged goods? Would he reject her as another man's leavings?

Staying here with Mitch Carter made an equally bad option. He knew she'd more or less used him last night. He'd used her too—taken advantage. Worst of all, he believed she despised him.

Well, she did. Didn't she?

Her increasingly maddening thoughts were interrupted then by a knock on the door. Her pulse leaped alarmingly. "Who is it?"

"Mrs. Carter?" The mechanical maid. Tessa's ensuing relief left her dizzy. "Mr. Carter asks you to join him in his office at once."

"Please tell him no."

"Yes, Mrs. Carter."

Ensuring silence fell, during which Tessa fought to master her breathing. What could he want? How could she possibly live like this?

The next knock sounded mere moments later and with greater authority. "Tessa, please come down. Your brother is here with his lawyer."

Tessa went to the door and opened it a crack. Her husband stood there, wearing a look of annoyed stoicism. She felt a twinge of sympathy; he wasn't having a very good day.

His gaze swept over her. "You've been crying."

"I was upset." She brushed at her cheeks with the heel of her hand; something in his hard gaze softened. The word *darling* chased its way through Tessa's head again.

"What does Gerald want?"

"You, I expect. But he refuses to discuss anything without you present."

"Why? He hates me."

"The fact remains you're his sister. Family relations, so I'm assured, are complicated, though"—another of those hurtful smiles curled his lips—"of course I wouldn't know from personal experience."

"I'll come down. Just give me a minute to—to repair myself."

"All right." He nodded at Valerie, close at her side. "Bring the dog if it affords you any comfort."

Chapter Seventeen

Tessa recognized the lawyer, one Mr. Bottering, whom her father had also employed. Tall and almost skeletally thin, Mr. Bottering always looked like he'd just caught a whiff of something nasty.

Not a man in whom Tessa could confide.

Her brother, as she saw in one glance when she entered Mitch's office, looked angry. At her or at Mitch Carter?

Both men focused on the little mechanical dog that trotted at Tessa's heels.

"Must you, Tess?" Gerald asked. "A toy? We're here on serious business."

Tessa said nothing. Did Gerald fail to see she walked on a fine wire from which she might, at any moment, tumble and shatter? That the presence of the dog might reassure her?

"Please sit down, Tessa," Mitch said. An array of chairs had been set up opposite his big mahogany desk. She lowered herself into one, and Valerie jumped into her lap.

Gerald and Mr. Bottering exchanged glances. Mr. Bottering said, "Miss Verdun, we've come about moving forward with annulling your recent marriage. Your brother wishes to pay back the sum of money your late father accepted from Mr. Carter and take you home with him."

"Yes?" Tessa clasped her hands on Valerie's cool neck and shot a look at Mitch. It did her no good; his face looked shuttered tight.

"In order for that to happen," Mr. Bottering went on, "I need your official agreement. Just a formality, as I understand it. You merely need to state that this marriage was, in fact, forced upon you and you wish for it to be dissolved. Is that not so?"

"Well, yes." Tessa couldn't look at Mitch at all now. But the truth was the truth.

Mr. Bottering went on more delicately, "Just as, I understand, anything of a more *intimate* nature that occurred following the marriage must also have been forced upon you."

"I—uh—" Honesty froze Tessa where she sat, while memory flooded upon her—the memory of opening herself to Mitch Carter there in the dark, the word *please* on her lips.

Gerald burst out, "Of course she was forced. Look at her! And look at him. My sister is virtually a child."

Mitch said in a voice like iron, "She's twenty-two years old."

"But a child nonetheless, in her heart and her mind, protected all her life, never—until now—subjected to a bully who would use and manipulate her." Gerald looked as if he wanted to hit Mitch Carter. "I'll bet it was you who kept her from going to our father that night, you who are in fact responsible for his death."

A way out, Tessa thought. She could jump on it, throw Mitch Carter under the tram car and claim that, yes, he'd kept her from going to Father when he needed her. She could return to the bosom of her family, hide there, and pretend Mitch Carter had never existed.

Of course none of it was true. And she'd promised him honesty. Did a man like Mitch Carter deserve honesty?

Mitch said in that hard voice, "The payment you're talking about, to your father, was not a loan. It was not, in fact, a payment. It was a forgiveness and, as such, can't be repaid."

Bottering said, "I am more than aware of the terms of that agreement. I was, as you will recall, Hugo Verdun's attorney."

"How could I forget?"

"You, in fact, bought up all his debts from his various creditors around the city—with aforethought—paid them off, and then called in Mr. Verdun's debt, transferred to you, in order to coerce him into an abhorrent action and force his hand."

"His daughter's hand, actually." The terrible smile twisted Mitch's lips again. "And it's all been made completely legal."

He opened the center drawer of his desk and extracted a paper, which he pushed toward the two men opposite him. "This has Mr. Verdun's signature on it, as well as Miss Tessa Nicole Verdun's."

Tessa's eyes widened. Gerald looked at her accusingly. "Do you remember signing this?"

She did, in a vague and distant sort of way. That had been the night she first met Mitch Carter, a meeting that had taken place in her father's parlor, after Father had spent hours alone with her, crying and pleading.

He will hurt me, Tess, if you don't agree. Or have me killed. He's the kind of man who does that. He has a reputation in this city, a dangerous one.

In the end, frightened and emotionally battered, she

hadn't been able to face the prospect of being responsible for harm befalling her father. Now look what had happened; that was precisely what she'd done.

Refusing to look at Mitch or at her brother, she stared at the paper. "I signed it."

"It doesn't matter," Bottering claimed. "We shall tell the court it was signed under duress."

Mitch said nothing.

"Was it, Tess?" Gerald asked. "Signed under duress?"

"Yes." The agony of witnessing her father's fear, her inability to refuse him.

"What about the money?" Mitch asked.

Gerald nearly spat. "Yes, that's what it comes down to for you, isn't it? It's all about the price. And yes, you paid a high one for my sister—very high. Don't worry, you'll get your money back."

Bottering cleared his throat. "I thought we might set up a series of payments."

"No," Mitch said.

"I beg your pardon?"

Mitch glared at Gerald. "You come here claiming I bought your sister? Well, then, I'm refusing to sell her back to you."

"An annulment—"

"Ask her. Ask if she was forced to my bed."

Everyone looked at Tessa. Bottering's inspection, cold and analytical, bored into her, beneath the skin. Gerald's, half horrified, asked a question. Mitch looked guarded as ever, but in the depths of his hazel eyes something burned.

Honesty, she thought she heard him whisper in her mind.

She threaded her fingers together, clenched them till they felt ready to break. In her lap, Valerie wiggled while Tessa struggled to think.

If she went home with her brother, she would have to face his condemnation, yes—even if she blamed Mitch for keeping her from her father that night. But she might have another chance at life, a chance with Richard after all.

Eventually it might even seem like none of this had ever happened.

All she had to do was lie.

"Tess?" Gerald said. "Speak up. You needn't be afraid of him."

And what would Mitch Carter do if she lied? Give her up? She didn't think so. He'd fight, and he had resources. He might destroy them all.

Still, she didn't fear him, not the way she had. How could she, after he'd touched her so carefully, so gently? When he'd called her his darling?

The Queen of Prospect Avenue. Wife of a child found in the gutter. Was that how she wanted to spend her life?

****

Mitch watched his wife as emotions played across her face and flickered in her green eyes. As he'd told her, he found it all too easy to read her. She struggled now between her honesty and the desire to be free. What did she want more?

To leave him, of course. For what earthly reason would she want to stay? Surely not for the way it felt when their lips met or when their bodies melted together in a storm of heat. When he entered her and damn near lost himself.

Choose honesty, he willed her, and her gaze flicked to him almost as if she heard.

But...but hadn't she come to this room, this very morning, and told him it could never again happen so, between them? That she didn't want him?

Oh, God, oh, Jesus, she was going to walk out of his life on her brother's arm. He'd never touch her again.

Tessa parted her lips. She spoke. "Gerald, Mr. Bottering, could I speak with my husband alone?"

Gerald flared. "I don't think that's a good idea."

"Nor do I," Mr. Bottering agreed.

"Please."

The same word she'd spoken when she asked Mitch to stay with her. All that had followed remained burned into him like a cauterization.

He jerked to his feet. "Let's step outside."

She followed him, leaving the little mechanical dog in the chair; they exited through the door that led to the yard. Outside it was bright and windy, with a sharp November bite off the river.

They stood facing one another, less than two feet separating them. Tessa's gaze fluttered to his and as quickly away.

"You want me to stay," she said, not a question.

He sucked in a breath. "Yes."

"Even if...what we did never happens again?"

Well, there it was, plain and simple. It would hurt him and badly, if he never had her again. But he didn't quite believe he never would.

"Yes."

"You'll make a lot of trouble for my family if I leave?"

"I don't want to make trouble for you, Tessa, but yes."

"Then I want to make a deal."

"A deal?"

"Just between you and me." She jerked her head at the house. "Nothing to do with them. It's what you do, isn't it? Make deals."

"Yes." His heart thundered and his thoughts raced.

"What will you give me to stay?"

"Anything," he said rashly. He'd never bargained so in the past, not once, but didn't care now. "Anything you want."

She smiled tightly, and he went cold.

"What do you want?"

"A measure of independence. Autonomy." She looked thoughtfully at the door behind which her brother sat. "He won't give it to me."

"No, he won't."

"He thinks I'm still a child."

"What would this autonomy include?"

"What can I have?" Her green eyes challenged him. Bargaining, indeed.

"I've just said, anything you want. Jewelry, clothes, a car of your own, a horse, servants."

"All that's fine, but I want something better. The freedom to come and go as I like, answerable to no one." Her chin came up. "I want leave to see Richard when I choose, to continue my relationship with him."

"Richard?" The expression in her eyes revealed exactly who that was. "Relationship?" Over his dead body. "You want me to approve you having an affair with the man?"

"I didn't say that. Just that you won't prevent me

seeing him if and when I wish."

"And if he'll agree to see you? Given you're married to me."

"Yes."

Mitch thought hard about it. The wind blew sharper, making Tessa shiver. Mitch reached out and caught her shoulders between his hands.

A devil's bargain, and no mistake. But if ever there existed a bargainer who might get the better of the devil, he was Mitch Carter. He looked her in the eye. "I agree."

"You do?" Her face lit. For Mitch, it felt like a stab to the heart.

"Yes."

"Then let's go back inside."

"Wait. What are you going to tell your brother?"

"I'm going to tell him the truth."

Chapter Eighteen

"Automatons," Dinty announced.

"What?" Mitch jerked his mind from the depths of dark thought and focused on Dinty, who stood in front of him. An almost impossible feat, to focus at all. His wife had ordered the car and gone out alone this morning. He could only wonder where.

He'd had her followed, but still…Richard. Was she with him now? What did they do together? Would he lose her after all?

He thought of what she'd said to her brother and the lawyer, Bottering, after they came back inside yesterday. She'd looked Gerald Verdun in the eye and told him her marriage could not be annulled because it had been consummated.

What did that mean for him, Mitch? Only that she prized the right to see Richard so highly she was willing to purchase it by staying with a man she detested.

Him.

It made him want to spit.

She thought she'd got the better of him in their bargain. But no one ever got the better of the King of Prospect.

"Boss? Did you hear what I said?"

"Automatons," Mitch repeated it. "What the hell are you talking about?"

Dinty waved a hand like a conjurer. "The secret

consortium—it's secret no more. It's made up of automatons, those fancy, hybrid ones and others in with them. They're buying up property all over the city, including downtown."

"They're the ones competing with Dwyer and me?"

"Yeah, Boss."

"Where are they getting their money?" In Mitch's experience, it always came down to money.

"They're pooling their resources, Boss, all the steamies in the city are. You know they're getting wages now, most of them, since the revolution."

"It wasn't a revolution." Just a crazy standoff in Niagara Square, between the city's mechanicals and the humans who opposed them. Mitch had no part in that and didn't want one.

But now, if he found himself in competition with the buggers, it affected him.

Dinty shrugged. "What do they have to do with their money, when you think about it? They don't drink, gamble, or whore."

"I thought they were trying to construct other hybrids." Mitch had heard as much. Creepy, but that didn't impact him the way them buying up property would.

"That too, Boss. They seem to have their fingers in a lot of pies."

"Do they have a leader, a head man?"

Dinty grinned his gap-toothed smile. "A steamie king, you mean, the way we got you? If they do, it'd be the one called Pat Kelly, one of the hybrids. He's a police officer."

A dim bell sounded in Mitch's overwrought mind. Right, the strapping police officer at Verdun's funeral.

He'd spoken to Tessa, who said she'd met him at the Meadows Club.

"Ah. Maybe I need to have a word with this Pat Kelly."

"With an automaton, Boss?"

"If he's in charge, yes."

Dinty now wrinkled his brow. "But what can you say to him? What pressure can you put on him? He's a machine."

"You leave that to me." The way Mitch was feeling, wondering where Tessa might be and what she could be doing, he just might rip the damn machine's head right off.

It would be a relief.

****

A steam unit answered the door at the Trask residence and stared at Tessa through blank, sculpted eyes. Its voice came through a grate located in its throat.

"Yes, madam?"

Tessa drew a breath. She'd asked Marty to let her out of the car a short distance away, near the park, and walked here in an effort to protect Richard. She'd been here before—once—when, among a group of people, she'd stopped by during a scavenger hunt. It felt far more daring now.

But, she reminded herself, she and her husband had a deal. She had his acknowledgement she could see whomever she wished.

"Is Master Richard at home?"

Please, please let him be here, she willed the automaton. Its expression, of course, did not change. But it inclined its head and swung wide the door, inviting her in.

"Of course, madam. Will you please wait in the parlor? Whom may I tell young master is calling?"

"Tessa Verdun." A lie, but she didn't feel like Mrs. Mitch Carter. Even though their marriage had most certainly been consummated.

"One moment, madam."

The steamie abandoned her in the parlor and rolled out. Tessa, left on her own, stared around the room, noting, with some dismay, subtle signs of decline. This house, when newly built on Bird Avenue, had been as affluent as her father's on Bidwell Parkway, but the Trasks, like Tessa's own family, had recently suffered a change in fortune. It seemed only the criminals in Buffalo prospered these days.

A soft sound from the doorway spun her around. Richard came into the room, staring incredulously, and shut the door after him.

He appeared disheveled, the collar of his shirt open, sleeves rolled up, and fair hair mussed. He blinked at Tessa as if he couldn't believe his eyes.

"Tessa? By God, you shouldn't be here."

"No?" She feasted her gaze on him, thinking of all she'd had to trade in order to manage it. "But tell me you're glad that I am."

"I'm glad. Oh, yes—but what has brought about this miracle?"

"I wanted to thank you for coming to Father's funeral service. I couldn't do so then. I…"

Richard's blue eyes kindled. "You were under guard by that cretin of a fellow playing watchdog to you," he finished for her. "Yes, I could see that."

"I'm relieved you could." She puffed out a breath.

"I didn't want you to suppose I no longer wished to be your…friend." She added deliberately, "Because I do."

"I'm happy to hear it. But you've taken a terrible chance coming here, haven't you? What if he finds out?" Richard swallowed, his Adam's apple sliding up and down convulsively. "I understand he's a very dangerous man."

"He is, yes. But I have his permission to be here."

"What!"

"Otherwise I never would have endangered you by coming. Richard, we need to think of a way we can see each other. A—a legitimate reason for us to meet that won't incur too much gossip."

Richard grasped her hands and towed her to the settee, where they seated themselves so close their knees touched.

"I'd like that, Tessa. I've missed you so much. And I have to say, I was overset when I heard the news of your marriage. I thought—well, that is, I supposed you and I had a kind of understanding. I know I hadn't spoken outright. Perhaps I should have, before all this happened."

If only he had. She never would have agreed to marry Mitch, no matter the pressure.

Tears came to her eyes. "I married Mitch Carter for Father's sake."

"The rumors say there was money involved." Anger sparked in Richard's eyes. "He bought you, didn't he?"

"Well—"

"But if you only married him for your father's sake, can't you get free of him now your father's dead?"

"There's a lot more involved than money." If she shared her guilt with Richard, the loathing her family now had for her, and which she held for herself, would it change how he saw her?

She dared not find out.

"But you will be able to get free of him?" Richard raised her hand to his lips and brushed the backs of her knuckles with a kiss. Tessa experienced a sudden flashback to the house on Prospect, and her husband planting a burning kiss on her wrist.

"I'm not sure."

"Please, Tessa. It would make me ever so happy."

Tessa's heart leaped. Would her marriage to Mitch prove the catalyst, the thing that pushed Richard to claim her for his own? Such a tangled mess of circumstance, but at least she had room for hope.

She held Richard's gaze with hers. "And if I do manage to get free of him?"

Richard didn't answer directly. Instead, still holding her hand, he said, "Remember all the fun times we've had together? The laughter and the silliness? I've been thinking about that a lot lately, since I believed I'd lost you. I want those times back, Tessa. No one can make me feel the way you do. If you can get free of that monster, I want us to be together."

Tessa went suddenly breathless. "Richard, are you asking me to marry you?"

"Can I?" he returned the question, with yearning in his voice. "You're another man's wife. But I've kicked myself a hundred times, wishing I'd spoken up when I had the chance. It's just that I supposed we did have that understanding." His gaze beseeched her. "Forgive me?"

All the doubt fled Tessa in a rush. "If you will forgive me in turn, for what I had to do."

"But how are we to see each other now?"

"I've been thinking about that, Richard. Carter has given me leave to engage in good works."

"Eh?"

"Charitable works. If you were involved also, it would give us a legitimate reason to be in contact. No one could object." Not even Mitch Carter, presumably.

Richard's nose wrinkled. "What kind of charitable works?"

Tessa thought of Mrs. Michaels. "The plight of orphans in this city is quite distressing."

"Orphans? You mean, someone else's unwanted children?"

Tessa assured herself she'd thrown poor Richard off stride, both with her visit and her suggestion—that explained his less-than-warm reaction. "Yes," she said patiently. Some of those orphans had even been plucked from the gutter. But she thrust that thought to the back of her mind. "I think I'm going to throw my weight—and Mr. Carter's money—behind that particular cause. Will you join me?"

A new look invaded Richard's eyes. "He's very wealthy is he, this husband of yours?"

"I believe so. That doesn't matter. I'll get in touch with Mrs. Michaels—the woman who's spearheading the effort to reform the orphanages—and send you a message where we're next to meet. Will you come?"

"Tessa, I will."

"Promise me?"

"I promise." Again he raised her hand to his lips.

"Then I'd best leave now. I don't want to do

anything that will risk me being able to see you again."

Richard leaped to his feet when she rose, still holding her hand. "Say it will be soon, Tessa. I can hardly wait."

"As soon as I can manage things."

He escorted her to the door and handed her out into the chilly sunshine, his gaze ardent.

Tessa, facing a walk back to the park and the presumably waiting car, didn't even mind. All had come right with her world.

Chapter Nineteen

"Afternoon, Mr. Dwyer."

The man lounging at the scarred table with a glass of black ale set before him glanced up lazily when Mitch spoke and then leaped to his feet. "Mitch Carter, here?" he marveled. "What in God's name's brought you to an Irish bar in South Buffalo?"

Mitch eyed the fellow carefully. Dwyer, tall and stringy, with rawboned shoulders, wore his shock of dirty-blond hair long and had enough freckles for a respectable appaloosa. Looked a bit like a horse, when it came to it, with big square teeth. But his eyes held evidence of a hard and canny intelligence.

"You and I need words together," Mitch told him.

"Do we?" Dwyer crooked an eyebrow.

"You leaned on one of my boys not long ago, roughed him up and broke his arm. I wanted to say if you have business with me you come to me, right? Because it's tit for tat—you hurt one of my boys, I'll hurt you back. But that's all water under the bridge now. I came here today to suggest we quit battling each other long enough to discuss a common problem."

"Well, I have to say you're a bold man, a brave man to come here onto my stamping ground. Takes balls, that does."

"You know me, Dwyer—ever one to take a risk."

Danny Dwyer grinned unexpectedly. "A calculated

risk, maybe. So is it a truce you're after seeking?"

"Maybe a temporary one."

"Then sit down. Meg, bring the man a drink. What will you have, Carter?"

"Beer's fine." Mitch, contrary to the talk about him, rarely drank. Oh, he might take a glass of whiskey—mostly Scotch—when he desperately needed to unwind. By and large, though, he couldn't afford to drink to excess and cloud his wits.

"Bring him a whiskey, Meg," Dwyer called to the barmaid, and she nodded. Everyone else in the bar stared. Mitch wondered how many of them were Dwyer's minions.

"I hear congratulations are in order," Dwyer said when the barmaid had brought the drink, "on your recent marriage. Beautiful girl is your wife."

Mitch bored Dwyer with a glare. "How do you know anything about my wife's appearance?"

"It's all over town, who you married. Or should I say who you bought?"

"You're an offensive ass, Dan Dwyer. No wonder I never do any business with you."

Dwyer didn't like that; his pale eyes narrowed. "We've never done business together because I don't want to associate with the likes of you."

"Well, I think you might change your mind."

"I doubt that." Dwyer raised his glass and supped some ale. "All I'm saying is, a pretty wife like that needs looking after. You wouldn't want anything nasty to happen to her."

Mitch stiffened in every limb. His first instinct bade him inform the cretin sitting across the table that if anything nasty even so much as winked at Tessa he,

Mitch, would tear Dwyer to bloody pieces with his bare hands. But it wouldn't do to reveal the depth of his feelings for her and hence his vulnerability. So he shrugged instead and said, "She's a status symbol—a mark that I'm moving up in the world, just like my house and car."

Dwyer seemed to find that amusing. "Your house and car?"

"All expensive toys."

"And you call me an ass."

"Meanwhile you're living down here in this rabbit warren."

Dwyer's eyes glinted with annoyance. "I prefer to spend my money on other things. I can tell you, I'm not much enjoying this conversation, Carter. So spit out whatever you came here to say."

"All right, I will." *But leave my wife out of it.* "You and I find ourselves in competition—for real estate, mostly."

"That could be."

"No 'could be' about it. We've outbid one another no less than six times. Oh, you tend to use agents to do your buying, but I always know it's you."

"How?"

Now Mitch smiled. "You buy in patterns, a property here or there and then fill in the neighborhoods with other purchases. You don't like to bid above a certain price, but you will, if you don't want me to have it. You're steadily encroaching on my turf."

"Your turf, is it?"

"Yes."

"So," Dwyer sneered, "you've come here to warn me off."

"No. As I said when I sat down, I've come to suggest we work together, repugnant as that prospect may be."

Dwyer stirred in his chair and sat up straighter. "The hell, you say."

"What do you know about a man called Pat Kelly?"

Dwyer's expression changed. "I know he's not a man. I know he almost got destroyed a couple months back. And I know he's a"—Dwyer sneered—"cop."

"And Irish. Just like you."

"Well, now, there's a question. Can an automaton actually be considered Irish? Kelly's a machine that might fancy itself as being Irish, so to speak."

"Involved with a lot of things in this city, would you say?"

"Aye, so."

"A mover and a shaker—just like us?" Mitch pressed.

Dwyer scowled. "Not like us. I sweat and I piss—I bleed and I know you do too. I'd say there's a difference."

Mitch played with the glass on the table, though he didn't take a drink. "What's your stand on these automaton rights?"

"You come here, on my turf, to ask me about my politics? Christ! The things are fecking machines, and dangerous ones at that. I say shut 'em all down. Give the employment to my fellow countrymen and women."

"That's not the way it's heading. They're gaining rights. Using our laws. Buying property."

Dwyer, not stupid after all, didn't take long to grasp the point. "The hell, you say!" he exclaimed again.

"So I've been informed."

"Well, I'm not the man to doubt your sources. Some of the best in the city, so I understand. You say Pat Kelly's in it?"

"He's their leader, isn't he?"

Dwyer shrugged.

"And," Mitch added deliberately, "moving in on your turf, and mine."

Dwyer grimaced hideously. "So what do you suggest, great King?"

"I thought we should pay a call on Mr. Kelly, advise him it might be prudent for him to focus his interests—and center his purchasing—somewhere other than downtown."

"Work together, you say. Us?"

"Look, Dwyer, I don't like it any more than you do. But if we don't act, we might both be cut out."

Dwyer pondered it while supping another measure of ale. "If I should agree to such a thing, Carter—and it would gall me no end to do so—I doubt our usual methods will serve. How do you lean on a bunch of machines?"

"Kelly has a wife. I understand she's human."

"Is that so?"

"Do your research. Get back to me. But, Mr. Dwyer"—Mitch leaned across the table—"you beat up another of my boys, you'll learn about hurt, understand?"

Dwyer scowled. "I thought that's what we do— hurt each other. Can't your boys take it, Carter? I thought they was tough."

"Tough as nails." His boys, most of them, had been

through hell and back.

"Well, then. And if we should dispose—together—of Mr. Patrick Fecking Kelly, what then? How do we come to terms between us?"

"I'm thinking we share downtown. A reasonable division."

Dwyer's eyebrows leaped upward. "Share, is it? Blow me! Well, I suppose stranger things have happened. Meanwhile, you look after that pretty little wife of yours, eh?"

Mitch got to his feet. "I intend to." And he did.

He went out into the autumn sunlight, where the car waited and a number of his boys with it. They'd been exchanging looks like daggers with an equal number of Dwyer's lads, though so far no trouble had erupted.

Mitch got into the steamcar; his men followed.

"Where to, Boss?"

"Home."

And would Tessa be there when he arrived? If not, where would she be? Off visiting her fancy man—again?

Mitch had no doubt that's where she'd gone last time. Marty had told him how she'd asked him to wait at the park and gone walking off south down Delaware. Being no fool, Marty had followed at a discreet distance.

And seen which house she'd entered.

A bit of circumspect investigation had told Mitch who owned that house, a family named Trask. Once wealthy, they'd invested in clockwork rather than steamworks and, when clockworks became secondary, lost big. Now, like a lot of other flashes in the pan, they'd spent beyond their means and were hurting.

It seemed Mitch would have to pay yet another call. On Mr. Richard Trask.

Chapter Twenty

"I am so pleased to see you again, Mrs. Carter," said Lily Michaels, gazing at Tessa with large, impossibly blue eyes.

"And I you, Mrs. Michaels. But please call me Tessa."

The automaton, so very difficult to identify as a mechanical, inclined her head. "Only if you will call me Lily, in turn. I hope we will be friends."

"I would like that." Tessa smiled, and meant it. She'd come to this second meeting at the Meadows Club as prearranged in hopes of encountering Richard, and found Mrs. Michaels instead. So far, Richard hadn't showed, but Tessa genuinely liked the automaton, and Lily's company would make a great cover till he did arrive—or didn't.

Politely she said, "Is Mr. Michaels not with you?"

"Rey is at work," Lily confided. "He has a very important job, you know."

"Oh?" Tessa thought of the big man with the careful brown eyes and tumbled shock of brown hair. "What's his line of business?"

"The transportation of corpses."

"I beg your pardon?" Tessa must have heard that wrong.

But Mrs. Michaels answered proudly, "It is his job to collect deceased clients—human ones—who have died at their homes or elsewhere, and carry them back to McMahon's Coffin Shop, where he is employed. They produce a wonderful product, as I can attest, having spent the night in one. Though, of course, I do not remember much, having been shut off at the time."

Tessa wondered if she'd slipped somehow, unnoticed, into a crazed, parallel dimension.

"As far as I know," Lily Michaels rattled on, "McMahon's has never built a coffin specifically for an automaton. We are usually scrapped when we cease to function—at least, the metal parts are."

Tessa could not help but stare. With her golden curls piled beneath a clever little blue hat and her trim figure in a simple dress, Lily Michaels could not look more human.

She wished suddenly she could hear Lily's whole story, how she'd ended up married to a human. Of course, the large automaton wedding that had taken place last June in the park on Delaware was still big news. But automatons married other automatons, right?

"I am glad, Tessa, you are here today. It is to be a very important meeting. Oh, and look—another new arrival."

So distracted had Tessa become by the paradox of Lily Michaels, she'd failed to notice the young man come in. Now her heart leaped alarmingly, and the breath stuck in her throat.

Richard.

He paused just inside the meeting room and their eyes met.

"Oh, ah," she said to Lily, "I know him, actually. An acquaintance of mine."

"How splendid. We need all the members we can

attract. Will you introduce me to him?"

"Of course."

They crossed to Richard's side while Tessa fought to disguise the extent of her relief at seeing him.

Her voice quivered when she said, "Mrs. Michaels, I would like you to meet Richard Trask. I spoke to him about your marvelous charity work and asked him to attend today."

"Very pleased to meet you, Mr. Trask." Lily shook his hand; Tessa wondered if he guessed she was mechanical. So far he'd spared barely a glance for anyone but Tessa.

"Charmed," he said, displaying some of the warmth that had first attracted Tessa.

"I was just saying to Mrs. Carter that today is very important to our mission."

"And exactly what is your mission, Mrs. Michaels? Mrs. Carter did try to explain, but as a newcomer I'd like to learn all I can."

"We aim to alleviate the suffering of orphaned children in this city, either through adoption or reform."

"Reform?"

"Of the orphanages. Did you know, Mr. Trask, there is no governing body for these institutions? No overseers? Anyone can set up and open what they call an orphanage and, henceforth, sue for funds both from the city and private donors. With very few exceptions, conditions in these houses are appalling. Children rarely see benefit from the money meant to feed and house them. It goes into the pockets of those supposed to care for them, instead."

"How—uh—admirable of you to take an interest." Richard shot Tessa an incredulous glance.

"Someone must," Lily said very earnestly indeed, for an automaton. "My husband first discovered the plight of these children when he went to collect the little ones who had died there. You would not believe how many perish alone and unloved."

"I see."

"My husband and I hope to adopt, since we will never have children of our own."

"Ah—" Richard faltered.

"Today," Lily announced, "we plan to stage a raid."

"I beg your pardon?"

At that moment an older gentleman whom Tessa had met at the previous meeting called them to order. Mr. Ellison had gray hair and tiny spectacles, but he spoke like a Roman general.

"Ladies and gentlemen, I ask you on this day to harness your sensibilities and marshal your courage. You will see things that cause you outrage and rouse your ire. You will want to act, perhaps to become physically violent. Please remember this is a fact-finding mission—a sortie, so to speak, a way to make aware those in charge of the heinous prisons known as orphanages that someone is watching them."

"What have you got me into?" Richard whispered in Tessa's ear. His warm breath tickled her neck and made her shiver.

"I'm not quite sure," she responded. What she'd expected to be another genteel meeting—an excuse to see him—seemed to have transformed into something quite different.

Mr. Ellison's audience responded to him with enthusiasm. Tessa felt a little frisson go through the room. Mrs. Michaels listened like a woman enrapt.

Or perhaps like an automaton.

"There seem to be eight of us here today," Mr. Ellison continued. "We will embark in two carriages and descend on the chosen orphanage unannounced."

"Which orphanage?" asked a middle-aged gentleman.

"I have selected at random from a list of the worst offenders. We shall, today, tour the Home For Abandoned Children on Elm Street."

A woman asked, "What if they refuse to let us in?"

"Mrs. Roberts, we are prepared for that eventuality. We have a police sergeant on call, one sympathetic to our cause. Since this institution takes donations from the public, we intend to impose our right to see just how those funds are being spent."

"My God," Richard breathed. "Tessa—"

"I'm sorry," she whispered. "I had no idea."

"Officer Fagan awaits us at the address. Shall we carry on?"

Tessa managed to maneuver herself next to Richard in the carriage. Under cover of her skirt, their fingers meshed and held; her heart thudded. Worth anything, she decided, to be with him this way.

Did he feel the same? She shot a look at him from the corner of her eye. Golden hair, perfect profile…there could be no one else for her.

Unexpectedly, an image of Mitch Carter superimposed itself over Richard's countenance. She jerked in reaction, and Richard turned his head.

"What is it? What's wrong?"

The other two passengers in their carriage looked at her also. She fumbled for something to say.

"I hope this will not prove too distressing."

The elderly Miss Carroll, who with her sister comprised their fellow passengers, smiled acerbically. "Courage, my dear. If we cannot stand to tour these places, how much worse for the wee ones forced to exist there?"

And Richard's fingers squeezed Tessa's in reassurance.

The building before which both carriages drew up had a grim façade of weathered wood and bars on the lower windows. A tall policeman clad all in blue waited on the pavement out front. Mr. Ellison disembarked to speak with him while Richard handed all the ladies from their carriage.

Even as they approached, Tessa could hear the officer's Irish brogue. "—want no trouble. Understood? Mr. Ellison, your attorney was after telling us you just want a tour of the premises."

Mrs. Michaels stepped forward. "Good afternoon, Sergeant Fagan."

He smiled at her. "Mrs. Michaels."

"How is your lovely lady?"

"Very well, indeed. And your husband?"

"Very well also. Are you certain the officials who run this place will let us in?"

"Quite frankly, I don't suppose they'll be too happy about it. But the law is the law in this city—institutions that accept public funds or donations must be willing to open their doors to inspection when requested. I'll do my best to enforce that and get you in. But as I said, there will be no trouble, mind?" The officer inspected them all through bright blue eyes. "Whatever you see in there," he jerked his head toward the building, "it's best to keep your opinions to yourselves."

The crusaders exchanged glances. "Understood," said Mr. Ellison. "Let us get on with it."

Chapter Twenty-One

"Out of the question."

The man who faced off against them in the grim front hallway of the orphanage had a healthy set of jowls and eyes cold enough to freeze alcohol. He'd appeared from the doorway of an inner office when Sergeant Fagan pounded on the door—Tessa could see that much through the wavy skylights of the entryway—but refused to allow them in any farther. "This is a private institution. I have no intention of admitting you."

Sergeant Fagan stared him in the eye—not an easy feat since the police officer topped the jowly man by at least a head. "*Sor*, there's a city ordinance says that any institution that accepts donated funds must be accountable to the public as to how those funds are spent."

"On paper, yes. Officer, we issue our annual report. I suggest any interested parties"—he swept the rest of them with a glare—"should peruse that information. Nothing in the law states I must admit a boatload of do-gooders without advance notice."

Mrs. Michaels stepped up onto the step beside Sergeant Fagan. "What, sir, would be the purpose of an inspector giving advance notice? You would quite likely correct what violations you could beforehand."

"We just want to see where your donors' money is

going, sir. Surely that is perfectly reasonable," Mrs. Roberts pressed.

The jowly man glared at her. "And are you a donor?"

"I have contributed in the past, sir, yes, and I demand admittance."

An angry flush rose to the man's cheeks. "No."

Sergeant Fagan spoke, "Then, *sor*, I am afraid I shall have to issue a citation and ask you to accompany me to the station."

"I can't do that. I have no one here to look after the children, except some steam units."

Sergeant Fagan tipped his head. "Then your easiest course, *sor*, may be to allow the inspection." He pulled a notebook from his pocket. "You are Mr. Agnostus Grupp? Administrator of the Home for Abandoned Children?"

"I am."

Sergeant Fagan made a notation on his pad. "Duly registered."

Grupp grunted and stepped back into the hallway; the rest of them followed.

The first thing that hit Tessa was the smell, a heavy fugue that thickened the air and nearly stoppered her throat. Second was the sound of sobbing at a distance.

Not so surprising, that. Children cried—often in anger or demand. But she heard a different note to this wailing—the sound of weariness or defeat.

These children did not expect anyone to respond to their cries.

Officer Fagan made a gesture and stationed himself at the door.

Mr. Ellison turned to Grupp. "Where are your

charges schooled? Fed? Where do they sleep?"

"They do not take lessons as such. I have a steam unit that instructs them in their A-B-Cs and 1-2-3s."

"Then," asked one of the Miss Carrolls, "how do they pass their time?"

"In learning a trade, of course, so they may be productive citizens."

"A trade?" Mr. Ellison cocked an eyebrow.

Mr. Grupp sighed. "Come along."

The house became more distressing the farther they penetrated. A large, cavernous room, now empty, boasted a few tables and led to a kitchen staffed by three battered mechanicals, all of which ignored their presence.

"How many children do you house, Mr. Grupp?" asked Mr. Ellison.

"It varies. Some leave. Or die. Others get dropped off like bundles of dirty laundry."

"Leave?" inquired Miss Carroll.

"Some run away," Mr. Grupp told her tersely. "Here is the gallery where the children work at their trade."

He opened a door onto a still larger room. Tessa, peering around Mrs. Michaels' shoulder, took a glimpse into what looked like a hell.

Long tables had been set up the whole length of the room. At these stood ranks of children aged from what appeared to be toddler to teen, all busy with their hands. Dim light and a lack of windows left them in dense gloom.

"What are they doing?" asked Mrs. Michaels even as every small head turned toward the door.

"Sorting metal."

"I beg your pardon?" Tessa surprised herself by asking.

"Scrap from disassembled steam units is brought here. The children sort and classify it by value and usability—"

"With their bare hands?" This from Richard.

Mr. Grupp laughed nervously. "Oh, there's nothing harmful in it."

"And this is meant to prepare them for a future career—how?" demanded Mr. Ellison.

"They might well become scrap collectors themselves, or even work in steam unit construction, since they are so familiar with the components."

Mrs. Michaels tipped her head in a characteristic fashion. "Mr. Grupp, I can hear children crying."

Indeed, the terrible drone continued somewhere, now closer by.

"Oh, that would be from the infirmary. There are always a few ailing, or claiming to be sick so they can get off work."

"I would like to see the infirmary," Mrs. Michaels said firmly.

"Out of the question," said Mr. Grupp again.

"I'm afraid I must insist."

"I cannot allow it. You might acquire an illness there."

Mrs. Michaels stepped up to him. "I, sir, am not human and therefore cannot contract human diseases."

"Eh?"

"I am, in fact, a hybrid automaton. Allow me to view this infirmary."

Apparently robbed of further objections by his surprise, Mr. Grupp led her off. The rest of them stood where they were, whispering furiously.

"What kind of place is this?" Richard asked Tessa, his blue eyes wide. "What have you dragged me into?"

"I am sorry, Richard, I had no idea it would be this bad. But you must admit there's reason to push for change."

He lowered his voice still further. "I'm no activist, Tessa. I only came along so I could be with you."

"I know. Now that we've seen conditions, though, surely you want to effect change. It's so awful."

"Awful? I'll have nightmares, and I haven't even seen the infirmary."

"I don't think I'd want to."

"Tessa, I…"

Richard failed to complete the thought when Mrs. Michaels came back down the hallway with her head high and Mr. Grupp at her side. The rest of the group waited for her to speak; she did not disappoint.

"Five children languish in the bare and comfortless chamber Mr. Grupp insists on calling an infirmary," she told the group, no emotion visible on her face. "Alone, without so much as a single steam unit in attendance." She paused and added concisely, "Their cries go unheard and unanswered."

Her listeners stiffened in outrage. Mr. Grupp flushed with annoyance. From down the hallway, Tessa could still hear a child crying.

What did that do to a child, she wondered—to be left wailing endlessly with no one to come? She could not remember a time when her mother, her nurse, or another family member had failed to comfort her in a time of distress.

She did not want to imagine weeping alone. Yet

had fate dictated differently, a life beginning in such a place as this might well have been hers.

The luck of the draw—that alone separated these children from others.

"Now, madam," Mr. Grupp began defensively, "you must sympathize with my position."

"Your position? Yours?" Tessa almost fancied steam came out of Lily Michaels' ears—quite possible, as it happened.

"I have no funds to assign a steam unit to the infirmary. It would not pay. Sometimes there are no children there—should I purchase coal for nothing? That, madam, would be poor use of funds, indeed."

Mrs. Michaels stepped up to him. "Coal? Do you not also pay your mechanicals a wage, sir?"

"I paid good money to purchase them. Why should I also waste funds on them? Do I pay the cooker in the kitchen a wage?"

Mr. Ellison quickly stepped in. "Sir, how many steam units do you employ? I have seen only those in the kitchen and the two serving as overseers in the work room."

"There is another, currently broken down."

"Five units for the whole house? That is all?"

"That's plenty—they can run all day and all night. Who are you people to come in here questioning me? I have very limited funds with which to operate this house and see to the children's needs."

One of the Misses Carroll laughed incredulously. "Is that what you call it?"

"You seem, sir," Mr. Ellison took it up, "to be well dressed and well fed. Funds enough for that, eh? And I assume you take a wage. How much?"

"I do not have to tell you that. Get out! You've had your damned tour. Leave before I complain to the police officer."

They returned to the hallway where Sergeant Fagan waited. He ushered them out, and they stood in a little flock on the sidewalk, heads together.

"Abominable!" seethed Miss Carroll. "Mrs. Michaels, tell us what you saw in the infirmary."

Lily Michaels' expression did not change, yet Tessa fancied she caught anger in her pale blue eyes. "A barren room, narrow cots with only a thin blanket each. Bars on the windows. The children appeared quite ill. I suggest, if we can afford it, a doctor should be sent in."

"We will afford it," Mr. Ellison declared, "even if I have to pay out of my own pocket. Officer," he turned to Sergeant Fagan, "what can be done?"

The tall sergeant looked sincerely regretful. "Not much, I'm sorry to say. There are few ordinances regulating such places."

"Then I suggest," said Mrs. Wright, "we organize to enact such ordinances. And I further suggest we meet at the Meadows Club in four days' time to launch another such raid. Mr. Ellison, will you choose our next target?"

"I will, Mrs. Wright. Meanwhile, any contributions to this cause are welcome."

Both Misses Carroll dug into their pocketbooks, as did Tessa; Mitch gave her a generous allowance.

Mitch. It hit her suddenly like a solid blow to the gut—her husband had grown up in just such an institution as this, and had escaped as soon as he could manage it.

So that was the answer to her question of what these places did to a child.

Richard, standing with his hands stuffed into his pockets, spoke in her ear. "I'm afraid I have no ready funds to spare."

"That's all right." Tessa gazed into his clear blue eyes. "You will meet me again at the Meadows Club? In four days' time?"

His expression became ardent, and his fingers once more brushed hers. "I will."

Chapter Twenty-Two

"You're very quiet tonight, Tessa. Are you feeling unwell?"

Mitch and his wife sat alone at their dining table, served by a single steam unit. So far, he'd watched her toy with her food, push the excellent roast around the plate, and do no more than sip her wine. Conversation had been nonexistent.

She raised her lovely green eyes to his face and seemed to study him anew. Even such simple regard from her heated his blood. He wanted her again, longed to snatch her up from the damned table, carry her up the stairs, and woo her till she moaned his name.

He didn't suppose such behavior would be considered completely civilized. And he was supposed to be civilized, wasn't he? He at least wore a veneer of civilization.

"Forgive me," Tessa said. "I was thinking about my day."

Her day. She'd gone out—he knew that much—to the Meadows Club. What else had she done? Had she seen him—Richard Trask?

"Ah." He pretended mere casual interest. "A pleasant day, I hope. What did you do?"

She continued to gaze at him in that disquieting way, as if she could see right inside him. "Charity work."

"You've decided, then? Chosen your—er—cause?"

"I have, or rather I think it's chosen me. Today, we toured one of the city's orphanages."

That, too, hit him like a blow to the gut. He tried not to let his surprise—his dismay—show. Very casually indeed, he said, "Oh? Which one?"

"It's called the Home for Abandoned Children on Elm Street."

Well, at least it wasn't bloody God-damned Carter's. "I'm not sure I like the idea of you going to such places."

"No, it wasn't pleasant, but it's necessary, don't you think? The underbelly of the beast must be exposed."

"Beast?"

"The atrocities must be brought to light, revealed."

"Atrocities."

"If what goes on there isn't brought out in the open, nothing can be done to help those children."

He laughed harshly. "They're lost souls. Nothing can be done for them. They have to climb up on their own feet and get out."

"Like you did."

There it was. The truth. "Yes."

"But some of them will never make it out."

"You're right."

"Many aren't as strong as you." She laid her fork beside her plate. "I will tell you frankly—may I speak frankly?"

"I wish you would."

"After what I saw today, I can't imagine how any of them survive."

Mitch tried to remember what he knew about the

Home for Abandoned Children and failed to come up with any specifics. Didn't matter—one of those hell holes was as bad as the next.

And now a bunch of do-gooders, that included his wife, thought they could go in there and—what? Change the parameters of hell?

The little clockwork dog came up to Tessa's chair, stood on its rear legs, and pawed her knee. She lifted it into her lap.

He waited till she had settled the toy before he asked, "What did you and your group hope to accomplish by touring one of those places?"

"It wasn't a tour so much as a raid. We plan to do it again and again at other institutions. And what we hope to accomplish, ultimately, is reform—improvement for those children, change to the way they're treated." Earnestly, she added, "We're having a physician sent in, for one thing. Mrs. Michaels said the children in the infirmary are in dire need of one, and that terrible man who runs the house won't pay."

"Mrs. Michaels—the automaton. How can an automaton have sympathy for anyone?"

Tessa stroked the head of the dog. "You'd be surprised. I was surprised. She's very warm and caring and—she means to fight for those children." She gave Mitch a close look. "I hope you won't object if I say I'd like her for a close friend."

Mitch's head spun. That's all he needed, his wife befriending one of the mechanicals like the ones he was up against for downtown. What had become of his life, since he first laid eyes on Tessa Verdun?

His single weakness.

"I've told you, I'm happy for you to have friends.

But I'm not sure I'm comfortable with this crusade you've chosen."

She looked him in the eye again, glaring now. "Too bad. You bade me choose an interest. I have, and it's one in which I feel completely invested."

Yeah, but why did it have to be the one that he, Mitch, had lived?

She tossed her head. "I should think you would take an interest, since you have personal experience with what these poor children endure on a daily basis."

Poor children. The last thing he wanted was her pity. Anyway, how could he explain to her without exposing vulnerabilities he'd spent a lifetime trying to conceal that he couldn't even bear to think about the orphanage? Just being reminded that such places still existed felt like poking a burning brand into a lurid wound. His best chance at survival came from forgetting what he could.

Except he got reminded every time he looked at one of the boys who'd been at Carter's with him. And now, when he looked at Tessa.

"I've no time for all that," he told her dismissively. "And I want you to be careful if you visit those places."

"Oh, I am in very good company."

Why did that assurance make Mitch feel even more uneasy?

And wasn't it ironic how his wife could feel friendship for some hybrid automaton and love for a mechanical dog, but none for him?

****

"It's a message, Boss. From Danny Dwyer. He wants you to come at once."

Mitch looked up from his desk into Tiny Haskins'

excited face. Morning sunlight bled through the windows, its dirty color predicting rain. He'd had very little sleep last night, and what he'd managed to snatch had been colored by evil dreams which left him in a foul mood.

"Since when do I jump to Danny Dwyer's demands?"

"He said it's important. And that you two have an agreement."

That caught Mitch's interest. "He send a messenger?"

"Yeah, Boss."

"The messenger still here? Send him in."

The fellow who sloped into the office wore a flat cap which he doffed in Mitch's presence; there ended any show of respect. With red hair and an ugly, cunning face, he had "Irish" written all over him.

Mitch fixed him with a hard eye. "What's this all about?"

"Danny has something to show you, Mr. Carter."

"To show me?" Mitch scowled.

"Aye. He asks you to meet him at the boathouse down at the end of Erie Street."

"What boathouse? There are plenty of sheds down there."

"I'll take you if you like, show you the one."

Mitch didn't like; this had danger written all over it. Still, if Dwyer wanted to lure him someplace in order to work him over, he'd hardly do it in broad daylight.

Curiosity chewed at him—what could Dwyer possibly have to show him?

He shoved aside the paper he'd been reading, a list of late rents.

"You go ahead," he told the man. "I'll follow with a couple of my boys."

"All right. But Danny says don't bring your car."

"Why not?"

"Everybody in the city knows that car, and you're not gonna want to be seen. Right so?"

"What am I supposed to do? Walk?"

"Heaven forfend the King of Prospect should have to hoof it anywhere. I've a steamcab waiting. We take it part way, get off and take a carriage, then walk."

Such secrecy—what the hell could Dwyer want? "All right. Tiny, you come with me. And fetch Lou." Lou—another alumnus of Carter's—never went anywhere without being armed.

It started to rain as they exited the first cab and, by the time they set out on foot for the waterfront, it was pounding down. The foul weather had no visible impact on Danny Dwyer, whom Mitch found lounging outside one of the boathouses that lined the pier. A number of Dwyer's lads also stood about; they eyed Mitch and his two men the way sated lions might size up antelope, with lazy interest.

Dwyer stepped forward and gave Mitch an indolent grin. "And how might you be, sir, on such a bonny morning?"

"Bonny? It's bucketing down."

"What I have inside makes it bonny." Dwyer laid his finger aside his nose. "But careful what you say, now. It has ears."

Ears?

"You just step inside with me, yeah?"

Dwyer cracked the door of the boathouse; the two of them stepped in out of the rain. The interior space—

maybe ten by twelve feet—lay littered with nautical trappings, coils of rope, oars and tools, even a crude winch. On a stack of folded tarps dead center sat—

A woman.

Perhaps thirty years old, she had light brown hair and wore a good quality dress of russet red, from beneath the hem of which peeked the toes of black boots. Mitch couldn't see her eyes or much of her face because she also wore a blindfold. Her arms were bound tightly to her sides.

Mitch swore with feeling and turned incredulous eyes on Dwyer, who grinned at him like a madman.

The woman perched on the tarps shuddered even though she couldn't see them.

When Dwyer spoke, he disguised his voice, making it rough and gravelly, and nearly losing the brogue. "My friend, I'd like you to meet Mrs. Patrick Kelly."

"Shit!" Mitch exclaimed.

"Is that any way to talk in front of a lady?"

"Who are you?" Mrs. Kelly demanded. She made an effort at composure, but Mitch heard her terror. "What do you want?"

"How—?" Mitch began.

"Snatched her last night from right outside her own house."

"My husband is a police officer. You—"

"We know that, missus. And nothing bad's going to happen to you. I just wanted my friend here to see you, wanted to show him what I can do."

A message, right enough, Mitch thought as his heart clenched in his chest. One meant for Patrick Kelly—and for him, also. It might just as well be Tessa

Ones she knew he could fulfill. Would it be so wrong? To go with him into her bedroom, take off her clothes, and let him make her feel all that again?

Yes. Yes, it would be wrong. For one thing, she must think of Richard, the man she truly did love.

"I'm sorry," she said with some genuine regret. "I have plans to go out this afternoon."

"Out? Where?"

"Another meeting at the Meadows Club."

"Ah." His eyes narrowed. Was he suspicious? He couldn't possibly know she met Richard at those meetings.

"Perhaps another time," she suggested. Later tonight he might come to her room. Perhaps it would still be raining. And in the dark she could once more forget who he was.

No.

"Of course. Enjoy your meeting."

"I will." Something made her add, "Thank you for the chocolates. But—you don't need to keep buying me gifts."

"You won't let me give you what I want to give you—what else can I do?"

And there it was right out in the open between them, the searing memory of that night when she'd let him give her what he wanted, what she could see he still desired every time he looked at her.

She trembled. For an instant the composure she fought so hard to maintain crumbled—she feared what he might see in her eyes.

"I—I must go. I don't want to be late." She fled out the door and never realized, until she climbed into the car, she still had the chocolates in her hand.

****

"Mrs. Carter, are you well? You seem out of sorts."

Tessa turned her head when Lily Michaels spoke in her ear. They'd just finished their meeting, making plans for the raid on their next orphanage target, and still sat side by side on the folding chairs.

"I'm fine, and please, I asked you to call me Tessa, or Tess."

"Of course, Tess. I would like to think we are friends."

"I like to believe so, too."

"Friends confide in one another. Such as when they feel ill."

"I do not feel ill. Really, I just have something on my mind."

"Is it Mr. Trask?" Lily directed a glance across the room at Richard, who stood locked in conversation with Mr. Ellison.

"Why would you ask that?"

"I am an automaton, highly trained in picking up nuances in humans and adapting my responses to them. Truthfully, I can't keep from doing it. And forgive me saying, but it would not require such abilities to notice how the two of you look at one another."

"Oh." Tessa flushed in dismay.

"Yet you are married to another man."

"It's quite complicated."

"Perhaps you would like to confide in me."

"Oh. I don't think…"

"I am quite reliable and was designed to keep secrets. I will, in actual fact, not breathe a word." Lily emitted what, for her, must pass for laughter, a soft fluttery sound.

"That's very kind of you."

"It is what friends do. Since the meeting has ended, I suggest we withdraw to a café and have tea. I cannot, of course, actually drink the tea, but I view it as a charming exercise."

"All right. Let me just say goodbye to—"

"Your lover? Right enough."

Tessa arose and went to Richard, who'd just finished his conversation with Mr. Ellison and turned to face her. They clasped hands.

"Mr. Trask, I will see you for the next raid, the day after tomorrow, will I not?"

"Tess"—he gazed into her eyes—"this is all well and good, but I wish to be alone with you."

Her heart thudded. "I'd like that too. I promise I'll think of something and let you know the day after tomorrow. Meanwhile, we must be discreet. Mrs. Michaels already suspects."

Richard shot a look at Lily. "She's just a machine."

"A very perceptive one."

"Don't worry about it." Richard's eyes burned. "Seeing you like this, not being able to touch you, will drive me mad. We need privacy."

Tessa couldn't misunderstand what he meant. But was that what she wanted to be? A woman who lied to one man, and went outside her marriage for sexual gratification from another?

One thing she knew for certain: since her night with Mitch, she wanted—no, needed—to experience such gratification again. Maybe Richard could soothe her desire.

****

No one in the busy tea shop looked at them

askance. No one, apparently, took Lily Michaels for anything but human. To Tessa's initial surprise, Lily ordered tea but merely played with the handle of her cup, her attention fastened on Tessa.

"Now, Tessa, you may safely unburden yourself to me. What is troubling you?"

Tessa searched Lily's pale blue eyes. "You promise you will say nothing to anyone?"

"I promise."

Tessa curled her fingers around her cup. "Mr. Trask and I have a friendship. It existed before I married Mr. Carter."

"Mr. Trask is your lover," Lily remarked, as she had before. At Tessa's look of consternation, she went on, "I understand about lovers. I have done much reading, and they are a common feature in literature."

"I see. Well, Richard isn't my lover—not in a physical sense. Not yet. That's the thing. There's a moral line, and I'm not sure I'm ready to cross it."

"Ah. But you want to cross it?"

Did she? She craved physical contact, that couldn't be denied. But how could she expect this automaton to understand such impulses?

"I'm not sure. Going outside my marriage would— well, it would change everything."

Lily tipped her head, apparently considering it. "You are a newlywed, just like me. Newlyweds are known for indulging their sexual impulses with their spouses. May I ask why you do not turn to your husband for release? Are you not attracted to him?"

Well, now, that was the question, wasn't it? Right out in the open, and no mistake. The automaton hadn't failed to zero in on the aspect of Tessa's situation that made her most uncomfortable.

She flushed as she replied, "Well...I must admit I never expected to be attracted to him. The marriage, if you must know, was thrust upon me. Not my choice."

"I understand."

"Do you?"

"Tessa, as I mentioned before, I once was forced to serve as a prostitute at a place called the Crystal Palace, before it burned down. I had many things thrust upon me, none of which I welcomed."

"Oh. Yes." Tessa blinked at her. "You did mention that." And it had been the talk of the city for a time, though her parents had tried to keep the details from her ears. "I'm so sorry."

"Do not be. You had no part in oppressing me, and I am now free, living with the man I adore. We must try and find you a similar happiness."

"I'm not sure we can."

"Do not give up. You do not love your husband?"

"No."

"But you are sexually attracted to him?"

Tessa wasn't sure she should confess this part, even to an automaton sworn to secrecy. "He and I— well, there was this one night we spent together."

"As lovers?"

"Yes. Now I can't seem to get it out of my mind. And I think—I fear—he loves me, or at least believes that he does."

"Ah. You do not wish to hurt him."

"I don't think it's that. He's a hard man, a tough man. I'm not sure that I could hurt him."

Lily corrected softly, "You do not wish to betray him, after sharing intimacy with him."

Tessa raised troubled eyes once more. "Perhaps that's it."

Lily tipped her head to one side for a moment. "Would you welcome advice?"

Would she? "Yes."

"As I see it, you have two choices: if you crave further intimacy, you must either break your restraints and go with your lover, or—"

"Or?"

"Seek intimate relations with your husband once again, and that may well be your safest course of action."

Chapter Twenty-Four

Tessa watched her husband's hand as he raised the glass of whiskey and sipped from it. An after-dinner drink—they'd just finished yet another awkward meal together and repaired to the parlor. She felt if she didn't break the silence between them soon, talk about something important, she'd lose her mind.

Instead she found herself focusing on his hand— the same that had once cupped her breast in the dark— and his lips that now gleamed with amber liquid. Those lips had been all over her body, in places she herself rarely touched.

She wasn't even attracted to him.

Why then did she burn at those memories and tremble at the thought of doing it all again?

He laid his drink aside. One thing she could say about Mitch Carter, he didn't drink much. Taking a whiskey, for him, seemed more like a social habit than a vice. But he had plenty of other vices.

From across the elegant, carved table that fronted the sofa, where she sat, he looked at her almost as if he heard her thoughts.

God forfend that he could!

"How was your meeting?"

"Productive. Afterward, I went for tea with Lily Michaels."

She wondered what would happen if she asked him

to go upstairs with her. Well, she was pretty sure what would happen; she could tell by the way he looked at her. Mitch always looked at her as if he was hungry. For the same thing she craved? Oh, yes. If they did go upstairs together, things could become explosive. She would come apart in his arms—like before.

But she didn't love him or like him much, or even respect him…and what about Richard?

Should she be worrying about betraying Richard, or her husband? And would it be such a sin, just one more night with Mitch?

She knew she had only to say the word. A heady feeling.

"The automaton?" he asked, and Tessa, who'd completely lost track of the conversation had to fumble over to what he referred.

"I think she's going to become a true friend. Odd, isn't it?"

"Not so odd, given the bond you've formed with the clockwork dog." Mitch nodded at Valerie, who sat at Tessa's feet. "But surely you have plenty of other friends."

"A few." She'd lost touch with most of those from her past life, as she now thought of it. She'd never been the sort of girl to surround herself with a crowd of silly gigglers.

"Why don't you see them? I hope you know, Tessa, you're free to invite anyone you wish to this house. Your friends will be welcome. I wish you to think of this as your home. I wish," Mitch added deliberately, "for you to be happy."

Happy. With him. The message resounded in the quiet room and shone clearly in his eyes.

Was there nothing for which she couldn't ask? For his time, his attention? To once more lie in his arms in the dark, while every inhibition flew away from her and those rough hands of his did wicked, wonderful things?

He pressed, "Why haven't you invited anyone here? Is it because you're ashamed?"

"Ashamed?" she repeated in surprise.

He met her gaze with honesty akin to what she'd seen in Lily Michaels' eyes. "Of our relationship. Of me."

Maybe that made up a component of what she felt. She hadn't wanted her friends from the past to know she'd been pushed into this marriage on her father's behalf—about his debts and the fact that he had, in essence, sold her. And Mitch Carter wasn't the kind of man any young woman of her circle ever imagined she'd wed.

But she shook her head.

A bitter smile twisted his lips. "We've been over this, Tessa, and I thought we agreed to be honest with each other."

"Honest, yes."

"I'm well aware that people in this city talk about me. How I came from the gutter—we talked about that too."

Yes, after he'd made love to her with that thrilling gentleness and fire.

"I've come up in the world. And I can make more changes—for your sake. Just ask me, Tessa." Raw hunger looked at her from his eyes. Tessa drew a breath to reply and at that moment heard a tap at the door.

It opened a crack and one of Mitch's men—Tiny Haskins—looked in.

"A woman to see you, Boss."

"What?" Mitch tore his gaze from Tessa with what seemed an effort and glanced at Haskins. "Not now, Tiny. I'm—occupied."

"Boss, I know. I tried sending her away till tomorrow. She's insistent."

"Give her an appointment."

"Boss," Tiny's eyes widened in distress, "she's out here crying."

Tessa rose to her feet. "You have business. I can go."

"No. Don't." Mitch looked at her again, that longing still bright in his eyes.

Before Tessa could respond, a small woman pressed past Tiny and burst into the room.

****

Damn it all to hell, Mitch thought as anger curled through his belly—the place where constant desire for his wife usually lodged.

Constantly lodged.

He sensed they'd been close to a breakthrough, that something he'd said had reached her at last. That she might even be willing to go upstairs with him and…

He focused, with distaste and outrage, on the woman who'd come pushing into the parlor.. Small and shabby, no taller than Tiny, she wore a brown bonnet and clothes so often washed they'd faded to gray. Mitch knew the look of poverty in this city—so he should— and hardened his heart to it. A reflex, a self-defense mechanism. Pity was a luxury he could not afford.

He, like Tessa, had risen at the interruption. The woman slipped past Tiny, around the table, and threw herself at Mitch's feet.

"Please, sir. You must hear me!" She clasped her hands and stared up at him. "For the sake of my children."

Mitch heard Tessa gasp but didn't spare a glance for her. He stared instead into the woman's worn face. Perhaps thirty years old, she already wore the signs of age; lines marked her forehead, and her reddened, chapped hands looked skeletally thin.

"Get up," he told her through clenched teeth. "Who do you think I am?"

"You're our landlord, Mr. Carter, and the man who holds the power of life and death over us. If we're thrown out into the streets, my children will never survive. They're just little, sir—eighteen months, three years and five years. And the youngest has been ill."

"Mitch," Tessa said.

He did shoot her a look then. She'd gone dead white, and her green eyes burned with dismay.

Again he told the woman, "Get up." He didn't want to touch her; she looked fragile enough to break. But he reached down gingerly and raised her by the elbow. "Who are you?"

Tiny, who lingered just inside the door of the parlor, answered for her. "Mrs. Keller, Boss, from Connecticut Street. Tenant."

"Mrs. Keller, please come back during business hours tomorrow. We'll discuss the matter then."

"I can't, sir. I'm working at the laundry all day long. If I don't show up I'll lose my place, see, and things will be worse than they are, though I can't imagine they could get much worse. So I come to beg you not to throw us out. I've nowhere else to go. My neighbor, Gert, watches the children during the day, but she has a full house, no room for us to stay. And with the baby sick, and the nights getting cold, what will happen to us?"

Mitch drew himself up and deliberately hardened his expression. The city, he told himself, was full of sad stories. He hadn't become successful by listening to them. And he hated scenes.

"Where is your husband, Mrs. Keller?"

"Dead. He died just after the baby was born. Till then he made a decent wage and I was able to stay home."

"How far in arrears is your rent?"

"Three months, sir."

Mitch flicked a look at Tiny. As evidenced in the past, Tiny hadn't lost all his pity and often let such things drag on for too long.

"Your man came this morning, came to the laundry where I work, and told me if I couldn't pay the rent they'd toss my belongings out and chain the door. Please, Mr. Carter, sir, I beseech you for time. For my—"

"My man is quite correct. Three months in arrears gives me more than just cause to evict you."

"Mitch!" Tessa said again.

He went on as if he hadn't heard her, speaking directly into Mrs. Keller's face and destroying all hope. Because, as he knew, false hope made a cruel master. "You've already had all the leniency I can afford."

"But, sir, I've been paying the rent up till now, even if it meant we didn't eat. Just, when Sammy got so sick, I had to use the money I'd put aside for rent in order to pay a doctor. I can give you part of the first month's now—" She broke off to dig in a pocket and came up with a few coins which she extended in the palm of a trembling hand. "Surely this will buy us more time?"

"Mitch," Tessa said for the third time.

He looked at her over little Mrs. Keller's head and nearly came undone. Unshed tears stood bright in her eyes, and her parted lips breathed distress. He wanted to take that look from her; more, he wanted her to think well of him. But he'd been down this road before, in the beginning. He knew one month's grace would lead to two, and thence many, and it would become impossible to toss the little family out.

"Sir," said Mrs. Keller, "without a roof over his head, my baby will die." Tessa stepped forward around the table, to Mrs. Keller's side. "Mitch, I will pay Mrs. Keller's rent."

Mrs. Keller's head whipped around. She stared at Tessa.

From the doorway, Tiny made a sound in his throat—protest, or appreciation?

Dismay seized Mitch, deep and black. "No."

"But why not? Surely my allowance is mine to spend as I choose. You said so. And it's the right thing to do."

"It isn't the right thing to do."

Tessa stamped her foot. "Have you no pity?"

"None. I can't afford it."

"You can. The price of this carpet alone—"

"I'm not talking about money." All too aware they argued in front of Mrs. Keller, to say nothing of Tiny, Mitch snapped, "Please keep out of it."

Tessa's cheeks flamed. She turned to the woman at her side. "Mrs. Keller, what's your address?"

"Number Two Connecticut Street, ma'am. But—"

"Go home to your children. Your back rent will be paid, or forgiven. But you must keep up with it in future. Understand?"

"I promise you, ma'am. Oh, bless you, ma'am. I can't express my gratitude."

Tenderly, Tessa repeated, "Go home to your children."

Tiny saw Mrs. Keller out. The air in the parlor quivered.

"Go ahead and holler at me," Tessa said then. "I know you want to."

"I do not."

"You're going to say I shouldn't interfere."

"So you shouldn't."

She looked him in the eye. He felt the impact all the way to his toes.

"If, Mitch Carter, you ever want relations between us to improve—"

"I do."

"You're going to have to change your ways. Become a different man."

"You want me different?" She wanted him?

"A better man. You could do worse than to take up the habit of philanthropy."

"Philanthropy? Me?" He swallowed. "Tessa, I'm the only man I know how to be."

"Not good enough."

Not good enough? He'd made himself better and better, starting from nothing, and she told him he wasn't good enough? God damn it!

She might as well stab him in the heart.

Chapter Twenty-Five

"A word with you, Mr. Trask, if you don't mind."

The young man who'd just climbed from the steamcab paused on the walkway and turned in inquiry. As soon as he recognized Mitch, his expression changed, brows drawing down and a cautious light invading his eyes.

So, Mitch thought, taking a good look at him, this was what attracted his wife, and held her affections. He had to admit, the last time he'd encountered the fellow, at Hugo Verdun's funeral, his anger and jealousy had kept him from making a fair inspection. Not so, now. The bright autumn sun shone down outside the Trask household, and they stood up close, and personal.

A good-looking devil, and no mistake. Just as Mitch had noted last time, a pretty boy. He had a couple of inches on Mitch—that was what starvation in youth did to a man—with a clear complexion, nearly beardless in the clear light, and golden hair any woman might envy. Long-lashed blue eyes completed the picture.

It fair turned Mitch's stomach that Tessa should prefer this sissy to a real man.

His opinion must have been visible in his eyes; Trask paled and backed up a step. Good healthy fear—well enough. Nice to know the boy had survival instincts.

To be sure, he was nothing more than a boy, surely no older than Tessa at twenty-two. From the hard age of twenty-six, Mitch sneered inwardly.

"Mr. Carter," Trask said, and swallowed convulsively. "May I ask what you're doing here? This is private property."

Mitch smiled. He'd learned from experience that his smiles tended to get people's attention. And they never seemed to provide comfort to their recipients.

"Just a word, as I say. A friendly word. Shall we go inside, or do you want to conduct this business on the street?"

Trask glanced at the house and back at Mitch. "What business?"

"So you prefer to discuss it here? Your decision. I understand you've been seeing my wife."

"No. That is—please come inside."

Mitch followed the young man into a foyer that, for all its grand proportions, had a barren feel to it. The young man shot him an uneasy look before he said, "We'll go into the library where we won't be disturbed."

For a library, the room boasted very few books. It contained merely a large desk, a couple of chairs, a sideboard, and bookcases, most of them bare. Trask crossed to the sideboard and poured himself a drink.

"Will you join me?"

Mitch shook his head. "Too early in the day for me. Besides, I'd like to keep my head clear for this."

"This?"

"Our conversation. It's overdue, don't you think?"

Trask gulped amber liquid from his glass and drew himself up. "Mr. Carter, nothing untoward has happened between your wife and me."

"But you'd like it if something 'untoward' did happen."

"What makes you say that?"

"Just look at her; what man wouldn't? She's the loveliest woman I've ever seen."

"She is very lovely," Trask agreed carefully. "But she and I are just friends."

"You've been meeting her on the sly."

"I haven't. We do meet in the course of our charity work, if that's what you mean."

"Charity work."

"Yes, sir."

"How long have you been involved in this charitable enterprise?"

"Not long. A few months."

"You mean, a couple weeks." Mitch smiled again. "Don't try to mislead me, Mr. Trask. I have sources. Information."

Thoughts—and panic—raced through Trask's blue eyes. "Very well. If you want the truth, Tessa and I were well acquainted before she married you. We did—and still do—hold one another in high esteem."

"I see."

"I daresay I would have asked her to marry me, had I been in a position to propose."

Mitch's heart sank. "You were not in such a position?"

"No, unfortunately. A family situation that included financial constraints."

"I see." Mitch glanced around the room again. "Whatever your connection with my wife—your former connection—I'm here to tell you it needs to end."

Trask bristled. "You can't tell her whom she may or may not see."

"I'm not telling her. I'm telling you."

"You want me to stop seeing her? And what if she finds out it's at your request? She'll hate you forever."

Too true, probably. But Mitch said, "She'll get over her upset. Women always do. I can offer her a good life, after all. Far better than you can offer."

Trask sneered; his lip actually curled up. "You can offer her money and trappings. None of that will win Tessa. And no trappings can disguise what you are."

"What am I?"

"A street tough. A bully. You badger, coerce, and lean on people to get your way."

"Quite true. Just like I'm leaning on you now."

Trask's eyes widened. "Are you threatening me?"

"If that's how you want to interpret my visit. Me, I'd call it a friendly warning. Break off your association with my wife, Trask. End it without letting her know why."

"And if I won't?"

"I don't think you'll like the consequences."

"You suppose you can attack me with impunity?"

"Certainly not. There are laws in this city to protect people from vicious attack. There are also any number of dark streets and alleys, and eyes to tell me where you walk, and when."

"I see."

"Not a threat by any means, just an advisement."

Trask thought about it. His face grew tight. "What reason can I possibly give Tessa for breaking off our friendship?"

"Think of something. Oh, and perhaps you'd like a

little spending money, just something for essentials." Mitch dug into his pocket and deposited a wad of money on the side table.

Trask flushed even deeper red. "You're buying me off?"

"Certainly."

"How dare you assume I can be bought?"

"There are very few men who can't be. Look at it this way, Trask—you get to keep your skin intact and you get to play the part of the upper-crust dandy a while longer."

"I'm not—"

"You are. You just can't see it. Trust me, you don't want to be involved with another man's wife. Especially mine."

Trask looked at the money and at Mitch once again. For an instant Mitch thought Trask would snatch up the pile and toss it back in his face. But he let it lie.

"I'll see myself out, shall I?" Mitch moved to the library door. When he looked back, Trask hadn't stirred so much as a muscle.

****

"Attention, everyone. The carriages have arrived, and we are ready to embark," Mr. Ellison called busily.

"Not yet," Tessa said under her breath. She glanced once more at the entrance of the Meadows Club, hoping to see Richard entering. She couldn't imagine why he hadn't yet arrived.

"What is it?" Lily Michaels leaned over and whispered.

"Richard."

"Your lover?"

"He hasn't arrived, and we're nearly ready to

leave."

"Today," Mr. Ellison announced, "we are planning a raid on Carter's Home for Boys."

That snagged all Tessa's attention. She stared at Mr. Ellison in dismay. He looked back at her.

"This, Mrs. Carter, should be of particular interest to you."

"Yes," she agreed faintly while her heart sank. She'd had no clear idea the place still operated.

"It is," Mr. Ellison went on, "one of the most notorious and worst-run orphanages in the city. We may have difficulty persuading them to let us in. Sergeant Fagan is, unfortunately, not available today. But fortunately Mrs. Michaels has put us in touch with her good friend Officer Kelly, who is meeting us there and may be of assistance. If we do not want to keep him waiting unnecessarily, we must leave at once."

"Where can Richard be?" Tessa asked Lily.

"Perhaps he was unavoidably detained. Here." Lily tucked Tessa's arm into hers. "We shall go together."

Tessa's first sight of Carter's Home for Boys, located on lower Tupper, nearly made her forget Richard. Its cold edifice—made of gray block stone— was not improved by the trails of rust running down from the barred windows, like tears.

Mitch had lived here. Mitch had grown up here from an infant, taken the place's name for his own.

Suddenly, Tessa could feel her heart breaking; she wanted to weep.

Officer Kelly, as reassuringly big, strapping, and human-appearing as the last time Tessa saw him, stood at the gate. Lily Michaels stepped from the carriage and hurried up to him.

"Patrick, how are you? And how is Rose doing?"

Before Kelly could answer, Lily turned to Tessa, still at her side and said, "You remember Rose, Patrick's wife? Recently she was abducted from her own front step and held for a short time on the waterfront. She was soon released, not much harmed but terribly frightened. But, Pat, how is she recovering from the ordeal?"

"She remains shaken, Lily. I have left her now with friends, including Ginny Landry. Rose cannot stand to be alone. Given her past history of imprisonment and abuse, it was perhaps the worst thing that might have befallen her."

"Are there any suspects?"

"Several suspects, yes, but as yet no solid proof. She was snatched from behind while entering the house and immediately blindfolded, you understand. She could give us little information. But I have all the members of the Irish Squad working on it." Something glinted in the automaton's eyes. "We will find the miscreants."

"She saw no one?"

"No, unfortunately. She had just returned from shopping with parcels in her hands and had no chance to turn before being subdued. However, she did hear voices."

"How terrifying," Tessa murmured, and the automaton switched his bright gaze to her face.

"Pat, you remember my friend Mrs. Carter?" Lily asked.

"Of course. Yes, Mrs. Carter, my wife Rose was quite terrified by her unfortunate experience. I have done my best to reassure her. But she has a past that lends her to fear that she may be snatched again."

Tessa murmured, "Everyone should feel safe in her own home."

"I tend to agree." Pat Kelly glanced behind at the ugly orphanage. "I doubt, however, any of the residents of this house feel particularly safe. This may be a distressing visit, ladies. Are you prepared?"

Was she? Tessa could only wonder.

Chapter Twenty-Six

Tessa let herself into the front hallway of the house on Prospect Avenue and stood for a moment with her eyes closed, seeking a measure of composure. The place seemed blessedly quiet after what she'd experienced at Carter's, and smelled clean and fresh.

The sights, sounds, and smells of the orphanage returned to her again in a staggering wave. How could anyone endure living there a single day?

How had her husband endured?

That place, that awful place.

Patrick Kelly had fought to get them in, using a combination of unflappable insistence and reference to the law. Unlike Officer Fagan, who'd waited at the outer door, he'd shepherded them around the institution, and she'd been very glad for his presence.

Grim, cold, and terrifying...Tessa did not have words enough to condemn Carter's. It should be burned to the ground, except she suspected Hell might not burn.

At parting, Mr. Ellison, no doubt sensing how shaken they all were, had said to them, "I know we have witnessed some terrible things today. But remember that kindness is a strength and that kind people, working together, can effect miraculous change."

For some reason those words stuck with Tessa,

echoing inside her head along with the whimpers and sobs.

The mechanical maid rolled out into the hallway; Tessa sought to pull herself together.

"Doris, is my husband at home?"

"Yes, madam, he is in the parlor."

How was she going to face him? How, knowing what he'd endured. It could not fail to change the way she saw him, now that she knew...

"Madam, this arrived for you earlier."

Doris held out a folded message, which Tessa accepted by reflex. "Oh? Thank you."

"Will you join Mr. Carter in the parlor, madam? Would you like supper?"

"I couldn't possibly eat anything."

The maid trundled out. Tessa unfolded the note and read.

Her knees wobbled, and she nearly fell.

From Richard. He said he'd rethought their association and found there was no future in it. He no longer planned to attend the Meadows Club meetings and believed they should not see each other again.

She backed to the bench against one side of the hall and lowered herself onto it, hands trembling. A succession of emotions tore through her—betrayal, anger, pain. How could he do this to her when they'd had an agreement? When she'd been ready to give herself to him?

Good thing she hadn't, if he found it so easy to abandon her this way.

The emotions, on top of all she'd experienced at Carter's, nearly shattered her. Anger let her blink the tears from her eyes, get up, and walk into the parlor.

****

Mitch glanced up from his newspaper when his wife came into the room. The little clockwork dog, which had been sitting near his feet—for company, he'd almost have said—got up and went to her, its tail wagging madly.

For the first time since he'd brought it to her, Tessa ignored it.

Instead she stared at Mitch, pale as milk, her lips trembling.

"What is it?" He half started up. "What's happened?"

She didn't answer. His gaze fell to the paper crumpled in her fingers.

"Is it your mother? She's unwell?"

"No. It's not Mother. It's…nothing." She shoved the paper into the pocket of her dress.

"Something's upset you."

Her eyes looked impossibly green in her white face. "We—we raided Carter's today. Oh, Mitch, how did you ever bear it? That terrible place! I can't even imagine…"

He felt the blood rush from his head, which left him dizzy on his feet. "You went there? By God! What possessed you?"

"Mr. Ellison arranged it. He selected it from a list of the city's worst offenders. He wanted us to—to—"

She didn't finish the thought, and Mitch couldn't finish it for her. His throat grew far too tight.

Carter's. He visited the place regularly in his nightmares but wouldn't send his worst enemy there, to say nothing of the woman he'd married.

He wondered if it had changed since old Fink left,

since Mitch had escaped and worked like a boy possessed to buy his companions free.

Judging by Tessa's expression, it hadn't improved much.

Bitterly he said, "Ellison must be a madman, taking you there."

"No, he's very kind, really—a kindly man. He says kindness is a strength, a sort of power. He merely wishes to expose these terrible places for what they are."

"The underbelly of the beast, yes. So you said before. Well, he certainly went for an ugly beast this time."

She said nothing; her lips trembled.

"Here, sit down before you fall. Mind the dog." Taking Tessa's arm, Mitch steered her to the sofa and eased her down. "Let me get you a drink."

"I don't want one."

"It may help."

"There isn't enough whiskey in Buffalo to cure what I'm feeling."

The mechanical dog jumped up on the cushions beside her. She patted it, but her attention remained on Mitch.

"Tell me. Tell me how—" Her voice failed.

"I got out?"

"How you survived."

A crooked, painful smile tugged at Mitch's lips. He sat down next to her and gave her a cool look. "I doubt you want to hear that."

"I do, because having seen the place, I can't imagine. You must be so very strong."

He shrugged; he'd rather have all his teeth yanked

out with pliers than talk about this subject, but since she asked, he'd force himself to do so. He'd give her anything she asked. Almost.

"You have to remember that in the beginning I didn't know any better. Having been there from an infant, I had no idea people lived differently. It wasn't till I grew old enough to talk to other boys—the ones who'd once had parents and lost them—I found out children didn't all exist that way, in the cold and the half-dark."

"Were you raised by mechanicals?"

"What makes you ask that?"

"Both institutions I've visited so far are staffed mainly by steam units."

"No. Mechanicals hadn't risen in popularity back then. I remember only one battered unit, barely functional. There was a succession of women—none stayed long—but mostly we boys did the work. Raised one another."

Rough and ready, it had been. Bullying, loyalty, and yes, a few glints of kindness. Pity, sometimes. Friendships that grew like weeds in an empty building lot.

Something had to grow, and weeds were pretty hard to eradicate.

"Don't trouble your head about it," he told her. "It's all in the past."

"But it's not; it's still happening today. I've seen— I can't tell you what I saw there."

She didn't have to.

"The children were all so thin, and half of them looked sickly, with these bleak, haunted eyes. Many of them bear marks—welts and bruises. The man who runs the place, a Mr. Grendan, insists they're never abused, merely disciplined.

Disciplined. That was what Fink had called it, too. The strap with three tails. Being forced to work all night with torn and bloody hands. Denial of rations.

The black room.

No, he couldn't let himself think of that. But he wondered if that room still existed, way at the back of the house.

Very carefully he asked, "Did you see the whole place?"

"No. Not even the officer we had with us could persuade the man to show us the infirmary. Or the cellar."

"Tess, best to accept it: such places merely exist."

"Well, they shouldn't."

"They do."

"Then it's time for change."

"I wish you'd drop this crusade. Involve yourself, if you must, in something else, something more genteel."

"And forget about those children we've seen? As you were forgotten?"

"Don't break your heart over them."

A new look flooded her eyes; her hand traveled half way to her pocket and withdrew again. "Then over what should I break my heart?"

"Don't break it at all, Tessa. Just stay here and be my wife—protected and cared for. Let me take care of you."

"Will you?"

"Yes. I promise it." He raised his hand to her cheek, which felt soft as velvet. All at once he could see that she—*she*—was the one soft thing in his life. He gazed into her eyes, and she swayed toward him.

"Hold me, Mitch. Please."

And just like that, after all the waiting and suffering, she came into his arms. Heaven. He tried telling himself she just needed comfort and he happened to be available. Nothing more than that. But every inch of him responded to her presence and cried aloud in gladness.

"Tessa," he whispered.

"Don't let me go."

"I won't."

"I need—I need..." She drew away far enough to gaze into his face. "Stay with me?"

"Eh?"

"In my room. Tonight."

"If that's what you want."

"I think...I think it's what I need."

And to think, Mitch marveled to himself, he'd once scoffed at miracles.

Chapter Twenty-Seven

"No, don't light the lamp," Tessa begged as Mitch half carried her into her bedroom.

"Why not?" Even to his own ears, Mitch sounded intoxicated. They'd shared a series of staggering kisses in the parlor and more on the stairs coming up. He could barely think straight. "I want to see you."

"Please, no."

Did she want not to see him? Did she perhaps want to pretend he was God-damned Trask? He didn't like that one bit but knew he'd take what she was willing to offer.

Whatever crumbs she threw him.

Enough light came in through the windows, anyway. The moon must be up, shining above the city like a great silver eye.

"All right."

"Undress me."

That he could do. His fingers, clever in their eagerness, went to work; his lips followed and kissed every place he touched. She made no protest.

That told him one thing—she wanted him. No lie, she trembled with eagerness for it. If he had any remaining doubts, they were allayed by her groan of pleasure as she pressed her bared breasts against him and clove her mouth to his, after speaking one word.

"Mitch."

Well at least she remembered his name. And, oh, God, she tasted so damned sweet. He wanted to live in her forever. His personal heaven.

"Here." He tore his lips from hers in order to speak. "The bed."

"Yes."

There, he trapped her on the side of the mattress, straddling her with his legs, while he pulled the pins from her hair. It fell down, curl by curl, to her white shoulders. Once more he let his mouth follow.

The breath hitched in her throat. She reached for the buttons on his shirt.

He licked the swell of one breast and then the other. She caught his face between her palms and guided him down where she wanted him. He latched on to one nipple.

Forget about the world. Forget about the past and who he had been. Forget every damned thing.

God, but he wanted her, wanted to pour himself into her. As simple and as consuming as that.

"Mitch. I want it to be like before. Just like before."

He could do that. A repeat performance.

She gasped again when he quit suckling and lifted her to the center of the bed. He stripped while he stood looking down at her stretched there like an offering. Did she know how much he could see by the moonlight?

Did she care?

Maybe not, because she reached for him as he climbed onto the bed, as naked as she. She planted her hands in the hair on his chest and slid them downward until her fingers curled around the length of him, standing upright. He nearly came off the bed.

"Careful, darling. I'll explode."

"Inside me."

She reared up and wrapped herself around him then—arms, legs. Her tongue wooed his into her mouth, and he slid into her below, just as easily. Holy, sweet Jesus, he couldn't ask more from life than this. It felt so good he wanted to weep.

Tenderly, he flexed himself inside her. He wanted to show her how he felt about her, make her forget everything else. Prove to her she was where she was meant to be.

"Tessa." He spoke into her mouth as he wooed her open body with his body, with his soul. "Say you want to be with me. Please."

She slid her hands from his naked back up into his hair and groaned. Her ankles locked behind him. "I—"

"Tessa, I can become the man you want. Only tell me what—who—you want me to be. Anything." He repeated the word as he pumped into her and felt her body quicken impossibly in his hands. "Anything. Anything."

She gave a gasping cry as they came together, and fluttered all around him, her body claiming his the way she'd already claimed his heart. For several minutes, all thought flew away. Then he realized she lay still beneath him.

Too still.

"Tessa? I didn't hurt you, did I?" He never wanted to be anything but gentle with her. But his passion had a mind of its own.

"No."

Good. "Are you cold?"

"Yes." He drew the covers up over her, over both of them, and cuddled her close. He'd never believed in words of love—they were for the soft—and had never uttered them. Now he wanted to speak them and, more than anything else, wanted to hear them.

If only she would say one small thing, a word spoken in tenderness.

She stirred at last, and he eased his weight off her onto the mattress, though he kept her close, within the circle of his arm. By the light from the window he saw she had her eyes squeezed tight shut.

Did she, after all, lie there pretending he was someone else?

Trask?

Oh, God, he couldn't bear it. He—

"Mitch?" His name on her lips. He closed his eyes in turn and pressed his forehead to hers.

"Yes?"

"You said…you said when we were making love, you'd become the man I wish."

Making love. "Yes."

"Did you mean that?"

"Yes. Just ask me, Tessa. Just…" He kissed her, pouring all his need into her.

"I think…I think we might be able to get along— like this—if you reformed."

Like this? More than one night? Nights without end?

Wait a minute, though. "Reform?"

"I think you should follow me in taking up good works, Mitch."

"We've talked about this before, Tessa. I'm not that man."

"You said you'd become the man I need. Mitch, I need—I need this city to see you differently, as a giver rather than a tough. As someone who helps rather than threatens. You have all this money; why not do something worthwhile with it?"

"Like what?"

"Reclaim and rebuild one of those orphanages. I know!" She gasped. "You could reform Carter's. Buy it and transform it into what it should be. *Carter's* in truth, do you see?"

"Ah, Tessa, I don't think—"

"And then," she breathed, "we might be together."

Together? She and he? What did she say, exactly? That she might be able to love him?

If he were different.

He shuddered at the magnitude of it. But he'd told her so, hadn't he, as he came inside her?

Whatever she wanted him to be.

Not giving him time to contemplate it, she fastened her mouth once more to his and stretched her body beneath him. His hand moved without his permission to cup her breast.

She stopped kissing him long enough to say, "If I remember correctly, last time we were together you made love to me twice."

Mitch didn't need reminding.

****

Morning came softly following the second night Tessa's husband spent in her bed. But this time when she woke, she found he lingered there beside her. Still asleep.

Ah, an entirely new proposition. It seemed one thing to indulge her wild cravings with him in the dark.

The light of day turned his presence into something still more immediate and inescapable.

She lay very quietly taking stock of how she felt, now, about him and watching the patterns the morning sun made on the ceiling—taking stock of her body also. She could feel entirely too much—Mitch beside her in the bed, the warmth of him, and the slow rhythm of his breathing.

A terrible intimacy. It reinforced what they'd shared the night before.

Oh, what had come over her? Throwing herself at him the way she had, virtually demanding he make love to her. Images of all they'd shared together swam in her brain, accompanied by the memory of sensations. How could she? She didn't love him; she certainly wasn't attracted to him.

Was she?

She stole a look at him, one of mingled wonder and disbelief. He lay sprawled on his back, with one arm bent over his eyes, sleeping quietly. She could see his chest, with that interesting pattern of black hair, rising and falling, could see his jaw with the stubble grown in and the fingers of his hand—long fingers with rough nails, square cut.

No gentleman, this. But he'd been gentle and careful with her. She couldn't complain of the way he touched her or, indeed, of the way his body fitted hers. Or how the things he did thrilled her physically.

But that had been in the heat of the moment, in the dark. Awakening to find herself in bed with Mitch Carter in the light of day altered everything.

He couldn't be less like Richard if he tried. Richard. A wave of pain and helplessness rushed over

Tessa. Richard, with his sunny smile and amusing personality might well be Mitch's polar opposite.

Tessa eyed the man lying beside her again. Beneath his bent arm she could just glimpse his features—no classic good looks such as Richard possessed, no. Instead a narrow nose with a wicked hook and those high, slanted cheekbones. Even in repose, he looked intent.

But he wanted her. He wanted her—something Richard apparently did not. And if she could tolerate being near him in daylight, Mitch had proved he could satisfy the terrible craving that built inside her, a veritable fountain of need that sprang up until he touched her and she lost all sense of decorum.

What had she said to him last night, in the throes of madness? She'd asked him to change, join her in her new vocation, become a different man.

She'd more or less promised she'd be with him, if he did.

Would he? Could he?

Oh, what had she done?

Chapter Twenty-Eight

"Do you remember me?" Mitch asked, and then corrected carefully, "Do you remember us?" He eyed the old man in the pushchair with a mixture of burning hatred and disbelief. Could this really be the same figure that haunted his nightmares? The source of all terror? This pitiful, bony wreck of a man?

Beside him, Tiny stirred. Mitch had pondered long before selecting whom he should bring along with him on this particular call. His lawyer, Mr. Gains, of course. They needed everything kept strictly legal, and Gains, used to Mitch's ways, knew to look the other way when he should, such as during the application of judicial pressure.

But Mitch had three of the boys with him also, those he deemed most deserved to come. Those who should see this—Tiny, Billie, and Tom.

Did they all feel as shocked as he at being admitted to Morton Fink's parlor and seeing what their old enemy had become? Old. *Old.* Frail. But perhaps, judging by the hard gleam in the man's eye, not entirely beaten. Yet.

Morton Fink eyed Mitch up and down, and his thick lips twisted. "I remember you. One of my boys."

His boys. God help the lad who found himself in this monster's hands. Discipline and harsh words— never a whisper of love.

Love. Mitch's mind darted to Tessa. Nearly a week had passed since the night she asked him, in the sanctity of her bed, to change. She'd spent every night since in his arms, her body cleaving to his in the dark. And he nearly dared hope her feelings for him might be changing. That, more than anything—even the desire for revenge—had brought him here today.

"And you, and you—and you." Fink's gaze moved from face to face, ignoring only Gains before switching back to Mitch. "You were the worst of them. Now I hear you've made a name for yourself."

"Yes."

"As a bully and a brute." Fink virtually spat the words. "Can't get more out of a gutter than you put into it. Scum, that's all you'll ever be."

"And you're a mean old bastard." Mitch caressed the words. "That's all you ever were. Why don't you ask us why we're here? It isn't a social call."

"I didn't expect it was. You ran when you were—how old? Thirteen?"

"Fourteen. Just after the last time you beat me. I still have the scars."

The old man leaned forward. "Well, bully for you. You come here to whine about it? Or do you want me to say I'm sorry? I'm not. A hard hand was the only chance you lot had of moving out of the slime where you were born. I tried. Obviously, in certain cases, I failed."

"I—we—didn't come for an apology."

"Good. You won't get it. Why are you here then?"

"This is my lawyer, Mr. Gains. He tells me you still own Carter's. The new man there's just an agent. You're still living off the funds that should be used to fill those boys' stomachs."

"What of it?"

"I want to put in an offer."

"I fail to understand what you mean."

Impatience joined the other emotions beating a tattoo inside Mitch's head. "I want to buy the place."

Beside him, Tiny, Billie, and Tom stirred. He hadn't told them why they were coming here today. He imagined they thought he wanted to rough Fink up. They liked that prospect.

"Carter's isn't for sale."

"Everything's for sale, Mr. Fink. Name your price."

Fink's eyebrow quirked, and his cold gaze moved over Mitch slowly. "That wealthy, are you? And how did you acquire such wealth? No, don't tell me—through blackmail, no doubt, usury and other illegal activities."

"Yes."

Fink gave a sniff. "As I said, the blood will tell."

Mitch kindled. "You don't know what kind of people were behind me." Even he didn't know.

"Oh, but I do." Fink sneered. "I've seen it over and over again. Dropped by a whore, no doubt—and got by some lowlife no better than he should be. I did my best to eradicate all that from you—from each of you."

Tiny, who tended to react readily, could stay silent no longer. "Is that why you whipped us bloody and raw?"

"Yes."

"Starved us?"

"No, Tiny," said Billie, beside him. "That was 'cause of his greed. The less coin he spent on food for us, the more he could put in his pocket."

Fink waved a hand. "Spare me your moaning. You all managed to survive, even if you have apparently sunk to your lowest natural levels."

"We are what you made us," Mitch stated.

"Wrong—you're what you made yourselves, in your case the self-styled King of Prospect Avenue, isn't that it? Ha!"

"I want to buy Carter's. If you don't sell to me, you'll regret it."

"What do you want with the place? I can tell you, it's not a good proposition, certainly no money maker. Not worth your time. Anyway, what could you possibly do to me?"

"I'll expose what goes on inside that place. I'll send somebody in to take a look at the books. I'll—"

"That's not what I meant. Anyway, inspectors have already barged in—some bunch of do-gooders who have no idea what it takes to ride herd on a bunch of evil-minded young criminals." Fink had no idea those do-gooders included Mitch's wife. "What I'm asking, King Prospect, is why you want to buy an orphanage."

The boys all looked at him; no doubt they wanted the answer to that question, too. For twelve years they'd done their best—singly and collectively—to get shed of the place. Why return to it now?

"I want to make improvements, bring the place up to nineteenth-century standards."

"Again, why?"

"My reasons don't concern you. But maybe I want to improve the lives of the poor sods stuck there."

Fink began to laugh, not a pretty sound. Mitch remembered him laughing like that when he beat the boys, as if genuinely amused. "That," he said, "is a joke. All of you get out of my sight before I call the police."

"Mr. Carter," Gains said, "we should leave."

"No," Mitch told the lawyer. "I'm not done. Fink, you can either sell to me now and get benefit from the money, or I'll wait—until you're dead."

"Is that a threat?"

"Just saying. You're not looking too good. How much time do you think you have left?"

"I'm not sick, just old. A few infirmities, mostly caused by rich living." Fink smiled again. "You'll have to watch out for that, given your lifestyle. I'll thwart you by living a good many years yet."

"You sure about that?" Mitch glanced at his companions. The boys all stared, rapt. Mr. Gains gazed away into the near distance. "Fright can kill a man, or at least hasten his demise."

Fink's lips pulled tight.

"Live here alone, do you?" Mitch asked.

"I have servants, as you've seen—both human and mechanical."

"There must be a whole lot of people besides us who hate you. Boys turned into men, those who survived."

Fink stared into Mitch's eyes for a long moment. Suddenly his composure broke. "Get out of my house. Get out. Get out!"

"We'll go. But you give my offer some thought. Send me a message when you're ready to sell. I'm on Prospect Avenue."

"You'll fry in Hell first."

"Mr. Carter." Gains touched Mitch's arm.

"Think on it," Mitch urged Fink again, and they filed out the way they used to leave the dining hall at Carter's after one of their meager meals, in a silent chain.

Outside on the sidewalk, the sunlight had faded. The three boys clustered around Mitch, and Gains stepped away to the car.

"Mitch," said Tiny, completely forgetting the title of Boss he normally used, "what was that all about?"

"Yeah," said Tom, "why in tarnation would you want to buy that rat hole? Or have anything to do with it?"

Mitch eyed them in turn. "Don't it bother you that it's all still going on? Sure, there's another man in place at the head, but from what I've been told, it's no better inside. And Fink's still in control, giving the orders, living off the fat those boys never see."

"Well, sure it bothers me," Billie said, squinting up his eyes like a boy in pain. "But to buy an orphanage, Boss. What you gonna do with it?"

"Hire somebody to run the place right, make sure the boys get fed and see a doctor when they need one. Maybe make sure they learn a trade."

All three of his employees stared at him like he'd caught fire there on the curb.

"But why, Boss?" Tiny emphasized. "You're no do-gooder."

"Well, maybe I should be. A man has to think about more than his future, you know, in the end. At least, he does if he wants to be proud of himself."

Chapter Twenty-Nine

Tessa entered her bedroom to find her husband there and waiting for her, something that had never happened before. In the past—the nights they'd spent together—they'd either come up here together or he'd followed her when he finished his work.

He, of course, had a bedroom of his own, which she expected him to use. On the nights they had marital relations, they also slept the balance of the night together. Sometimes he left before she woke; sometimes he didn't.

She still found the mornings awkward, but not as awkward as walking in to find him lying on her bed, even if still fully clothed.

What did he expect?

What did she expect? The skin all over her body prickled, and pertinent areas tightened at the idea of just what might happen. He must want what she wanted. Suddenly, she fought for breath.

Valerie, at her heels, ran into the room and jumped up with her front feet against the mattress. Mitch reached down almost lazily and stroked her head.

"Oh," Tessa said. "I didn't see you at dinner, didn't know you were home."

"I was out. Just got back a short while ago." He gestured to the room. "Hope you don't mind. I…thought we might talk."

Talk. That, heaven knew, wasn't what she wanted from him. In truth they spoke little enough. Their intimacy all took place beneath the blankets.

But she stepped in and shut the door carefully behind her. The thick carpet muffled her footsteps as she crossed to the bed.

"Talk about what?"

He shrugged. He lay propped against the pillows, the collar of his shirt unfastened. Tessa thought about unbuttoning it the rest of the way, and her fingers tingled.

"Whatever you'd like."

Tessa puffed out a breath.

He inspected her with careful eyes, starting with her hair, lingering on her mouth, and moving downward slowly. It felt like he touched her everywhere; she shivered.

"Are you chilly, Tessa? Would you like me to light a fire?"

Or he could warm her—start a fire indeed. The last few times they'd been together, he barely needed to touch her to set her aflame. A single caress, a single kiss—or, like now, one glance.

She sat on the edge of the bed. He reached out and touched her hand. "Lie down and talk to me."

Unprecedented. Not a step she felt sure she wanted to take.

Gingerly she positioned herself against the pillows beside him, the green satin coverlet soft beneath her, and searched her mind for something to say.

Before she could find it, he asked, "What did you do today?

"Me?" She tried to think. "We had another meeting

at the Meadows Club."

"Oh?"

"You should come with me some time and hear Mr. Ellison speak. And Mrs. Michaels. She's quite eloquent."

"For an automaton." His usual response when she mentioned Lily.

"But not like you'd think."

Mitch took Tessa's hand in his. "Would you like it if I came with you? Because I meant what I said, Tessa—I'll do whatever you need, be whatever you need to make you happy."

Whatever she needed? Would he take her in his arms? Kiss her until she forgot who she was—who he was?

She turned on the pillow and looked at him. Bright hazel eyes gleamed a question at her, black hair ruffled against the white linen.

She didn't know what he saw in her eyes, but he lifted her hand to his mouth and pressed a kiss into the palm. "Tessa, tell me—do I have a chance?"

Caught like a fly in a web, she repeated, "A chance?"

"With you."

She didn't want to answer that, didn't even want to think about it. Instead she moved forward into his arms.

For the first time ever, she gave herself to him with the light still burning. There could be no pretense when he stopped kissing her and gazed into her face. She could see the emotions in his eyes when he reached for the buttons on the front of her lacy white blouse. As he unfastened them slowly, one by one, another shiver traveled all the way to her toes.

"Tessa, Tessa, let me have my way with you."

His way? And what had they been doing all these nights?

As if he heard her thoughts, he whispered, "There's more. More than we've already shared."

"More?"

"Let me show you."

Oh, God. Could she stand more? Could she stand not having more?

"Yes," she breathed. "But put out the light first."

"No, I want to see you. All of you."

He shifted and cupped her breasts one after the other through the open front of her blouse. "Beautiful. You're so beautiful."

"The light. Please."

He froze and gazed again into her eyes. "I want you to know it's me."

"I do."

"I don't want you pretending I'm somebody else."

Tessa whimpered. She wanted him so much she could taste him. But she wanted the light out.

He reared up on the bed and began shucking his clothes, his gaze on her all the while.

He had a nice body, she decided, now that she could see it properly. Well-muscled yet lean in all the right places. Nothing like Richard, but Richard was a rat of the first water who wouldn't recognize loyalty if it rushed up and bit him.

She liked the way her husband's black hair tumbled over his forehead when he bent to kiss both her breasts. Loved the way the hair on his chest narrowed to a line which led downward to…

Oh, mercy, she'd never seen *that* in the light either.

Heaven help her.

"Put yourself in my hands, Tessa."

Nearly lost, she uttered the agreement, "All right."

After that they abandoned all need for words. She watched through half-slitted eyes while he sampled the skin of her shoulders, her neck, and both her breasts. He planted open-mouthed caresses on her arms and hands, and on her belly, removing her clothing as he went and making his way ever downward. When he kissed her thighs, pushing her ruffled petticoat aside, and urged them apart, she stiffened. But only for an instant—she'd placed herself in his hands, after all, at the mercy of his mouth, and that was where she wanted to be.

Still, the light changed everything, made it more immediate and, somehow, twice as intimate. When she felt his hot breath and then his mouth at her most private place, her fingers curled into the coverlet. For an instant she feared she couldn't bear it.

Then, a woman surrendering, she opened herself to him.

****

"There, I told you. Didn't I tell you? Tessa? Tessa, look at me."

After she shattered, he'd worked his way back up her body, fastened his mouth to hers, and slid inside her, where he'd released his seed. Now he cuddled her close against him, his arms tight around her, his cheek against her hair.

She drew away just far enough to look into his eyes. She felt embarrassed, half ashamed of her body's response to him, and at the same time so satisfied it shocked her.

But she said, "I'm looking."

He cradled her face between his hands. "Do you see? We're good together. Good."

That word couldn't begin to describe what her body had just experienced. She whispered, "I didn't know—I never thought men and women—"

"They do. We will. It can be like this for us always."

Oh, lord.

"Tessa, I love you."

She stopped breathing entirely. Again she gazed into his eyes and for the first time—the very first time—saw him.

Not the King of Prospect Avenue, not the tough, not the hard man, but one with a spirit that flared like light, who sought to disguise his vulnerability and yet let her see it now. A man who, more than anything, wanted to love.

Wanted her love.

"Oh, Mitch," she groaned. She placed her palm against his cheek and said again, "Oh—I can't…"

"Hush. I know you can't say it back to me."

She almost wished she could.

"It doesn't matter. I can wait. Wait till you're able to say it, until I become the man you need me to be. I want you to know I'm trying to buy Carter's. If I succeed, we can improve things there. You and me together, we can."

"That's wonderful."

His face quickened with gladness. "You think so?"

"Oh, yes. It's only right that you should make things better for the children there, boys like you were."

"Tessa, does it matter to you that I came from there, from nothing?"

"No," she answered truthfully. "Only what you do with your life."

"The man who owns a controlling share in Carter's—Morton Fink—is refusing to sell, so far. But I'll get 'round him."

The expression in Mitch's eyes changed when he spoke the name Fink—they narrowed, and their light dimmed.

"Isn't he—"

'He ran the place when I lived there, was the master."

"And cruel." Suddenly she could read him, feel his emotions the way she never had before. She caught her breath. "If he refuses to sell—"

"I'll persuade him."

"How?"

"Never you mind about that, Tessa. I will. And if not, after he's dead it'll pass to someone else who'll be bought. You'll see."

"Mitch, it doesn't have to be that orphanage."

"Yes, it does."

"You might acquire any of them. The important thing is that they get improved, one at a time."

"No, you were right when you said it should be Carter's. Look at this."

To Tessa's surprise he moved in the bed, rolling away from her until he could show her his naked back. The golden light from the steamlamp washed over his skin and revealed a network of scars. They criss-crossed in a pattern of ridges, some deep, all thick with age.

She gasped. "Oh, Mitch. Who—Fink?"

He turned back and lay in his former pose, forearm

across his eyes. "He gave me the worst of those the day before I ran away."

"Why? Why would he beat you so badly?"

"He wanted to break my spirit." Mitch seemed to ponder it an instant before he added, "But it wouldn't break."

Emotion flooded over Tessa such as she'd never before felt toward this man. How could anyone grow up in such a place, face such harsh discipline, yet keep his spirit intact? Come out of it to make a success of himself, fetch his fellows out after him, give them employment.

By whatever means.

At that instant she believed she understood him better than she ever had, even wondered if she might, some day, come to love such a man as this.

Despite what he might do to Morton Fink? Ah, but what did Morton Fink deserve?

"Mitch, I'm sorry for what happened to you. It shouldn't happen to any child. But that's the past, right?"

He lowered his arm; they gazed into one another's eyes. "You're my future, Tessa."

She crawled on top of him, fitted her body to his. Another first—she'd never before showed herself as eager for him. She'd also never imagined being anyone's future—his world. But the very idea went to her head.

Perhaps, she thought, she couldn't save all the orphans in the city. Just this one.

Chapter Thirty

"You look happy," Lily Michaels told Tessa as they sat down at their table in the tea shop. "Much happier, so I have to say, than when we first met."

Tessa shot her friend a look of surprise. It couldn't be denied that Lily Michaels, automaton or not, had become one of her closest friends. They'd fallen into the habit of meeting like this for tea and confidences.

Neither could it be denied that Tessa felt happier. Nearly a month had passed since her husband told her he loved her. Life had acquired a pattern she could only deem satisfying, even comfortable, sharing meals with him in the evenings, and kisses at parting. Marital relations most every night, so searingly hot she could barely stand to think about it. The things they did together got left in her room, during daylight hours.

Or did they? Perhaps they colored everything else. And brought warmth to her cheeks now.

"You are blushing," Lily observed. "Is it because your husband has become your lover?"

"How could you possibly know that?"

"I am remarkably observant. As I have said, I was constructed to respond to nuances. In addition, the first book ever I read was called, *The Adventures of Miss X*. Therein, Miss X learned many fascinating intimacies from her lover. I still use them on my husband, Rey." Lily tipped her charming head. "He never seems to tire of them despite the repetition."

"Really? Do you—er—still have that book?" And what might Mitch do if she acquired new skills and practiced them on him? Her skin tingled, just thinking about it.

"Yes, I still have every book I ever owned. They are like friends. Would you like to borrow it?"

"I believe I would."

"Lending books is a noble practice. I have borrowed many books from my good friend Pat Kelly."

"How is his wife, Rose, doing?" Lily spoke often of her friends, and Tessa couldn't help but sympathize with Rose, given her kidnapping ordeal.

"Better. I sit with her sometimes while Pat is away. He does not like leaving her alone."

"I can understand why. Has he discovered who snatched her?"

"Not yet. There are only a few clues. But Pat will not give up. He is very protective of Rose."

Tessa tried to imagine being married to an automaton, even one as sophisticated as Pat Kelly, and failed. Lily's husband, Rey, and Rose Kelly certainly didn't seem to mind their unusual matches.

"And"—Tessa lowered her voice—"how go your efforts to adopt?" She'd quickly learned that Lily's dearest wish was to either adopt or foster a child, since she would never be able to give her husband one of his own.

"Our application is still being reviewed, so we are told. Usually it does not take this long. I fear the delay presages a refusal."

"You don't know that for sure." Tessa covered Lily's hand, which rested on the table, with her own.

"No one who's met you could doubt you'd make a wonderful mama, warm and nurturing."

"I keep thinking of them shut into those terrible institutions. I know what it's like to be shut away, and powerless."

"I know." During their shared afternoons Lily had confided certain details of her past as a high-class and high-priced prostitute.

"But let us speak of more cheerful things. Since your husband has become your lover, you yourself may soon conceive a child. I am given to believe that often happens during the first year of marriage due to the frequency of sexual relations."

Lily, as Tessa had learned, usually spoke with frankness bordering on the blunt. She'd come to not mind.

But a baby—Mitch's baby...Tessa couldn't say the idea hadn't crossed her mind lately, especially considering all they'd shared together. And yes, she did happen to be late, but that could be due to emotional upheaval, or so she assumed.

She wondered how Mitch would react to news of an impending child. He must have thought of it too, when he came to her again and again.

"It's rather soon for that," she hedged. "Besides, if Mitch succeeds in buying Carter's, he'll have lots of children under his care. Say, Lily—if that happens, perhaps he could see to it you're given one of those poor boys."

"You think so?" Lily's blue gaze went wide.

"I don't see why not. But remember, you can't tell anyone he's trying to acquire the orphanage."

"I will not, Tessa. As you know, I am excellent at

keeping secrets."

****

"Boss, I think he's ready to sell." Tiny stood in front of Mitch's desk with his flat cap in his hands and several of the other boys at his back. Tiny's eyes gleamed.

"Come in," Mitch told them. "Shut the door."

They filed into the office the way feral cats might. To be sure, the boys who'd come from Carter's always had an edge. And these four had all come from Carter's.

"Tell me."

Tiny exchanged sidelong glances with his companions. "We been doing like you said, Boss—hanging 'round his house, making sure we can be seen from the windows. He knows we're there because he sends his steamies out to shoo us off. We go. But we always come back a while later. And at night—" Tiny paused.

"At night, what?"

A ripple passed through all four boys. Tiny closed his eyes for a minute like a man savoring something. "He knows we're there then, too."

Lou offered, "He's a hard nut to crack, old Fink. But we found a way in, see, Boss—through the coal chute." Lou held out his hands, the palms of which still showed black dust. "Good thing he starved us in our youth, eh? Else we'd be too big to fit through."

Another of the boys, Harry, spoke in turn. "He had his servants check all the doors and windows but automatons aren't too imaginative. Neither are the police, sometimes. If they were, we wouldn't still be in business, right?"

"Good job, boys," Mitch said.

"We try harder. That old bastard deserves a fright—and more."

"So"—Mitch played with the pen on his desk—"how do you know he's ready to sell?"

"He got all shaken up last night," Tiny replied. "His servants had to call the doctor for him. I reckon a suggestion—posed in the proper way—should about finish the job."

"Do it," Mitch told them. "Whatever it takes."

All four boys grinned—sharks now, rather than mangy cats.

Lou mumbled, "Our pleasure, Boss."

Chapter Thirty-One

"I wondered if you would mind skipping our usual visit to the tea house today," Lily Michaels proposed. An almost eager look appeared in her blue eyes. "I'd like to suggest something else."

"Oh?" Tessa adjusted her hat and pulled on her gloves. They'd just left a meeting at the Meadows Club that she'd found deeply upsetting. Mr. Ellison had proposed raids on three more orphanages—considered among the worst in the city—and had taken them over a disturbing list of statistics, citing the numbers of children who had died during the last year in such institutions.

Lily had stood up to corroborate the information, much of which her husband, Rey, had contributed.

"It is part of Rey's job to collect these poor little corpses from the orphanages. They are destined for paupers' graves but, at McMahon's Coffin Shop, where as most of you know he works, we do for them what we can. I often go in to help dress them properly, wash them, and groom their hair.

"These children, my friends, all too often die alone and uncared for. Worse yet, they are very often left alone while they are ill, rarely feeling the touch of a kindly hand."

Her words had brought tears to Tessa's eyes. Yet now Lily seemed to shrug off her sorrow, far more easily than Tessa could. Was it because Lily Michaels was, after all, an automaton? Yet Tessa had no doubt that Lily cared.

"Where are we going?" she asked as a horse-drawn cab drew up.

"To visit the Kellys. Pat is off work today and invited some good friends to tea. He hopes to cheer up his wife, Rose, and provide a diversion."

"That is very thoughtful of him," Tessa said as they climbed into the cab.

"There is nothing Pat will not do for Rose." Lily tipped her head, apparently reflecting on it. "Or she for him. A perfect marriage," she declared.

"But—" Tessa bit her tongue. What did she know about it? Her own marriage was so conflicted she no longer knew what to think. She both resented her husband's presence in her life and desired to be with him, so much it shocked her. When they were together, everything felt so intense and immediate, she couldn't bring herself to contemplate her still-absent monthly, and the fact that she might in fact carry his child. She hated what had brought him into her world, but loved what they did in the night.

She even found herself missing him from time to time.

"Rey is unable to attend," Lily said. "He is needed at his job. Nor can our good friends the Kilters be there. Jamie is busy with his sanctuary, and Cat is very pregnant—yet again." She beamed. "But there are others I would like very much for you to meet."

The cab made its plodding way from Delaware to Bryant Street, where it eventually stopped in front of a tall, narrow house painted blue. Lily descended and turned to pay the fare, but Tessa forestalled her.

"Allow me." Mitch gave her a generous allowance; Rey Michaels, as she knew, worked hard for his pay. Not that she could say Mitch didn't. He spent an inordinate amount of time—all hours—laboring in his office.

She wondered what he was doing now and how late he'd work tonight…and whether he might come to her room once she turned out the light.

"Tessa, you remember Pat Kelly?"

Derailed from her distracting thoughts, Tessa looked up—and up—at the automaton that stood on the doorstep. He was in fact a very handsome automaton, with that dark reddish hair and very human-looking green eyes.

"Yes, of course." She extended her hand. "We met at the Meadows Club, and you were there on our second orphanage tour—the one that took place at Carter's."

"So I was. Mrs. Carter, welcome to our home. I'm pleased you could come."

He drew them into the foyer of the house, where he bent his head and said in a slightly mechanical whisper, "My wife, Rose, is still having a hard time recovering from her ordeal."

"I'm not surprised, Officer Kelly. Shocking that such a thing could happen in our city. And I certainly don't blame her for being overset."

In a whisper also, Lily asked, "Have you discovered who snatched her, Pat?"

"We have been working tirelessly on just that, I and the other members of the Irish Squad, and have narrowed it down." His gaze moved to Tessa. "There is little in this city that does not come under observation by someone—be he human or mechanical."

"I wish you every success," Tessa said, and meant it.

"Thank you, Mrs. Carter. This is my city; I will defend it and everyone in it."

He led them into the parlor, where a group of people had gathered. Two extremely lovely, dark-haired women sat on the settee, in animated conversation. One Tessa recognized as Topaz Gideon, whom she'd met during her initial visit to the Meadows Club. The other, whom she'd never met, wore her hair in a fat braid down her back and sported a leather skirt and vest, the latter worn over a plain white shirt.

A fair-haired gentleman lounged near the windows. Slim and not overly tall, he had intelligent blue eyes and a deceptively casual air.

But the center of attention was unquestionably Pat's wife, Rose. She sat in a high-backed chair, reminiscent of a throne, separated by a side table from a larger overstuffed chair. A strained, rather worried expression marked her pale, oval face and invaded her mild brown eyes.

Lily stepped forward to take her hand and kiss her cheek. "Rose, I'm sure you remember Tessa Carter, whom you met some time ago at The Meadows Club. And Tessa, I know you recall Pat's wife, Rose."

"Of course," Tessa murmured—the woman who had endured the fearful abduction.

Lily went on, indicating the lady with the long braid. "And this is Ginny Landry. You met her fiancé, Brendan Fagan, during out first raid."

"Pleased to meet you." Tessa shook Ginny

Landry's hand. "Your fiancé was most helpful that day."

Ginny Landry had frank brown eyes that inspected Tessa without guile. "He's a helpful sort of fellow, all 'round."

"And"—Lily turned to the other woman—"I'm sure you remember Topaz Gideon, who gave an inspiring talk during your first visit to the Meadows Club. This gentleman is her husband, Rom." She turned to the fair-haired man by the window. "They are ever such good friends of the Kellys."

Topaz Gideon gave Tessa a measured nod, rather like one delivered by a queen. Her husband looked curious.

"Mrs. Carter, I've heard a great deal about your husband." He slanted a look at Pat Kelly. "Big man in this city, isn't he?"

Tessa experienced a mad and heretofore unprecedented impulse to defend Mitch. "He's achieved a great deal, yes, worked his way up from nothing to the owner of considerable properties around town."

"And bent on purchasing still more, the way I hear it," Pat Kelly said mildly.

"Most likely. Truly I don't concern myself much with his business."

"And indeed, why should you?" Topaz Gideon asked. "Lily tells us you're becoming quite involved in the campaign to improve the city's orphanages. It's a very worthy cause. It seems"—she raised an eyebrow and looked around the group—"we are all involved in something."

"That is because we are the ones who can improve

this city, change things for the better," said Lily with passion rarely seen in an automaton. "We are the only ones who can."

Mrs. Gideon smiled at Lily fondly. To Tessa she said, "Lily's correct. It's only right we've championed various causes. Rom and I work together to alleviate the struggles of the girls in Buffalo, on the waterfront and elsewhere." Her brilliant amber eyes clouded momentarily. "We've had a few setbacks, as Lily can attest, but some successes also. Ginny," she went on, "has taken up the fight, along with Pat and Rose, for automaton rights."

Ginny Landry smiled. "I'm afraid I collect aging steam units the way other women take in stray cats. Given the new ordinances requiring mechanicals to receive a wage, many owners are casting off those that are old and damaged, rather than repairing them. Turned out into the streets, they have few options other than to subsist—at least until their coal supplies dwindle—or take themselves to the scrap heap."

"How awful," said Tessa, thinking of Valerie. Clockwork or steam powered, she never wanted to imagine her pet ending up there.

"Yes," Ginny agreed, "because as anybody with a lick of sense knows, even the most basic units have feelings. I have personally experienced more love and loyalty among steamies than among most humans."

"Hear, hear." Rom Gideon raised his teacup in a salute.

"And now," said Lily enthusiastically, "you, Tessa, have taken up a cause so dear to me and Rey."

"Yes."

Rose Kelly spoke for the first time. "Please, Mrs.

Carter, will you take some tea?" She reached out to pour from the ornate, rose-figured teapot that rested on the table between their chairs, and Tessa's gaze fell on her wrists, both of which bore livid scars, barely healed over.

Startled, her gaze flew to Rose's. Color came and went in the woman's face, and her eyes dropped.

"Mrs. Carter, you will be wondering about these marks you see on my wrists." She glanced at Lily. "You did not tell her?"

"Rose, it is not my story to tell."

Pat Kelly laid his broad hand on his wife's shoulder. "Last summer, Mrs. Carter, during an uprising at the park, I was attacked and heavily damaged. It seemed for a time my artificial intelligence had been destroyed and would not be recovered."

Rose shuddered and reached for her husband's hand; his fingers enfolded hers tenderly.

"During that time," Pat stated flatly, "my beloved Rose tried to take her own life."

Tessa's lips parted in horror. Just like her own father—the victim of despair.

Rose's brown eyes flooded with tears but met her gaze. "What you must think of me, Mrs. Carter. But I couldn't bear the thought of living without Pat—I just couldn't."

"Of course, I understand," Tessa said on a rush of compassion. But did she? Could she imagine feeling that way about her own husband? Did she want to imagine?

She turned to Pat Kelly. "I'm very glad you survived."

He made a soft, grinding sound in his voice box.

"As am I, if only for Rose's sake. But let us speak of more cheerful things. Tell us, Ginny, about the repair shops you've been setting up."

Ginny Landry did so, describing them as part shelters for unwanted automatons and part hospitals where, often times, they rebuilt one another.

"Afterward, they're often able to go out and get other jobs, as opposed to being scrapped," she concluded.

Rom Gideon mused, "Now if the powers that be would only smarten up and allow some of these available automatons to look after the city's orphans properly, we might make real progress." He turned to Tessa. "Tell me, Mrs. Carter, is your husband involved in your philanthropic activities? Unless I am mistaken in what I've heard about him, he came from a foundling home, did he not?"

"Yes, from Carter's, as a matter of fact." Very thoughtfully, Tessa gazed around the room, looking from face to face. "And yes, I do believe he will become involved—so long as I ask him to."

Chapter Thirty-Two

Mitch came down the stairs and saw his wife hovering in the foyer at the bottom, almost as if she waited there for him.

The morning light sifted through the sidelights that framed the big front door, turning her hair to flame and picking out the intense hue of the suit she wore. A blue suit it was, with a hat, tiny little heeled shoes, and white gloves.

She looked good enough to eat. The fact that Mitch had only recently come from her bed, where he'd done just that, didn't make him feel particularly satisfied. Instead, the mere sight of her made him hungry all over again.

"Another meeting today?" he asked in an effort to disguise his completely unreasonable need.

"A tour of another orphanage." She bent to pat Valerie, who'd darted out from the direction of Mitch's office, before she looked up at him from under the brim of her hat. "Actually…"

She let her voice trail off and bit her lip, an action that elevated Mitch's heartbeat.

"Yes?" he prompted.

"I—uh—wondered if you'd agree to come with me. Many of the women's husbands are involved, at least peripherally. And I thought…"

He came down the last step and crossed the floor to

her, drawn like a wasp to honey. "You thought what?"

She raised her eyes to his—clear green in the morning light and seeming to hold a reflection of every intimacy they'd shared not so long ago. *His mouth at her breast, between her legs, tasting heaven. Her small fingers wrapped around him...*

"I thought it might make us feel—well, closer."

How could they be closer than when he was inside her? When he searched the inside of her mouth with his tongue and she melted for him, opening herself in that delectable way she had. When she begged wordlessly, with her body, for what she would not say.

But she was saying now—asking him, telling him. She wanted something more than physical closeness. This represented a real hope for him to get near her heart.

He had a dozen things to which he should attend today, not the least the problem of Danny Dwyer who, by all accounts, continued to throw his weight around in a dangerous fashion. But when Tessa looked at him that way, how could he say no?

****

At first, Tessa didn't realize how tense her husband had become. They took the long black steamcar with Marty at the wheel and met the other members of the party outside on the steps of the Meadows Club, as prearranged.

To say they appeared surprised to see Mitch would be an understatement. The Misses Carroll whispered together, and Mr. Ellison raised his eyebrows high.

"Mr. Carter? Well, I did not expect you, sir, to concern yourself with our small affairs."

"Not small, surely, Mr. Ellison." Mrs. Wright

stepped forward. "And if what we've heard of you proves true, Mr. Carter, I should think you of all men would take an interest." She nodded at Tessa. "Well done, Mrs. Carter, in persuading your husband to attend."

Mitch, nearly expressionless, offered the use of his car, which would reduce the number of steamcabs needed to one.

He asked Mr. Ellison, "To which institution are we bound, sir?"

"The Waifs, on East Ferry."

Did Mitch's lip quiver? The Waifs had not made Mr. Ellison's list by accident; it had a loathsome reputation.

Mitch gave the address to Marty, who stared. They set off, Lily and the Misses Carroll in the car with Mitch and Tessa.

Lily immediately leaned over and placed a hand on Mitch's arm. "Mr. Carter, I am so pleased to have a chance to become acquainted with you. Tessa speaks of you often."

"Does she?" Mitch swept Tessa with an incredulous look.

"Oh, yes. We women have our little confidences. By the way, Tessa, I have that book you asked to borrow."

Tessa's lips parted; no words came. She hoped Lily would not confide the nature of that book to Mitch.

She need not have worried. Instead, Lily spoke of how happy she was to find, in Tessa, a friend who shared her interests.

Tessa twisted her fingers together in her lap and wondered what Mitch thought. At least he didn't voice his usual reminder that Lily was, in fact, just an automaton.

The orphanage proved to be located in a shabby wooden building covered by molting green paint, its windows shuttered and its façade sad. A sign out front read *The Waifs*, the letters all but worn away by weather.

Not until they climbed from the car and formed one group on the sidewalk, and Tessa took Mitch's arm, did she gauge the intensity of his tension. Though his face still showed little, his body fairly vibrated, the arm beneath her fingers like iron.

"Remember we are mere visitors here," Mr. Ellison cautioned. "As before, when we toured the other institutions, we must keep our opinions to ourselves, no matter what horrors we may observe."

He shot a look at Mitch. "I daresay only one of us here is completely prepared for what we will see."

God help her, Tessa only fully realized at that moment what she'd asked of her husband. To accompany her into hell. Back into a hell he'd once been forced to occupy.

She looked into his face, searching. "I don't know what I was thinking. This isn't a good idea, Mitch. You wait here with the car—there's no need for you to come inside."

His smile looked almost ordinary, wry and controlled. But she saw the slick sheen on his skin and the shadows in his eyes.

"Don't be foolish, Tessa. Of course I'll come with you."

"No, really. Please stay with the car. It won't take long."

He tucked her arm inside his. "Your Mr. Ellison is right; I'm the perfect man to inspect the place. I know what to look for, don't I?"

Tessa's stomach turned as they filed in through the front door. The overseer of The Waifs had agreed to this visit in return for a monetary donation. The woman—big, rawboned, and middle-aged—came forward to meet them now and shook Mr. Ellison's hand.

"Welcome to The Waifs," she rasped. "I'm Mrs. Bains."

Tessa shrank closer to Mitch's side. These places, as she'd learned during the earlier visits, had a smell. Part stale air and even staler food, part urine and, in the best cases, disinfectant.

She smelled disinfectant here, but the shabby surroundings made of it little advantage. Dark olive walls, streaked with damp, a yellowed ceiling, a sad flight of stairs that led upward into gloom.

Mrs. Bains proved apologetic and seemed sincere. "This orphanage opened in 1862 when the house and property were donated by an elderly patron." She twisted her hands in her gray apron. "There was, however, no provision for funding. We have housed up to two dozen children here in the past—boys and girls together. At this time we have fourteen. We take them in off the streets, mostly children tossed out by landlords after their parents have died. We do for them the best we can."

Her cheeks flushed defensively even though no one else had spoken. "I'm aware it likely doesn't look that way."

Lily Michaels stepped forward and said, with

compassion, "Will you let us see your facility?"

"Yes." Mrs. Bains looked at Mr. Ellison. "You said something about a payment. It's just that I've no money for food, and several of the children are sick."

Wordlessly, Mr. Ellison passed her an envelope.

"Oh, thank you. Come this way. And please, believe I would do more for my children if I could."

The group, with Tessa and Mitch at the rear, entered a room on the left. It should have been a parlor, but Tessa saw rows of cots, bare but for one blanket each, in a chamber as gray and cheerless as a rainy day. Several of the cots were occupied by small children, their wan faces stark against the thin pillows. One tossed restlessly.

Patricia Carroll asked, "What is the matter with them?"

"Oh, the usual—cough, fever. They're always sick."

"You have not called a doctor?"

"Of course not," Mitch muttered under his breath.

Mrs. Bains shot a look in his direction before she answered. "I had no funds. I will be able to, now."

Another member of the party asked, "Where are the rest of the children? At their lessons?"

Mrs. Bains hesitated. "I'm afraid not. Most days, they do piece work."

"Piece work?"

"We assemble wooden boxes for a local man who uses them in his business. It's very simple work, but it does provide a small income."

Mrs. Wright asked, "Have you not applied to the city for supplementation?"

"I have. I was refused."

"Why?"

"I was told we're not large enough. If I took in more children I might get funding, but I wouldn't be able to provide adequately for them."

"It does not seem, my good woman, you're providing adequately for them now. Please show us the kitchen."

Now grim and silent, Mrs. Bains led on. The kitchen, a dank cave of a place, housed a handful of children struggling to fill a large pot with water from a rusty pump and scrubbing a long, plank table.

"Say good morning to our visitors, children."

"Good morning," they chorused. Tessa, leaning forward from the shelter of Mitch's arm to peer at them, decided none looked well. Cautious eyes returned her stare from pinched and chapped faces. Their clothing, though reasonably clean, appeared shockingly shabby.

"By God," said Brenda Carroll. "Something must be done."

She went on speaking, her ire at the fore, but suddenly Mitch interrupted her. Holding up his hand he growled, "What's *that*?"

His tone was such it caught the attention of children and adults alike. Mrs. Bains turned to him with a look of horror.

"It's—" one of the children began.

"Hush." Mrs. Bains slapped the girl on the head. "I don't hear anything."

Tessa did. A muffled thumping, it seemed to come from the hallway off the kitchen.

Mitch spun on his heel, releasing his grasp on Tessa.

"Mr. Carter," Mr. Ellison cautioned, but Mitch

disregarded him. They stood near the doorway; mere steps took him to what looked like the door of a broom cupboard out in the passage.

"No, sir—" Mrs. Bains bounded after him.

Tessa could hear the thumping much more clearly now that they stood in the passage. It most certainly came from the tiny closet. A rusty hook and hasp held the door shut. Tessa saw Mitch's hands tremble when he reached for them.

The door swung open with a creak. The dim light from the passage barely reached inside but Tessa's horrified eyes saw—

A child. A boy, she thought, crunched into the suffocating, small space with his body bent nearly double and his head tucked down.

Before she could even draw a breath, Mitch reached inside, lifted the child with careful hands, and set him on the floor of the passage. Everyone surged forward.

Tessa saw the truth then. Throughout the tour she'd been willing to give Mrs. Bains the benefit of the doubt, assign her the role of struggling housemother with good intentions.

But the small boy on the floor, surely no more than eight years old, had been shoved into a closet with his hands bound behind his back and a gag tied over his mouth.

As everyone watched, Mitch gently removed the gag. He loosened the boy's hands even as the party began to argue with the housemother.

"How could you, Mrs. Bains?" Mrs. Wright demanded, turning on the woman.

Mrs. Bains' face had turned bright red. "That is a

very naughty boy. He does nothing but cause trouble and grief. I could not let you see him, could I? What would you think of me?"

"Better to wonder what we think of you now! Madam, this institution needs to be closed down."

"Yes?" Mrs. Bains shrieked. "And then what will happen to these children? Tell me that."

Tessa, listening with one ear, watched her husband help the child to stand, ask him a question, and feel him over gently, touching his back with gentle hands.

He raised his head, and Tessa got a look at his face—eyes burning, lean cheeks drawn tight, mouth hard with anger.

He stepped up to Mrs. Bains, interrupting her defensive tirade. "This child has been caned."

Once more everyone went silent. Except Mrs. Bains. She screeched.

"Of course he has! I told you he's a very bad boy and will not obey. What else was I supposed to do?"

"You might," Mrs. Wright said indignantly, "try love."

"Love? I have no time for love."

"So," Mitch gritted through clenched teeth, "your answer is to whip him and shut him—bound and gagged—into a dark closet?"

Tessa had never seen Mitch look so dangerous. At that moment, she believed him capable of anything.

"What if the child had smothered?" Mrs. Wright demanded.

And Mrs. Bains, all pretense of warmth and caring fled, answered, "It might well have benefitted this world."

"I have to get out of here," Mitch muttered and

pushed past everyone in the passageway. With Tessa at his heels, he marched straight outside, where he stood inhaling great breaths of air.

"Boss, you all right?"

Marty stood outside the car, looking concerned.

Ignoring him, Tessa faced her husband and seized his hands.

"I'm sorry," she said. "That was my fault. I never should have asked you to come here with me."

He glared at her, and in his eyes she saw—memories. Shadows and old horrors. A flare of pain.

Never had she imagined seeing the composed and controlled Mitch Carter look this way. The truth tumbled upon her.

She said, "That happened to you, didn't it? You were shut—shut in somewhere. Just like that boy."

"It doesn't matter." As if he convinced himself, he repeated it. "Doesn't matter anymore."

"Mitch, what will happen to that boy?"

"If he's lucky, he'll grow up and make something of himself. Then it won't matter for him, either."

Chapter Thirty-Three

Tessa lay in her bed with but a single light burning in the room against the darkness, wondering if her husband would come to her this night.

He'd been quiet following their visit to The Waifs, far too quiet. Upon their return home, he'd shut himself into his office, saying he had business matters to which he must attend, and had not emerged.

Not even for supper, which was a meal they almost always shared.

He'd still been in his office behind the closed door when Tessa came up to bed. Where she tossed and turned—and waited.

That had been hours ago. He must have come up to his room by now. But not to her, at least not yet.

She lay on top of the coverlet, wearing one of her most fetching negligees, while stroking Valerie's smooth hide. She thought again of the words her husband had spoken to her outside The Waifs, that once grown, what one suffered as a child no longer mattered.

She didn't believe it. She, who'd experienced life in her father's household, knew it for a lie. How much worse for a man who'd lived through what that young boy today had.

Tessa had seen the look in that boy's eyes when Mitch pulled him out of the closet. She'd also seen the look in Mitch's eyes.

For the first time ever, Mitch Carter—master of keeping his composure and schooling his emotions—had appeared vulnerable.

And it changed how she felt about him. Maybe, she reflected as she stroked Valerie and the little dog wiggled closer, because she felt responsible for what had happened today. She should have thought, before she asked, about what a visit to such a place would do to Mitch.

He might be tough, but he wasn't made of stone.

Now she had an overwhelming impulse to make that blunder up to him, to get close to him in his vulnerability, and maybe even mend his hurt.

Here, in her bed.

But the minutes continued to tick by on the white enameled clock that sat on her dresser. The little dog went to sleep, or shut herself down. When the hands on the clock read one a.m. she sighed and pushed herself up in the bed.

It had been a long day. She should crawl in under the covers beside Valerie and go to sleep. But that wouldn't ease the longing inside.

She wanted Mitch, his touch, and the taste of him. She could go to him. But she'd never done that before—all their clandestine meetings had taken place here, on her territory.

She'd never realized what courage it must have taken for him to come here. What if she went to him and he rejected her?

She would go away humiliated. And aching for him.

Or she might make him an offer he could not turn down.

231

She slipped from the bed, turned off the bedside light, and padded on bare feet from her room down the hallway.

****

Whiskey never helped. When Mitch had nights like this—ones crammed so full of dark memories he had no hope of sleep—drinking only seemed to make it more painful. The liquor unleashed the emotions he always strove so hard to contain.

They'd been allowed far too much freedom already, today.

But he didn't think he'd sleep this night. Finding that boy crammed into the closet, trussed and able to do no more than thump his feet, had brought far too much back. He'd wanted to strangle that woman, Bains.

He wanted to go out and kill Fink, now.

When he'd felt the welts under the boy's shabby shirt, his anger had nearly exploded. He knew how it felt, being strapped and shut away into the dark—uncomforted, unwanted, unloved.

It had made him tough. At least he thought it had. So why did he lie alone in the dark now, just like the boy he had been?

He needed to do something about that place, make sure Ellison reported that woman, maybe get that boy out of there and—

He broke off when his ears caught a whisper of sound. The knob on his door turned and the door swished open. In the dim light from the hallway, he beheld a vision.

She wore a pale-colored gown rife with lace that swirled all around her body, and her hair streamed loose, tumbling down across her shoulders in a riot of auburn curls. The breath caught abruptly in Mitch's throat.

His wife. She had come to him. Unprecedented.

What could it mean?

"Tessa?" His voice sounded hoarse in his own ears. "Is something wrong?"

She froze, her hand still on the doorknob.

Don't go, he begged her silently. *Please.*

She seemed to hesitate where she stood, on her bare feet. Then she glided in and shut the door behind her.

Darkness ensued. Mitch wanted to reach for the light, wanted with all his being to see her, but he scarcely believed she was here and feared he might spook her.

Instead, he lay where he was, barely breathing, and tracked her by sound alone as she approached the bed.

"Mitch?"

"Yes?"

"I—" She hesitated again, almost within his reach. "I couldn't sleep. After today."

"Neither could I." His heart now pounded so hard in his ears, he didn't suppose he'd ever be able to sleep again.

Her voice came once more, still closer, and breathy. "I didn't want to be alone. I—I thought...rather, I expected you'd perhaps come to me."

Emotions speared through him and spun his head. She didn't say she *hoped* he'd come. Yet he heard the word anyway.

"Tessa, I thought you'd be tired, and I wasn't sure I'd be welcome."

She reached the bed; he felt her knee bump the side of his mattress. She stood there, and he cursed inwardly that he couldn't see what lay in her eyes.

Before she could comment, he asked, "Tessa, what do you want?"

Her only reply came in a whisper of sound. Mitch had very good hearing, honed by the instinct to survive. She, apparently, had very good night vision, for she reached out and unerringly captured his hand, lifted and guided it.

To her breast.

The sound he'd heard must have been her shrugging the silky bed gown from her shoulders, for her breast lay bare, a warm and tempting mound of softness. Mitch tensed where he lay, stiffened from head to foot, and splayed his fingers, palm against her skin, his delight like pain.

She didn't need to say. Oh, no, she did not.

"Tessa," he groaned.

"Mitch."

At least she knew his name. She moved still closer, putting a knee on the mattress, and bent to cradle his face between her hands. With no further words, she guided his mouth to her naked breast.

No need to ask questions then. He heard her breath catch, there in the velvety dark, as they connected, felt her skin ripple at his touch before she began to melt. Ah, his Tessa always melted so swiftly for him.

His Tessa.

He could give her what she'd come for, what she needed. All of it.

He suckled her there, head against the pillow while she bent to him, sight unseen. When he planted both hands at her waist and tried to lift her onto the bed, though, she pulled away a fraction.

"Wait."

No. he couldn't bear it if she left him now.

But her fingers moved in the darkness—he could see the faintest outline of her and saw when she gave a twitch that caused the gown to fall all the way off and pool at her feet. She stood clothed only in that glorious hair.

"There," she whispered.

He would have lifted her then, but she climbed into the bed, climbed up onto him, and lay with her mouth just above his mouth.

He couldn't breathe, but not for her weight. She weighed nothing, to contain his world. At that moment, the possibilities seemed endless. More suckling? His tongue, his member inside her? He'd offer her all that, and his life if she wanted it.

For answer she kissed him, the kind of kiss that blasted a man's nerve endings and left him gasping. He wore very little, never did for sleeping; she'd smashed herself against his bare chest, and it felt wonderful. But that word fell woefully short for description.

Her tongue plundered his mouth and had him standing below, so hard he knew she must feel it. When she broke the kiss, he could have bellowed in protest.

"I'm sorry," she whispered.

"For—?"

"I'm sorry I ever asked you to go to that place with me this morning. It must have been awful for you. I should have thought."

"This makes up for it." He wound his fingers in her hair and brought her mouth back down to his. This time the kiss became a long, leisurely demand.

One she broke determinedly again.

"Mitch?"

He managed a moan in reply.

"Usually when we're together, you give me whatever I want. You make sure I get all the pleasure."

"Not all of it." But yes, her sweet pleasure had become his pleasure.

"It's going to be different tonight. I'm here for you, understand?"

At first, he didn't. Then he felt her lift herself up from him, felt her tongue against his skin, there in the dark. At his throat. Across his shoulder and plowing into the hair on his chest. Her mouth followed a determined trail that led ever downward.

"Tessa," he said very hoarsely indeed.

"Hush."

A woman on a mission, she glided her mouth over him, unstoppable. Mitch felt the tension—that provoked by memory—leave his body even as a new tension curled through his belly, through his balls and every muscle, making him vibrate in anticipation.

She wouldn't. They had never before crossed this line. She simply would not.

He knew she would when he felt her fingers on the buttons of the short pants he wore, his only garment. By then he already lay like a man slain, flat on his back in the bed, arms out flung. She freed him from his confinement and curled her fingers around him as she had before.

"Does this feel good? As good as when you put your mouth on me?"

Her voice sounded different, thick with desire. The

very sound of it made his member twitch. She put her tongue on him and he nearly rose off the bed. Here, in the quiet dark, he'd found heaven, or it had found him.

"Yes."

"Um?"

"It feels good."

"I want you to feel good tonight. I want to make up for—"

He'd venture into a thousand orphanages in exchange for this. He'd spend a night back at Carter's if she asked it of him. He'd give her his heart, his soul.

She took him in her mouth, tentatively at first, not sure about it. Her mouth, a deep cavern of heat, enfolded him, and he promptly lost his mind.

She worked her way up and down the length of him, taking him in and out, leaving a trail of wet that cooled where she breathed.

"Yes. Tessa, oh, God."

He didn't believe in God. Only he might, if she asked it.

He wound his fingers into her hair and arched his body up into her. She took him deeper and he began to quiver like a man who'd run too far.

He knew he had excellent control. It had been honed in the very harshest of conditions. But those conditions had never included pleasure.

Never this.

It shattered when she lifted her mouth from him and said, "You taste wonderful."

"Tessa, oh, God. You'd better stop. I don't want to release myself into your—" Only he did, more than anything.

"Why not?" Her voice still sounded thick with

arousal.

"You'll find it—disgusting." Women did.

"I don't think I will." She began to lick his thighs, his balls, and then worked her way up the standing length of him again. Just before she took him back into her mouth, before the night exploded and the dark turned bright with stars, she whispered, "I want to please you."

She did. Oh, she did.

Chapter Thirty-Four

Tessa, poised on the curb, glanced around for a steamcab, having left both Marty and Mitch's big car at home earlier in the day. Before meeting Lily Michaels for tea, she'd gone shopping, had even done something unprecedented and bought her husband a present—a silk shirt she fancied might look well on him. Now, loaded down with packages, she saw a cab approaching and turned, raising a hand.

Only to collide with a gentleman bent on hailing the same cab.

The minor collision succeeded in making her drop all her packages. The man in question scrambled to help her retrieve them, and they both lost the cab.

"Oh, I'm so sorry," she gasped, looked into his face, and faltered. "Richard?"

Sure enough, she found herself staring into that very young man's eyes. Accustomed, now, to Mitch's rather rough appearance and even rougher edges, she found Richard Trask almost shockingly handsome. Shining fair hair and a complexion that looked like it had never seen a razor...

His blue eyes immediately cooled. "Mrs. Carter." He looked around frantically, as if searching for another cab. None appeared; the two of them stood marooned on the curb.

But why was Richard looking at her that way?

He'd been the one to break off their friendship, reject her without so much as a decent explanation.

She wanted that explanation, and she wanted it here and now. "I got your message," she said. "How could you, Richard? I thought we were friends."

"Your husband doesn't want me to be your friend."

"What's it to do with him?"

Richard twitched, a full body motion; fear flashed in his clear eyes. "I don't wish to speak of it."

"I do. We had an understanding, or I thought we did. You've even stopped coming to the meetings." She added with emphasis, "Where we were supposed to meet."

He faced her fully. His gaze widened and enfolded her. "I only attended those meetings because of you, so I could see you."

"So, what's changed?"

"Look, Tess, we can't talk about it. Not here in the open where anyone might see—"

"Then let's go somewhere. A café, or a tea house."

"God, no. You can bet he has you watched. He'll know."

"He? Who?"

"Don't be stupid, Tess."

"Mitch? You're talking about Mitch? But he wants me to be happy, he's said so over and over again."

"He wants you to himself." Now anger kindled in Richard's eyes. Odd how easy it seemed, reading Richard's emotions, after learning to decipher the mysteries of Mitch's shuttered face.

Richard rushed on. "He's like a dog. Can't you see that? Some big, ugly, vicious street mongrel in need of a good kicking. He's found a morsel he wants and now won't let anyone else near it."

Tessa shook her head. "I don't know what you mean."

"Then I'll tell you, shall I? He came to see me, Mitch Carter—your husband. Paid me a call at my home. Told me I'd better stop seeing you, warned me if I didn't I'd better not walk down any dark streets in this city, not unless I expected some terrible harm to befall me."

Tessa reeled. She blinked rapidly. "But—the note you sent..."

"He ordered me to break it off, or else. Now, I daren't stand here talking to you any longer. If one of his toughs sees us, it will be me, not you, who pays the price."

"You're afraid of him."

Richard's fair face flushed. But he replied, "Damned right I am. Do you know what a man like that could do to a fellow? Tess, you're his wife."

"Not by choice." True, but once uttered the words felt like a betrayal. She'd married Mitch at her father's behest, yes. But she'd slept with him, these many nights past, for her own sake.

"You married him," Richard said almost nastily. "So in future, please leave me out of it."

A long steamcar with glossy black sides purred up to the curb in front of Tessa. The nearest window cranked down, and she saw the face of Marty, her husband's chauffeur.

"Mrs. Carter, do you need a ride?"

Richard made a strangled sound in his throat and hoofed it with more haste than grace. Marty left the car running while he got out, opened Tessa's door for her, and ushered her inside.

Not till they turned onto Prospect Avenue did Tessa realize the car hadn't appeared by chance, or even providence. Richard had been right—her husband was indeed having her watched.

For how long? And why?

What could she do with the emotions the knowledge raised?

****

"Good news, Tessa," Mitch told his wife as she entered his office. She rarely ventured here uninvited, but they'd become closer since that night when she came to his room, and quite likely she'd come looking for the little dog, which tended to stay with Mitch when she went out.

He didn't care; just seeing her enter the room brought him almost painful pleasure, akin to that when he made love to her. And how lovely she looked, having obviously just come in from outside. She still wore her hat and carried a number of shopping bags in her hands. Her cheeks looked flushed, and her eyes unusually bright.

But she failed to pat the little clockwork dog when it ran up and pawed at her skirt.

"Good?" she repeated the word. "Good news? What could be good about it?"

Mitch frowned at the edge in her voice, but he answered readily, "The old man who owns Carter's is ready to sell. I figure it will take just a bit more persuasion."

"Persuasion."

She sounded like an automaton. Perhaps she'd been spending too much time with that new friend of hers. Glaring at him, she jerked to life; the bags fell from her hands and hit the carpet.

Only then did Mitch realize how angry she was, aflame with rage.

She stepped up to the desk where he sat and leaned both hands on the surface opposite him. Her eyes glowed like those of an incensed tabby. "What sort of persuasion would that be?"

He tensed as he tended to do in the face of any strong emotion or personal threat. "What is it? What's the matter?"

"You frequently persuade, don't you? You coerce. You threaten. It's what you do best."

Mitch got to his feet slowly. He walked around the desk, around the dog which stared at Tessa as if it had never seen her before. Mitch sympathized; he'd never seen Tessa in this mood either. He shut the office door and turned to face her.

"You're angry."

"Oh, how perceptive he is—for a tough."

Mitch flinched inwardly, though he didn't let it show. Disappointment touched him. He'd hoped they were past all that and she'd accepted what he was—and wasn't.

"Maybe you should explain why you're so upset, Tessa."

"No, maybe *you* should explain." Her eyes narrowed. "Do you have me watched?"

And where had this come from? When he failed to answer at once, she grimaced and barreled on.

"By your boys? By Marty, maybe? Big man in this city, aren't you? You can have things any way you want."

"What's got you so fired up?"

"Marty appeared with the car this afternoon, out of nowhere—just after I'd bumped into a *friend*."

"So?"

"The friend was Richard Trask."

Oh. Anger combined with dread in Mitch's stomach. This couldn't be good. It couldn't possibly—

"Richard said you warned him off me. Threatened he might meet with a mishap down some dark street in the city if he didn't break things off. That's why he dropped our association. Is it true? Is it?"

"Tess, you don't need associations with other men."

"How dare you?" she howled. The little clockwork dog dove under the desk. "How could you banish a friend from my life and then act as if you care about my welfare?"

"I do care about you." If she only knew how much.

"So you show it by making me friendless?"

"He was more than just a friend to you, and you know it. You wanted relations with him. What chance did I have, with him in the picture?"

"You might have spoken with me about it, told me how you felt."

She had no idea how difficult he found it to express his feelings.

"Instead you went behind my back. Got Richard to drop me with no explanation, so I thought he didn't care about me anymore."

"He didn't care." Just like hers, Mitch's voice rose. "If he cared—if he really loved you—he'd have done anything for you. Whatever he had to. He'd move heaven and earth to be with you." This Mitch knew to his very soul.

"He's afraid of you. Most people with any sense in this city are afraid of you. Why did I ever think anything else? Why did I imagine you could change?"

"I *can* change," Mitch said desperately. "Tessa, listen to me."

"I'm done listening to you. You're nothing, Mitch Carter—nothing but a brute, a bully, and a manipulator. You thought you could manipulate me, didn't you, with your gifts and your kisses? Well, it's over. I'm finished with you."

"Tessa, don't say that." He reached for her the way a man overboard might reach for a life preserver. Frantically, she batted his hand away. "Don't touch me, never again. I hate you. Do you hear me?"

He heard. *He heard.* He also heard the door slam as she went out of the office, the worst sound since a similar heavy door used to slam on that room in the back, at Carter's, where Fink would put a boy alone.

It all rushed upon him then. What had he done? Lost her.

Lost her.

She hated him.

Groping like a blind man, he found his way back around the desk and sat in his chair. Something nudged his hand. The little clockwork dog had ventured out from under the desk and stared at Mitch with earnest glass eyes, as if reading his mood.

He touched its head, and it scrambled up over his knee and into his lap, where it cuddled close. It stayed with him as he sat on into the night.

****

"I'm sorry, Mrs. Carter, ma'am, but I have orders

not to offer you the car. From the boss."

From the boss. Of course. Tessa's anger, which had eased only marginally during the interminable night, roared back to life. He thought he could keep her trapped here, did he? The monster.

And Mitch Carter was a monster, just as she'd thought at the beginning of their association. He might have fooled her for a time with touching confidences, after worming his way into her bed, but she saw the truth about him now. And she needed to visit her brother, Gerald, as soon as possible, so she could tell him she wanted her marriage dissolved after all—by whatever means possible.

That was the truth she'd realized in the depths of the night after she wept and raged and grieved—for she had grieved the loss of trust and belief in Mitch Carter. If he could go behind her back that way, he might do any damned thing.

She couldn't stay with such a man. She certainly couldn't love him.

But when morning came and she pulled herself together, put on her most stylish clothes, curled her hair, and ventured downstairs, Marty refused to let her use the car.

Now she stared at the chauffeur in outrage. He looked back at her impassively, all but for what might be a hint of sympathy in his eyes.

God knows how she must appear—she hadn't managed to erase all the tearstains and still felt ill.

But she said, "Very well. I'll hail a cab. Or walk."

Marty reached out for her. "Ma'am, I—"

She stiffened. "Oh, are you going to keep me here by force? Are those his orders? And you do whatever he tells you, right?"

Marty withdrew his hand as if she'd slapped it. He seemed to battle some strong emotion. "I'd do anything for the boss. He's been good to me. He came back and got me out of Carter's."

Tessa thought of that terrible place, of the courage it would take to go back at all, once sprung. But that couldn't overwhelm her anger or make her trust Mitch again.

"Please, ma'am," Marty said earnestly, "don't hurt him."

"Me, hurt him?"

"He cares so much for you. I can tell."

"You're mistaken. Now, unless you mean to make a captive of me, please step aside. I'm going out."

Looking miserable, Marty shuffled to one side. Hand on the doorknob, Tessa looked back at him. "I suppose as soon as I step out this door you'll go running to him."

Marty shook his head. "He's in a meeting. An important one."

"Good."

Still watched by the chauffeur, Tessa slipped out the door and stood for a moment in the fading sunlight, trembling. The chilly autumn day promised rain, and Prospect Avenue looked busy. No cab to be hailed.

Very well, then, she'd walk to her brother's house on Bouck Avenue, if she had to.

Whatever it took to dissolve her marriage and free her from Mitch Carter.

Chapter Thirty-Five

"We have a problem. Seems that fecking hybrid automaton has quite a number of informants, likely more than you and I put together. He probably hears from every tin servant in this city, and there are a lot of them."

Mitch turned his head to glare at Danny Dwyer, who'd invaded his office early that morning and now lounged in the big chair opposite the desk.

Mitch had never made it out of the office all night and still wore the clothes he'd donned yesterday, now creased and far from fresh. He'd consumed more whiskey than he normally did in a year, grieved, argued, and raged in his head.

He wanted to go up to his wife's room. He longed to take her in his arms and tell her—no, show her— what she meant to him. He didn't quite dare—him, the frigging King of Prospect Avenue, who didn't dare face a small, slender woman.

Instead, around midnight, he'd summoned Tiny and given him orders for the other boys.

Watch her. Protect her. Guard her life as they would his, Mitch's, life.

If she found out, he supposed it would make her hate him more than ever. If that were possible.

The last thing he wanted or expected was an appearance from Danny Dwyer. He fought to marshal his thoughts as he paced behind the desk, unable to keep still.

"You're talking about Pat Kelly."

"Of course I'm talking about fecking Pat Kelly. The bastard's like an octopus, I tell you, damned mechanical fingers everywhere."

Mitch paused in his pacing to eye Dwyer again, and rage licked through him. "I suppose you're telling me he's on to us—the fact that we've teamed up to outbid him downtown."

"No." Dwyer sneered. "I'm after telling you he suspects we're the ones who snatched his wife."

"What?" Mitch glared. "I had no part in that business. You were supposed to talk to him, reason with him, Irishman to Irishman. Instead, you terrorized that woman."

"Ah, she wasn't hurt, was she? Just frightened a wee bit. And how was I to know Kelly's obsessive about the woman? He's a fecking machine, for God's sake."

"You don't mess with a man's family, machine or not."

Dwyer snorted. "You going soft, Carter? Or maybe you're developing sympathies for the steamies, like that piece o' trash under your desk?"

Mitch, all too aware that the little dog which had kept him company all night rested there, didn't even glance down.

"I have few sympathies for anyone."

"That's not what word on the street says." Dwyer smiled. "It says you've taken up philanthropy, planning on buying up orphanages."

"What's that to you?"

Dwyer shrugged. "Only that you're supposed to be such a hard man, but I'll bet Kelly's harder than you, and he's not even a man."

"You think I care about your opinion of me, Dwyer? I don't give a damn. You're a fool—you never should have snatched that woman. It was business, but you've made it personal with him. Now he likely won't rest till he and his army of steamies bring you and me both down."

Dwyer shrugged again, this time uneasily. "It was you gave me the idea, mentioning he had a wife. Anyway, I didn't have to come here and warn you he's on to us."

"Not us—I never suggested you should grab her."

"You were there in that shed, though, weren't you?"

"I'm not afraid of him." Mitch had far bigger problems.

"You should be. Yesterday he bought that property on Chippewa right out from under us. He has bids in on both Swan and Huron. I don't know where he gets the money."

"I told you, they probably pool it—the automatons. What else are they going to do with it? Listen to me, Dwyer. Our association, yours and mine, is over."

"What?" Dwyer shot up in the chair.

"You heard me. You went beyond the terms of our agreement, snatched that woman, and queered the deal. I'm done."

"You can't do that, man. He'll beat us both. We'll lose downtown."

"Then we lose it."

"To fecking automatons? God damn it, Carter,

they're not even real."

"They're real. They're just not human."

"What the hell's happened to you?" Dwyer got to his feet. "We had an agreement. It's not a good idea to go back on any agreement you make with me."

Mitch stepped up to him. "That a threat?"

An ugly look invaded Danny Dwyer's eyes. "You've got a wife too, right? A damn pretty one."

Mitch moved without his own volition, his body leaping before his mind could react. In a blink he'd seized Dwyer and forced him up out of the chair and against the wall beside the door, his forearm across Dwyer's throat.

"Don't even think about it. You touch a hair on her head—you even look at her—you're a dead man."

Dwyer gurgled; his eyes spat hate.

"Now…" Mitch released him with an extra hard thump. "Get out of my house. I don't want to see you again. Like I said, our association's done."

Dwyer, nearly too furious to speak, straightened his jacket. "You'll regret this."

"I don't think so."

"Anybody crosses Danny Dwyer learns how to regret."

"I didn't cross you, you stupid bugger. You ruined the deal."

Dwyer raked Mitch up and down with a glare. "What in hell happened to you? Ain't you supposed to be the fecking King of Prospect? Pitiful."

Valerie crept out from under Mitch's desk; Dwyer aimed a kick at the unit that nearly connected.

"Steamie sympathizer," he spat before he shot from the office, stormed down the hallway, and slammed out the front door.

A series of heads appeared—some human and some mechanical—and eyes peered at Mitch.

He gestured to the nearest, which happened to be Marty, lurking for some unknown reason at the side of the foyer.

"Where's my wife? Upstairs in her room?" It still being very early, no doubt she hadn't yet emerged. She might not emerge at all, if she remained angry with him.

"No, Boss. She went out."

"What?" Mitch's head reeled. "But I gave orders she was to stay put."

"Yeah, Boss, I know."

Tiny appeared from the direction of the kitchen. Mitch, still glaring at Marty, barely noticed. "I told you not to let her have the car."

"I didn't, Boss. That's why I'm still here." Marty hesitated. "But she was real determined on going out somewhere."

"Where?" Mitch demanded, his throat going tight.

"Don't know, Boss. If I'd been driving her—"

Mitch could have kicked himself. Marty was right. In the chauffeur's company, at least Tessa would have some protection. Now she could be any damn place.

Where might she go? Too early for one of her meetings. Might she go to a friend? That Mrs. Michaels she spoke of so often, the hybrid automaton. Or had she left him?

His chest grew as tight as his throat. Had she run to Trask?

He lowered his voice and stared Marty in the eye. "You saw her leave?"

"Yeah, Boss—while you was in with Dwyer."

"She take anything with her? Was she carrying a suitcase?"

"No, Boss. Just that little bag of hers."

A gentle bump against Mitch's ankle reminded him Tessa had even left Valerie behind. Surely she wouldn't leave for good without her pet.

To all the staring faces he said, "Find her. She might have gone to see someone called Lily Michaels."

"I know where the Michaels live. I dropped her off there once," Marty said. "I'll go."

Tiny asked, "But Boss, if we find her, you want us to bring her back even if she doesn't want to come—by force?"

"No." God, no. That's all it would take. "Just keep an eye on her, make sure she's safe. Let me know."

So he had some hope of going on, of living.

Chapter Thirty-Six

Tessa hadn't walked four blocks before the weak morning sunlight faded and it began to rain. A cold rain, it contained a touch of sleet and battered her hat in a manner that rendered it useless for protection. She cut down an alley from Prospect, and on the corner of Massachusetts and Niagara she searched in vain for a cab before walking on, her anger making the very idea of returning home impossible.

She never wanted to see Mitch Carter again. She intended to throw herself on Gerald's mercy, ask if she could stay with him and Dorcas until the marriage was dissolved. After that...

For the life of her, she could see nothing beyond that point. She'd once thought she loved Richard and wanted to spend the rest of her life with him. Now, though, what Mitch had said last night haunted her mind.

If he loved you, he'd have done anything for you. Whatever he had to. He'd move heaven and earth to be with you.

Was that true? Yet threats were threats, and Richard was a decent young man, not used to facing intimidation from the likes of Mitch Carter, a virtual savage who would say or do anything to come out on top.

A savage with whom she'd shared her bed—

repeatedly—and whose child she might now carry. A man who'd made her feel emotions and sensations such as she'd never imagined and made her crave him the way she suspected some poor souls craved opium. And who had lied to her all the while, manipulating her life.

Over. Done. All those nights now were like a dream from the past. She would never return to the house on Prospect Avenue. Gerald could send for Valerie and her other belongings.

She stepped off a curb into an icy puddle, caught her heel between a grate and a brick, and felt it snap. With a bitter curse she swayed and foundered, fighting for balance.

To her relief, a cab drew up in front of her. At last. The driver must have seen her standing here and thought she hailed him.

However, a back window rather than a front cranked down.

"Ma'am, you seem to be in some difficulty." The voice issuing from within sounded warm and Irish. "Would there be something I could do to help?"

"No, thank you. That's all right." For the life of her, Tessa could find no other words. She stood with the heel of one shoe clutched in her hand, the rain pelting down, and wondered how she'd ever make it to Bouck Avenue.

The passenger leaned forward so she could see him. About thirty years of age and wearing a workman's coat, he had a shock of light hair and a disarming smile.

"Surely, ma'am, you'll allow me to be of assistance?"

"Assistance?"

"I don't think you'll be finding a cab in this weather. But you're welcome to share mine."

"Oh, I couldn't inconvenience you."

"It's no inconvenience, I assure you. I'm certainly in no hurry. And I believe, don't you, there's no such thing as happenstance."

Tessa, no longer sure what she believed, hesitated one more moment. Then she hobbled forward two steps and climbed into the cab.

Her rescuer reached across her lap to shut the door. She caught a whiff of bay rum—and whiskey. Her stomach muscles tightened.

"I don't think…" she began and drew a breath. "I think I'd rather walk after all."

"No, you won't."

The cab glided off from the curb. Tessa's companion sat back against the cushions and examined her with pale blue eyes.

He said, "I know who you are. You're the fecking Queen of Prospect Avenue."

****

"Boss, she seems to have disappeared for the moment. Two of the boys followed her away from the house. They lost sight of her in the rain and went in different directions, hoping to pick her up again. One of 'em did, but there was a lot of traffic. He dodged between some cabs, and she was gone."

Tiny brought the ill news and stood with wide eyes, flat cap in hand, while he delivered it.

Mitch, desperate to distraction, raked his fingers through his hair and glared. "How could he lose sight of one single woman?"

"Like I say, there were a lot of carts and steamcabs,

Boss, and it was raining pretty hard."

"Which way was she headed?" Again, Mitch cursed himself for depriving Tessa of the car. With its use, at least he'd know where she was.

"She headed pretty much due north along Prospect, Boss. Maybe she was on her way to the Michaels'. Want me to call there?"

"Yes. No. I'll go myself." Mitch drew a breath and struggled to regain his composure. "What's the address? Have Marty bring the car around."

"Already standing by, Boss."

Mitch assured himself he'd find Tessa drinking tea with Mrs. Michaels, possibly telling her friend how much she despised him.

But he had excellent instincts and knew damn well he wouldn't.

****

The woman who opened the door of the apartment looked almost impossibly beautiful. Golden hair tumbled from a knot gathered on top of her head to kiss a pink cheek, and wide, ice-blue eyes regarded Mitch in cool examination.

As the last time he'd encountered her, he marveled at how little she looked like an automaton; then again, the hybrids rarely did.

"Mr. Carter," she greeted him. "How lovely to see you again. What can I do for you?"

"I'm sorry to intrude, Mrs. Michaels." Mitch had made a concerted effort before he left Prospect Avenue to tame his wild appearance. He'd combed his hair, crammed himself into a clean shirt, and donned a respectable jacket. But he couldn't hold back the anxiety that made him blurt, "I'm looking for my wife.

257

Is she here?"

The automaton tipped her head. "I am sorry, Mr. Carter, but Tessa is not here. I was planning on seeing her later, at one of our meetings, and perhaps sharing tea, but that would not occur until later this afternoon. Is something wrong?"

"I'm not sure. I—I think so."

"Please, come in."

The apartment, large and located at the top of the house, appeared modest in the extreme. Mitch had no idea what Lily Michaels' husband did for a living; he'd never bothered to ask Tessa. The place looked clean, though, and surprisingly homey, with touches like lace curtains at the windows and frilly cushions on the chairs.

He turned to look at the automaton. Sparing nothing, he said starkly, "We quarreled yesterday."

"Couples do quarrel, I am given to understand. She speaks of you often—"

"She does?" Mitch couldn't hide his surprise.

"Of course. I am privileged to be the recipient of your wife's confidences. We are friends."

"But she hasn't been here today?"

"No, I have not seen her since after our last meeting at the Meadows Club, when we shared tea at a café." Lily Michaels tipped her head to one side. "Was this quarrel you mention a serious one?"

"Yes." Mitch took a deep breath and plunged forward. "She's left me."

"I am sorry to hear that. Are you certain she didn't just go off for a while in order to calm her emotions?"

"Well, no." Mitch listened hard to his instincts again. "Yes."

"How very unfortunate. But she did not come here. I am certain, Mr. Carter, she will soon cool down, as people say, and return home."

"I'm not. She's quite upset with me."

"Do you think she's fled to her lover?"

"Eh?" Mitch nearly choked.

"Her former lover, I should say. I believe of late she'd transferred the bulk of her affections to you."

"What?"

"She spoke of you in the way a woman speaks of a man for whom she cares deeply."

"I'm sure you're mistaken." Mitch's heart began to thud in his chest sickeningly.

"I am rarely mistaken, Mr. Carter. I have a deep reference bank built up by all the reading I have done. Tessa herself may not realize how much she had come to rely on your presence in her life, but I could tell."

Mitch reeled. "Listen, I need to find her. Where do you think she will have gone? To him? Richard Trask?"

"He rejected her."

"But she'd recently found out why—that's the reason we quarreled. Mrs. Michaels, if you can think of anything—"

Again she tipped her head. "When upset, women frequently return to their families."

"Her mother? You think so? I'll go there directly. And thank you. If you come up with any other ideas, will you let me know?"

"I will. I will also go out and look for her at the Meadows Club, inquire of the other members, and check at the cafés we frequented. If I find her, I will advise her to return to your house."

"Thank you. I can't express—"

"No need. I told you, Mr. Carter, I'm very perceptive. I can tell exactly how you feel."

Chapter Thirty-Seven

"Who are you? And what do you want with me?" Tessa asked sharply.

The man lounging opposite her on the seat of the cab retained his casual pose, seemingly at ease, but even in the dim light Tessa saw how his eyes quickened with emotion.

"With you? Not a thing, though I will declare you're tempting. I must say, Carter has fine taste in women."

"My husband, then. This is about him."

"Smart cookie, as well as lovely. He broke off a deal with me. Nobody does that after they've given me their word; it means he's got to pay. And what should I see while I'm nursing my anger but yourself, standing there in the rain. I'm a lucky bastard sometimes, and no mistake."

Fear mingled with the dismay clogging Tessa's throat. What a fool she'd been to enter this cab! Fool, fool, *fool*. This man, whose voice had sounded so reassuring, proved dangerous as a snake. She might as well have crawled into a sack with an adder.

Swiftly she strove to calculate her odds. The cab now moved quickly through the rain-drenched streets, and she had no doubt the door beside her was locked. She possessed no weapon save the heel of her shoe, still clutched in her right hand.

But Mitch—Mitch always had her watched. Her heart steadied and rose a bit. Surely his men had seen what happened to her. They'd follow, they'd tell him.

She said almost involuntarily, "He's going to be furious with you."

"Carter? No doubt. But he needs to learn some respect, right? Thinks he's fecking royalty, when he started out no better than me. He values you, missus. And I always take what's of greatest value."

"Who are you?" Tessa asked again.

"Now, you can't expect me to be telling you that."

"Where are you taking me?"

He grinned, like a shark. "Can't tell you that either. Wouldn't be safe for you to know. No need for you to fear, though."

As if she believed that.

"I'll just hold you a wee while, send a message to your husband. Let him see how he's underestimated me."

Mitch. For an instant, Tessa longed for him so intensely she ached. She wanted to be with him, in the safe harbor of his arms. Then her anger returned, and she remembered why she'd left the house on Prospect Avenue in the first place.

Her fellow passenger moved for the first time since he'd leaned over to close the door for her. He seemed to coil, gathering himself; from a pocket he produced a length of fabric, with a flourish.

"Now, Mrs. Carter, if you'll just cooperate with me and keep quiet, we can make this easy."

"What—"

"Did I not tell you to hush? Do you want me to gag you as well?"

"Gag me?"

The length of fabric came at her, caught between the man's hands. Ah—he meant to strangle her. She'd never get out of this cab alive.

But she wouldn't die without a fight.

He flung himself on her, using all his weight, and pinned her between the door and the back of the seat. In response, Tessa erupted—she manipulated the broken heel in her hand so the point faced outward, brought it up and struck at him repeatedly, all while thrashing and kicking.

"Ah, feck! You shouldn't have done that, Mrs. Carter. You truly shouldn't."

"Don't touch me. Keep your hands off me. Keep away!"

Something came at Tessa from the gloom of the cab's interior. When it made contact with her face, it felt very hard, with both weight and power behind it. The force of it tossed her back against the side door, where her head made contact with the window. Darkness descended on her, thick, black, and utterly complete.

****

The house on Bryant Street looked neat and well-kept, even in the filthy rain. The front door had been painted red, and a large pot of copper-colored chrysanthemums sat on the stoop. The place didn't appear at all like the home of an automaton.

Mitch shook his body like a wet dog and told himself he didn't care. He'd left Prospect directly after a last powwow with his boys, during which the opinion had been expressed that Tessa had been snatched. Her trail had ended among the thick traffic on Niagara near

Massachusetts. No sign of her anywhere. Definitely not at her mother's house, though she'd been heading roughly in that direction.

Mitch had no choice but to reach for logic, his ultimate resource in times of difficulty. It seemed logical to him that if someone—even an automaton—suspected you had snatched his wife, he might well snatch yours in return.

He'd brought three of the boys with him to Pat Kelly's, but now he signaled them, and they took off on a turn around the block. He approached the red door alone.

When it opened to his knock, he saw a woman, but not the one he'd expected. He'd had a look at Pat Kelly's wife down on the waterfront, and even though she'd been blindfolded at the time, he knew he'd recognize her.

This woman, just above medium height and ramrod straight, had brown hair and intelligent dark eyes. She carried a very small steam cannon in her right hand.

Not the customary way to answer the door in a nice neighborhood; Mitch, completely overset, barely noticed.

"Yes?" the woman said, just a bit aggressively.

"I'm looking for Patrick Kelly."

"He's at work." The dark eyes narrowed. "Does he know you?"

"We've never met, but I think he has something that belongs to me. May I come in?"

"I told you he's not here."

"I'll wait."

"You won't." She began to swing the door shut. Mitch blocked it with one palm against the red paint.

"Is his wife at home?"

The steam cannon swung up and aimed directly at the center of Mitch's chest. "What's it to you?"

"I need to speak with her."

"You need a lot of things. Rose isn't seeing anyone."

"Look, Missus—"

"It's Miss. Miss Landry, actually."

"When will Mr. Kelly be back?"

Before Miss Landry could answer, a voice sounded from behind her. "What is it, Ginny?"

A woman stepped into view, the woman Mitch had last seen captive in Danny Dwyer's company. Taller than her companion, she had soft brown hair piled into a loose knot, a face rigid with tension, and worried brown eyes.

"Who is he, Ginny?"

The steam cannon didn't waver. "He hasn't said, but if I had to guess, I'd say trouble."

"What does he want? Are you going to keep him standing in the rain?"

"Yes, until he explains why he's here. He says he wants Pat."

"Mrs. Kelly, I'm Mitch Carter," Mitch began and the woman recoiled. "Ginny, I've heard that voice before. On that day—"

Miss Landry released the safety on the cannon. "Well, then, Mr. Carter, I expect you'd better step inside."

****

Tessa came awake slowly to thick, choking darkness. She didn't have a clue where she was, but the blindfold remained in place and had now been accentuated by a gag, tied uncomfortably tight, which made it difficult to breathe.

She lay on her side with her wrists bound behind her, upon a blanket that smelled of horse. Indoors, but she could hear the rain still falling at a distance, and her damp clothing had chilled enough to start her shivering. The left side of her jaw hurt like a fierce toothache.

That man, that horrible man, had hit her. Punched her. Never before in her life had she been so much as swatted. Her father might have had his faults, but they didn't extend to harsh discipline of his children.

Harsh discipline. Those words made her think of Mitch. She saw again the stark ridges on his back, felt them beneath her questing fingers when they made love, when he entered her with breathless tenderness. Emotion swamped her, and tears rushed to her eyes.

Oh, Mitch. Where was he now?

Deprived of the sense of sight, she stretched her ears and listened. Was she alone? Hard to tell—a whole crowd of people could be standing and staring at her, but if so, she couldn't hear them. No breathing other than her own gasps, fighting against the gag.

The man who'd lured her into the cab hated her husband, maybe even more than she did. For surely, surely she still felt angry with Mitch. And surely she hated him.

She'd told him so.

And what had she seen in his eyes when she spoke those words? Best not to think about it now or she'd lose her mind.

No, she needed to think. *Think.* Terror made that a difficult proposition. The man with the Irish accent had a beef with Mitch. Would he kill her, Tessa, in some terrible act of revenge? Would she die here alone, never having seen Mitch again?

She trembled where she lay, and the tears overwhelmed her, trickling from her clenched eyes to drench the blindfold. A sob caught against the gag, and her nose filled, making it impossible to breathe.

No, she couldn't weep. If she did, she'd lie here and suffocate in her own tears.

Desperate and sweating, she fought back the emotions and struggled to discipline them. Was that what Mitch always did? Was that how he'd endured the leather strap biting into his flesh, the starvation, and the loneliness?

Ah, yes, a sharp and hungry loneliness raged inside her husband. She'd felt it, caught glimpses of it behind that wall he usually kept up.

But why did she persist in thinking of him now? She would need all her wits, all her concentration, to survive.

She listened again and decided she must be in a large space because the crashing rain echoed at a distance. And the air, even when she cleared her nose, tickled the back of her throat.

She scrabbled around where she lay and flexed her wrists in an effort to loosen her bonds. Before she could succeed, her ear caught sounds other than the rain—what might be the slam of a door and footsteps. She froze.

Someone approached the place where she lay, and he came humming. A jaunty little tune, it too seemed to echo in the space she couldn't see, just like the footsteps. A man's voice.

Her stomach twisted with fear, and she thought

surely she'd retch. If she did, she would choke—so she fought her emotions down once again.

She didn't want to die here. More than anything else, she wanted to go home.

Chapter Thirty-Eight

"Explain yourself, Mr. Carter," said the woman with the dangerous dark eyes. After admitting him to the ground floor flat, she'd backed him into a straight wooden chair, where she kept him captive by force with the steam cannon. Rose Kelly perched on a second chair, the anxiety fairly streaming from her.

In his time on the streets, along the way to becoming the King of Prospect, Mitch had faced any number of weapons, including side arms, broken bottles, and knives of all descriptions. He didn't think any of them rivaled a steam cannon—even a small one like this—in the hands of a defensive woman. If her finger so much as twitched, significant portions of his anatomy would cook instantly and he'd die on the spot.

What would happen to Tessa then?

He looked Miss Landry in the eye. "Can you please aim that weapon somewhere else? I just want to talk."

"I'm afraid not, Mr. Carter. Mrs. Kelly here says she's heard your voice before, at an unfortunate moment in her life."

"Mrs. Kelly might be mistaken." Mitch shot a look at the woman in question. The agony in her wide eyes called up an unexpected measure of sympathy.

"Mrs. Kelly, I'm just looking for my wife. She disappeared this morning, and we've been unable to locate her. I very much fear she's been abducted."

Mrs. Kelly trembled. "And you think Pat has her? Why would he do such a terrible thing?" She leaned forward, displaying strength beneath her anxiety. "Why, unless I'm right about hearing your voice before, and you had a hand in abducting me?"

Why, indeed?

Mitch said, "I had no hand in snatching you, ma'am, but I know who did."

"And you were there that day."

"I might have been brought there by the person who abducted you. If your husband's after revenge, I'll give him the culprit's name, just so long as he releases my wife safely."

Rose Kelly gave a brittle smile. "You don't know my husband, do you? He doesn't believe in revenge. Mr. Carter, Pat isn't holding your wife."

"How do you know? She may not be here. That doesn't mean—"

"You're not listening to me. Pat would not put a woman—any woman—through what I endured. He's a finer man than that."

He wasn't a man at all, but Mitch didn't point that out. Rose Kelly seemed utterly convinced.

Miss Landry waggled the steam cannon at him. "Seems like you're barking up the wrong tree, Mr. Carter. Pat didn't snatch your wife. I suggest you concentrate on whoever did."

And in his mind's ear, Mitch heard Danny Dwyer's voice. *You have a wife too, a pretty one.*

Damnation!

"I see by your expression you may have arrived at a possibility," said Ginny Landry dryly.

Had Danny Dwyer grabbed her? But how? And for

what reason? Kelly had the motive of revenge. Dwyer...

Dwyer, a brute and a bully, got what he wanted out of life through thievery, cajolery, and intimidation. He might have snatched Tessa just to get back at Mitch for breaking off their deal. Men like him—and Mitch himself—always went for the weak spot.

And no one could deny Tessa was Mitch's weak spot, possibly his only one.

"Mr. Carter, do you think your wife's been snatched by the same man who abducted me?" Mrs. Kelly urged, "Give me his name. We'll send a message to Pat, and he'll help you hunt the villain down."

"His name's Danny Dwyer. You can tell your husband so, but I'll need no help hunting him down. I have my own boys."

Miss Landry's eyes widened. "You mean to start a turf war, Mr. Carter? I don't think Pat would approve. That's what the police are for."

"Miss Landry, men like me don't turn to the coppers for help."

The two women exchanged glances. Miss Landry held out her side arm. "Do you need to borrow this?"

"No, thank you, Miss Landry. I've weapons of my own."

Mrs. Kelly leaned toward him. "Then go find your wife, Mr. Carter. Find her as quickly as you can."

****

The cheerful, hummed ditty ceased just above Tessa's head. She could feel the man standing there, and goose bumps broke out all over her body. He might do anything to her—beat her, brutalize her, or rape her.

And what about her child—Mitch's child—then?

Oh, Mitch, she cried in her mind.

Without warning, hard hands seized her and drew her up. Fingers dug at her mouth—the horrid gag came away.

"Don't scream. It will echo something fierce in here and I'll be forced to silence you."

Tessa sucked in a deep breath and coughed. "Where are we? What is this place?"

His voice warmed, the Irish accent oozing charm. "You, my dear, are privileged to occupy the interior of Mr. Dart's great invention."

"What?"

"You're not familiar with Mr. Dart? And you native to this great city. Tsk, tsk."

Tessa fought to keep from screaming; she believed her captor would follow through on his threat. "I don't understand."

"This, Queen Carter, is the interior of a grain elevator, one of many here on the waterfront. The bin you're in happens to be empty at the moment—cleared out into canal boats earlier today. The Irish boys who work here did a good job, didn't they? Got nearly every scrap. If not, I daresay you'd smother."

"Take off the blindfold so I can see."

He ignored the request. "Of course, Queen Carter, this bin won't stay empty long. The lake freighters are standing by waiting to unload. As soon as this rain stops, that process will begin, and then you *will* smother."

"Take off the blindfold!"

"Not a good idea, pretty lady."

"I already got a good look at you in the cab," Tessa reminded him, perhaps unwisely.

"Very well." Cruel fingers tore the blindfold away, catching a handful of Tessa's hair in the process.

Tessa looked wildly from the man poised in front of her—dirty blond hair, narrowed blue eyes, and a twisted smile—to the space that surrounded them. *Bin* made a good description of the place, at least from what she could see by the light of the single lantern set on the floor at her captor's side. Made of wood, like a giant crate, the building stretched out around her. Far overhead she could see a shuttered opening. A chute? Grain littered the broad floor.

No hope of escape, that was the important thing, especially with the man standing so very close to her.

With difficulty she focused on him. "What did Mitch do to you, to make you abduct me?"

Again he ignored the question and spread his hands. "Did you know I worked here a short while? Not for long, it's true. Moving grain is damn hard work, and I wasn't born to work hard. In the old days, before Mr. Dart had his grand idea, all the grain that came down the lake was moved on the backs of Irish laborers. They were cheap, see. Cheaper than horses, and people cared even less what happened to them. Now they just have to break their backs shoveling. Things get better for some, not so much for others. I've found we make our own fortune. Point is, the grain's moved up from the holds on a conveyer powered by steam. When you hear that big steam engine fire up, you'll know you're about to die."

"Why?"

"I told you, your husband—the self-styled King of Prospect—needs to be taught a lesson in respect. I've sent him a message. We'll see what he's willing to trade for your safety, just how highly he values you."

Tessa thought of the look in Mitch's eyes when she told him she hated him. A deep shudder wracked her body. How might a man like Mitch Carter—one who'd been through the hell that was life in the orphanage, where love never showed its face—react to a declaration of hate?

Might he decide he was done with her? Sure, he'd whispered the words "I love you" when he held her in his arms, but did he even know what love was? Might he not wash his hands of her, leave her here in the clutches of this dire bully?

To smother beneath a load of grain. To die.

"Let me go," she advised. "You don't want to cross him. He's a dangerous man."

"You think I'm afraid of fecking Mitch Carter? Ah, no."

"Just let me go."

"You mean to beg? That might be interesting. You're awfully pretty." He grinned. "It might be entertaining to find out just what you'd do to ransom yourself."

Tessa recoiled, and he laughed. "We'll save that for later, eh? Just before you die. Meanwhile, let's see what your husband decides to do."

Oh, Mitch, Tessa's heart cried again. *Please, please come.*

Chapter Thirty-Nine

"A note's been delivered, Boss. Not ten minutes ago, right here at the front door." Tiny, who'd greeted Mitch on the steps when he arrived home, searched his face, eyes full of anxiety. "Think it's about the missus?"

Mitch, his instincts working overtime, felt sure of it. He only said, "Where?"

Tiny produced a single, folded sheet of paper. Mitch fairly snatched it from his fingers. He read and the blood drained from his head. "Christ! He does have her."

"Who does?"

"Danny Dwyer."

"Dwyer snatched your wife? But how? And why?"

Mitch fought to breathe against the weight of dread sitting on his chest. He thought again of Mrs. Kelly— her terror when Dwyer had dragged him to the waterfront to view her.

The boathouse. Could that be where Dwyer had Tessa now?

Tessa.

"I don't know how he got hold of her. He and I had a meeting here, and he left... Damn it all, I should have let Marty drive her." His fault. It was all his fault.

Marty, climbing from the car, joined them on the steps. Others of Mitch's boys filtered from various points around the house. It reminded him of the old days at Carter's when they would gather—a ragged and desperate band just looking for some way to fill their bellies.

A family.

Family, for those who'd never had one, consisted of those you favored closely, those whom you'd never abandon. That had always been enough for Mitch, till he laid eyes on Tessa Verdun. Then, for the first time ever, he'd wanted something solely for himself.

And now Tessa was paying the price. King of Prospect? He was a damned slave, lying at her feet.

"Boss?" said one of the boys. "You all right? Only, you don't look so hot."

Mitch didn't feel very well. There were moments, he'd found, when his life ground to an ugly halt—just like that last time Morton Fink beat him—and started up again, spinning in a new direction.

Such as now.

"We need to find her." If he couldn't find her, he might as well slit his own throat. Because even though she hated him, he couldn't live without her.

"What's Dwyer say?" Tiny demanded and nodded at the note in Mitch's hand.

Mitch's lips twisted. "He requests another meeting."

"Here?"

"No." Mitch glanced at the laborious printing on the paper, which blurred before his eyes. "He says he requests the honor of the King's presence down on Commercial Avenue. Some freight office there."

"Now?"

"Six p.m."

Tiny spoke. "Dwyer used to work shifting grain on the docks before he took to buying up properties. You think he has a bolt hole there, Boss?"

"I think he has half a dozen of them. Rats usually do."

"We'll get some weapons," Lou said, "and all go together. If he wants a war—"

"Don't you get it? He has my wife—and that's every weapon that matters. He can name his terms, and he knows it."

The boys exchanged uneasy glances, there in the pouring rain.

"What do you think Dwyer's gonna ask for?" Tiny wondered aloud.

And Mitch, his stomach clenching inside him, said, "Don't know. I suppose I'd better meet up with him and find out."

****

After her captor left, Tessa lay on her side and tried to think about her odds for survival. The Irishman with the dangerous voice and deadly eyes had neglected to replace the blindfold. But he'd planted a sloppy kiss on her cheek before tying on the detested gag, drawing the fabric far too tight. When he touched her, Tessa had, indeed, feared she'd gag.

"I promise you, bonny lass, I won't leave you alone too long. If your husband decides he can't be bothered to ransom you, maybe I'll take out another sort of payment before you die, eh?"

An idle threat, or a credible one? Impossible to tell. Tessa lay aching inside and out, trying to decide what her fate would be.

From outside she could still hear the echo of the

rain, which she figured meant she'd be kept from death another short while.

Until the rain stopped.

She'd already had a taste of what it would be like to smother—every time tears gathered in her eyes and her nose clogged, she had to fight all over again for discipline. And every time she thought of Mitch Carter, she wanted to cry.

Would he come for her? Even though she'd told him she hated him? Who could tell?

Did she hate him?

No, no, *no*.

His image rose in her mind's eye, complete with supporting sensations. The way he looked at her when he was aroused, with such protective, possessive hunger. How safe she felt in his arms. Oh, if only she could be there now.

But…but she should still be angry with him. He'd gone behind her back and warned Richard off.

Just, part of her brain argued, *as you went behind his back in meeting Richard. Did he condemn you for that? Did he say he hated you?*

What else should a man do, to keep the woman he loved?

At least Mitch Carter had once loved her. He'd told her so, in the heated throes of passion, while he set her body alight and touched her soul. Maybe she'd killed that feeling for him, she didn't know. Couldn't tell.

She'd tossed his love back in his face. Lying there half choked by tears, it seemed clear that was exactly what she'd done.

And, every instinct told her, Mitch Carter's love wasn't an easy thing to win. She didn't suppose, knowing what she did about him, he gave his heart easily. Oh, he felt deep loyalty for his "boys" and had gone to great lengths to win them free of their shared hell. But the yearning she sometimes glimpsed in his eyes argued love had not found him.

Until he found her, and expressed the most secret sentiments of a very private heart.

Suddenly she knew she wanted to live not only for herself but for him. She wanted the chance to see him again, touch him, and gaze into his eyes. To tell him she regretted her words and wanted to make all the past hurt up to him.

If he'd only give her that chance.

Did she love her husband? Could such a thing be true? Had she fallen for him after all, without knowing? She couldn't say, but her fixation on Richard now seemed like a child's game.

She didn't care if she never saw Richard Trask again. But her very being tottered on the need to see Mitch one more time.

Suddenly she realized the rain had tapered off outside. Oh, God, no, not that. How long did she have left to live?

****

"You have my wife." Mitch stood on a bleak, near-deserted stretch of the waterfront at the canal side, staring down Danny Dwyer. The rain had at last begun to ease; out over the lake the clouds cleared, admitting shafts of late afternoon light. He fought to master his anger, a vicious, violent commodity he'd determined to use like a weapon when he needed it. Long ago, in his youth, he'd learned to harness his emotions. He expected the ability to serve him well now, but he balanced on the brink of turning into a madman.

Danny Dwyer grinned at him. "So I do. What will you give, great King o' Prospect Avenue, to get her back?"

Anything. But it wouldn't do to let Dwyer know that.

"Is she here? Which building?" This area, at the foot of Commercial Street, lay crowded with buildings both great and small—grain elevators and any number of shack-like storage sheds, all with the lake freighters moored beyond. Not his patch, clearly out of his ken, though Dwyer appeared all too much at ease here. In a voice like stone, he added, "And what do you want for her?"

"Now, there's an interesting question."

Mitch's clenched fists twitched. He longed to swipe the self-satisfied smile off the man's face, but that would do Tessa little good.

His heart yearned toward her. In which of these buildings might she be shut away? He saw a thousand possibilities.

"You and I, Carter, share many of the same desires. We both came up from nothing. Did you know I used to work at this place? Me dad did also, for years, till the hard work of it killed him. I followed in his footsteps for a little while, shoveling the grain, till I felt it starting to kill me, too. I stood here one day and swore to meself I'd do anything—anything—to get a better life. Lie, cheat, steal, intimidate—sure, what's abduction compared to all that?"

"Spare me the sad stories. I've plenty of my own."

"I don't doubt it. Only, see, there's a wee problem. You decided to break that deal with me. And because we both want the same things, that puts us at loggerheads. Two big bucks contesting for the same territory, right? One of us has to back down. And now I have your wife, it ain't going to be me."

"Just tell me what you want. We can deal. But, Dwyer, if you've hurt her in any way, I'll hunt you down. And I won't stop till I make you pay."

"Hurt her? Sure, do I look like that sort of man? She's tucked away all safe and sound. Tell me, Carter, would you trade your life for hers?"

That was an easy one. But Mitch said, "Is that what you want? You want me dead?"

"'Twould certainly make my days easier, wouldn't it, having you out of the game. Then I'd only have to compete with fecking Kelly and his metal crew, and I daresay since he's had a taste of how I operate, he may show a wee bit of respect. He won't want to endanger his wife again."

"You think so? But it wouldn't be wise to underestimate him. Or me."

The rain abruptly ceased. Above their heads the clouds parted and a shaft of sunlight pierced the air, bathing both men in radiance.

"Ah now," Dwyer crooned, "you'll see this place spring to life. The men will work all night if they have to, to get those freighters unloaded. Tell me, Carter, do you know what those big buildings out there are for?"

"I don't care."

"You should care, bucko—you really should."

Mitch gave the huge structures an impatient glance. "They hold grain."

"You're right. But, you know, that may not be all they hold."

Mitch's eyes flicked once more over the many structures. "You've put her in one of them." But was she safe?

"I have. But which one? It's like that old game, isn't it? Eeny-meany-miney-mo."

Here. Nearly within Mitch's reach. The breath came a touch more easily in his lungs.

"Enough of the games, Dwyer." He spread his arms. "You want to attack me, do it. Let's finish this."

Out along the shore, men appeared and began hurrying about their business, much the way birds emerge after a storm. At some distance, a steam engine fired up and then another, making a din.

Dwyer had to raise his voice when he said, "You offering to fight me for her, Carter?"

"If that's what it takes."

"That's an old-fashioned kind of chivalry. And on a certain level it appeals to me, I must admit."

Mitch shrugged out of his coat. "Let's have at it, then." He couldn't wait to get his hands on the man.

"But if you knock me for six, lad, how will you find your wife? You see, she's in danger. Safe for the moment, but once those conveyors start transferring the grain, it'll be the worse for her."

In one of the grain elevators that would soon fill. Mitch's heart leaped sickeningly. *But which one?*

"Damn it all, Dwyer, stop playing the fool. You want to be responsible for the death of an innocent woman?"

"As if you've never done the same, to get what you want."

Mitch hadn't, actually, though he'd come close a few times. He wasn't proud of the things he'd done in the past, but survival, as he'd learned early, was survival.

Trouble was, he was no longer sure he could survive without Tessa.

"Spit it out," he barked. "What do you want from me?"

"Nothing less than your fortune." Dwyer smiled like the devil. "I want you to work for me."

Chapter Forty

Tessa, half sunken into a stupor caused by exhaustion and lack of air, jumped violently when a steam engine suddenly burst into life close at hand. The sound of it echoed fearfully in the empty grain bin, making such a racket it set her heart racing full bore.

What was happening? How long had she been here, shivering in the near darkness?

Where was Mitch?

Once again, her longing for him rose up like a tiger, filling her inside—a strong, transformative emotion. She struggled against the gag in her mouth, her entire being at last acknowledging the truth.

She loved him. She loved Mitch Carter the way she'd never imagined loving any man. Somehow, amid the anger and the dismay, the distress at being forced to marry him, he'd wound up becoming a part of her— bone of her bone and heart of her heart. She wanted to be the one to ease the great loneliness inside him, wanted to live the rest of her days as his wife.

But she might have no more days.

Oh, Mitch, I'm sorry. Sorry I wasted our time together thinking I wanted something else. I didn't, I didn't. What I imagined I felt for Richard was just that, a silly girl's imagining. I wish I had the chance to tell you so.

A second steam engine roared to life. Tessa's ears

fairly rang. How long did she have before grain started filtering down from the chute above? Surely only a miracle could bring Mitch to her in time.

****

"Actually," Dwyer drawled, "I'm in the mood to be generous. I have to respect a man willing to do anything to save his missus. So I'll require only half your properties signed over to me. Everything south of Chippewa Street. I figure if I get that bastard Kelly surrounded, he'll have to yield to me."

"Everything south of Chippewa?" Despite himself, Mitch hesitated. "That's more than half my properties."

It had taken him ten years to build all that up, and the rents represented most of his wealth. Without those properties, he'd be lucky to keep his house.

A tough prospect.

"Or," Dwyer tossed at him, "you can let her die."

Mitch growled deep in his throat, like the animal to which he'd sometimes been reduced back at Carter's, while locked in the black room. There, he'd learned the only thing gained by throwing himself at the door and beating on the walls were bloody fists.

But Danny Dwyer was no wall.

Abruptly, the restraints he'd kept imposed on himself for so long broke. He leapt at Dwyer, fists swinging.

The world that was Buffalo might well underestimate him—Dwyer might. He wore good suits and kept the fine house and steamcar. Mitch knew the truth though; under it all he remained the scrapper who'd fought his way out of the gutter and on up through sheer determination.

Dwyer never stood a chance. He went over

backward under Mitch's assault, and Mitch battered him relentlessly. Dimly, he heard voices exclaim at a distance, but he saw only Dwyer's face in front of him, increasingly bloodied.

"Here now, what's this?"

The voice of authority broke through, or made it half way through. Mitch, seized and hauled backward, flew up as if he weighed nothing. He found his feet and tried to leap at Dwyer again.

"No, sir, I think not. Do you want to kill him?"

"Yes."

Breathless, his lungs working like bellows, Mitch continued to stare Dwyer down. "He has my wife."

The hands gripping his arms eased just a titch. "So I understand."

Turning his head, Mitch caught a glimpse of blue—a dark blue uniform. A policeman. A second, incredulous look informed him he stood in the grasp of the hybrid automaton, Patrick Kelly. Behind Kelly stood other...men?...none of them in uniform. Behind them stood Mitch's own boys, who'd crept out from hiding.

Kelly's green eyes engaged Mitch's. "Despite that, Mr. Carter, I'm afraid I can't let you kill him."

Mitch looked at Dwyer again. The Irishman lay sprawled on the ground; though his eyes remained open, he appeared to see nothing. Beyond him, a crowd of what might be dockworkers—mingled with Dwyer's men—began to gather, staring.

Mitch kicked Dwyer's leg. "This bastard's hidden my wife in one of those elevators—he wouldn't tell me which." He switched his gaze to Kelly. "What are you doing here, anyway?"

"My wife, Rose, sent for me and explained your predicament. She didn't want another woman to endure what she had. I got a few of the lads and, since we've determined Rose was held hereabouts, I thought this the logical place to begin looking."

"He says she's in an empty elevator but when the grain starts loading in, she'll die."

Kelly released Mitch, bent down, and hauled Dwyer up with ridiculous ease. Dwyer, no small man, dangled from the automaton's fist like a rag doll.

"Mr. Dwyer?" Kelly inquired in a polite tone, as if making a routine inquiry from a suspect, "where is Mrs. Carter?"

Dwyer's bloodied lips stretched in an ugly grin. His eyes rolled back in his head, and he passed out.

"Damn it," Mitch said as hard regret swamped him. How many years had he kept his discipline and his temper? The first time he let himself off leash, and it cost him.

No, it cost Tessa.

"Here, take charge of him, Terry," Kelly called to one of the other hybrids. "The rest of you, gather 'round. You too," he gestured to the staring dockworkers. He raised his voice to be heard above the increasing number of steam engines firing up.

"There's a woman being held here, quite likely in one of the elevators," he called. "I ask you to spread out and search. The more of us the better—look every place you can."

Controlled chaos broke out even as the breath whooshed from Mitch's lungs. Kelly meant to help, even though he had no reason to trust him. And a dozen or more searchers beat one.

The squad of hybrids, along with Mitch's boys, moved away, mostly in pairs. The dockworkers began asking questions, and Kelly waved them off. Then the automaton stood motionless for an instant, surveying the scene like—well, the way a machine might.

Many of the workers, not close enough to pick up on the commotion, continued to go about their work. At a distance, another steam engine fired up, fueling Mitch's panic. Out over the lake the sky continued to clear; beautiful light shone down, illuminating the scene.

A sudden sweat broke out all over Mitch's body. "She's going to die," he groaned. "I know it." Why had he thought differently? How had he supposed he could have in his life a lovely creature like Tessa Verdun— the one desire of his heart? Especially considering the fact that he'd forced her into the marriage and she said she—

Hated him.

Patrick Kelly looked at him with calm green eyes. "There is no reason to think so, Mr. Carter—not yet. Come with me."

****

Tessa's entire body tensed when, with a loud scraping sound, the grate far overhead opened. Bright sunlight flooded in, giving her another good look at the place where she lay. A bin, indeed a huge one, and she rested at the very bottom like a roach in an empty kettle.

She began struggling then, straining every muscle in an effort to inch her way toward the door where her captor had entered and exited. A fine dust rose around her when she moved, and it stung her eyes. Her efforts made her gasp against the fabric covering her mouth; her senses swam.

She collapsed with a sob; even if she reached the opening she wouldn't be able to open the door, with her hands bound. She would die here after all, and Mitch's child with her.

Oh, Mitch!

She closed her eyes on an intensity of longing and felt something touch her cheek. It felt like rain, only softer. Opening her eyes, she saw it was raining.

Raining grain.

It appeared almost beautiful at first, fluttering down to land all around her, swirling through the light. Then it began coming faster and faster, and it hurt, pelting against her like hail, striking her exposed skin. And the racket of it, combined with the throb of the engines outside, stopped her ears to any other sound.

Except her own inner screams.

Chapter Forty-One

"Here, Pat—over here!"

One of the hybrid automatons gestured to Patrick Kelly as Mitch and he jogged by in tandem, on their way to examine yet another of the elevators. The automaton, in company with another like himself, stood in front of one of the huge structures, facing a door. Above it—high above—a conveyor steadily lifted grain from one of the moored freighters to the roof of the structure.

"It's locked, Pat. None of the others has been locked. Suspicious."

Kelly thought far more swiftly than Mitch ever could. Without hesitation, he waved a hand. "Tim, get them to shut off that engine."

"Why—?" The other automaton questioned.

Kelly shot him a look. "It's dropping grain. If Mr. Carter's wife is in there, she'll smother."

Oh, God, Tessa!

The automaton hustled off. A small crowd of dockworkers once more began to gather.

"Does anyone have a key to this structure?" Kelly asked.

"Only the boss," supplied one of the men, "and he's at home up on Nottingham Terrace."

"We will need to break it down." Kelly turned to the remaining automaton. "Terry, please assist me."

"Careful," warned a second dockworker, one with a sweaty face. "We been dropping grain in there. You strike a spark, the whole place will explode."

"Don't care." Mitch muscled Kelly aside and put his shoulder to the door. "Have to get her out of there."

"Mr. Carter, we're not even sure she's in this elevator." Kelly asked the men, "How much grain has dropped in?"

"Enough."

Mitch threw himself against the door. The stout panels resisted. He battered it a second time.

"Hey," shouted one of the workers, jogging up. "Whatcha doing? You beat that door in, it'll blow. I've seen it before. Doesn't take much."

"Mr. Carter, please allow us."

Kelly jostled Mitch aside in turn. He and his companion applied themselves to the door; most of the workers withdrew with haste, some hollering.

The thick oak panel cracked beneath the automatons' combined strength. The lock held, but the wood around it shattered. The door swung open onto darkness.

Thick, choking darkness.

Mitch bellowed, "Someone bring me a light!"

"Can't," objected one of the workers, brave enough to remain near the building. "No sparks, understand?"

"Mr. Carter, let us go." Kelly imposed himself. "We see better in the dark, and we don't need to breathe."

Ignoring them, and despite his unreasoning fear of dark, airless spaces, Mitch dashed in.

He knew immediately he'd made a mistake. The interior of the bin felt cavernous, but he could see almost nothing. Grain covered the floor to the height of his knees—not too deep but enough to kill a woman lying down. Was Tessa lying down? Particles filled the air and rose with his every step, a fine, choking mist.

Somebody hollered from outside. Mitch's senses swam.

"Tessa!"

No response. She might not even be here. Yet he knew she was—instinct told him so, the same that had let him survive so long against daunting odds. That instinct had led him, always, to what he needed in order to live.

Now he needed Tessa.

"Mr. Carter, please exit the building," Patrick Kelly called from behind.

Mitch closed his eyes for an instant and listened to his heart.

He stumbled forward.

****

Mercifully, the clamor of the steam engine thundering loudest in Tessa's ears ceased. She could no longer see anything and she could barely breathe, her lungs on fire. Her consciousness flickered in and out like the flame of a guttering candle.

Darkness, then hazy light. Deep blackness before sudden brightness burst upon her. She saw a vast field of it, pure white, and it beckoned. It would be so easy to go there and end all her distress and terror.

No! her heart cried. *Mitch isn't there.* She said it over to herself, and to the light, in determined refusal. No. I need a chance to tell him I love him. I need—

"Tessa!"

Ah, and now she thought she heard his voice. She

must be hallucinating, fearfully close to death. Because she almost thought she could feel him also, the way she could when they lay together in the dark. Her heart leapt, and her head cleared on a shot of pure energy.

Here I am, Mitch. Here!

But the hallucination continued. For even though he couldn't possibly hear her through the sodden gag that covered her lips, she imagined him touching her, hands lifting and cradling, his voice giving a very unlikely whoop as he caught her high in his arms. The grain that covered her fell away in a terrible shower, and the hard contact with Mitch's chest was the best thing she'd ever felt.

Real. It must be real. But she still couldn't breathe.

His cheek pressed against hers. "Tessa, Tessa."

From somewhere behind him came an order. "Mr. Carter? Please get out of there at once."

The command sounded urgent, yet Mitch disregarded it. Instead his fingers fumbled with the gag, soaked with spittle and sweat, and coated with grain; he pulled it away.

She gasped, and so did he. "You're alive... Alive! Oh, thank God."

She wanted to tell him she still couldn't breathe. The air all around them danced with chaff and felt too thick to enter her lungs.

"Mr. Carter?" The voice came again.

Mitch turned and, with Tessa held high in his arms, pelted out into the light.

****

Tessa came to herself in the hands of the doctor and had a brief, if meaningful, conversation with him. When next she awoke, some indeterminate time later, she heard only silence. Her throat felt raw and her lungs seemed to be on fire, but the breath came more easily—one of the sweetest sensations she'd ever known. Her body hurt all over as if she'd been pummeled, and her eyes, when she struggled to open them, seemed to be full of grit.

She opened them anyway in an effort to determine her location.

She recognized the room—her own, back at the house on Prospect Avenue. A single lamp burned on the table beside the bed where she lay. Was she alone? No. Somebody's hand clasped hers tightly, and she could feel Mitch's presence in every part of her body.

He lay beside her, half collapsed onto the bed, where he'd fallen asleep. Tessa examined him the way a woman in a dream might, slowly and with rising delight. Black hair, no longer neat but mussed all over his head and still containing flecks of yellow grain. Hazel eyes closed, lashes fanned out—a frown creasing his brow even in sleep.

Her husband, her man. The one who, against all likelihood, she'd come to love on a level so deep that just being here with him now felt profound.

How had that happened?

Did it matter how?

Perhaps he didn't sleep after all, for when she drew a deep breath his eyes opened and his fingers clenched on hers so tightly it hurt.

"Tessa? My God, Tessa. How are you?"

She gazed into his eyes. "Better. Better, now."

He smiled at her. Oh, to be the recipient of a smile from Mitch Carter! Not one of his tight, calculating smiles—the sort he gave others—but one like this that lit his face.

And illumined her world.

"Are you all right?" he asked. Without waiting for an answer, he told her, "You passed out in my arms, and I feared the worst. Thought I'd been too late." Agony filled his eyes, a look such as she'd never seen there before. "Marty broke every law getting you to the quack on Fillmore. Doctor says—he says you'll recover, given some time. Your body will heal. I only hope your spirit will, too."

"I'll heal," she assured him. She'd discovered a wealth of strength inside herself since becoming Mitch Carter's wife, a veritable bedrock of stubbornness, tenacity, and compassion she'd never suspected existed. Here, in the intimacy created by the circle of light and Mitch's fingers on hers, she believed she could overcome anything. But she had to tell him what lay in her heart.

Abruptly her eyes filled with tears. "You came for me."

"Of course I did."

"You saved me. Even though I said—I said…"

"Hush, it doesn't matter."

"It does, though. It does. Because, Mitch, I lied. The whole time I lay in that awful place waiting to die, I just wanted to tell you one thing. I wanted the chance—"

"To tell me what?"

"I love you. I do, Mitch. I don't know how or when it happened, but—"

Pure astonishment shone at her from his eyes. "Eh? What did you say?"

She leaned up and caught his face between hands

that hurt, and drew him to her. "I—love—" the phrase ended in a kiss that, she hoped, said all she couldn't in words. Soft and gentle, it was both a question and a pledge. It ended with her tears.

"Can you ever forgive me, Mitch, for saying such a terrible thing?"

"Here! Here, don't cry. Please don't."

He kissed her tears away, gathering them with his lips in a gesture so tender it made her gasp. When his mouth returned to hers, she felt the deep well of his loneliness, his very heart open to her, an offering.

Her heart wanted nothing more than to fill that emptiness. But how? How to convince this man, who had lived on so little for so long and whose love she'd thrown back in his face, of just how desperately she needed him?

Constancy.

Devotion.

Giving herself to him again and again, forevermore.

"Mitch," she whispered when the kiss ended with a lingering sweetness of lips on lips. "I don't suppose you can believe me yet. But I'll prove it to you. You'll see—I want to be yours and yours only. I promise you, you'll never be alone again."

He buried his face in her bosom. Did he weep?

She lay there, swamped by tenderness and the desire to help him heal, at least as much as love could— this hard man, this starved boy, this tough prospect.

"Mitch?"

He raised his face, dazzlingly bright. "Tessa, I no longer want to be the King of Prospect—though I still want you to be my queen. I told you before, I'll become the man that you want, whatever you need me to be."

"Oh, yes?"

"Oh, yes, my darling girl, my beautiful wife."

"Do you know what I truly want you to be, Mitch Carter?"

He shook his head.

"The man you are—strong and brave and determined. The boy you were, loyal and courageous, who never stopped reaching for a future he couldn't even see. That's who I love."

Tears came to his eyes then. "I never dreamed you were my future. Else I'd have reached harder."

"I'm your present, your future, and your always. Let's try and forget the past. Let's go on from that moment I felt sure I was dead and then your arms lifted me."

"Yes, let's."

She tipped her head on the pillow. "You still mean to buy Carter's?"

"I do. More than ever, now."

"Good. We'll run it together—the way it should be run. And we'll rescue that boy from the closet and make sure he gets the opportunities he deserves. See if we can't find the others loving homes, maybe with people like Lily and Rey Michaels. Meanwhile, we'll turn Carter's into a place where the children feel safe. And then there are the other orphanages. We can take a look at those, too. After that, we'll sit down together and go over the rents on the properties you own, to see if we can't build a little mercy into your margin for success."

"Mercy, eh? Am I to suppose, Mrs. Carter, that you mean to take up a position as my conscience?"

"No." She laid her hand on his chest, just over his heart and gazed into his eyes. "But if you let me, from time to time I'll remind you about the conscience you already have."

His gaze kindled. "I'll let you do whatever you please."

"One more thing. If we mean to adopt, this house is going to be terribly full." She bit her lip. "I never had a chance to tell you, with all that's happened, but I'm carrying your child."

His eyes widened with pure astonishment. "A child? By everything that's holy, Tessa! Are you sure?"

"The doctor just confirmed it, when I saw him a little while ago."

"But—is the baby all right? After all you went through…we'd better call the doctor back again."

"The child's fine and so am I. I've discovered I'm a lot tougher than I thought, Mitch Carter—tough enough to be your wife."

Their third kiss heated rapidly, only to be interrupted by scrabbling at the side of the bed. Valerie stood there, her front paws on the coverlet.

Without hesitation, Mitch reached down and lifted the little mechanical dog onto the bed.

"There you go, darling. I think she missed you."

"You kept her wound up?"

"Yes."

"Even though I wasn't here?"

"It seemed the thing to do. Couldn't let her run down and—and die, could I?"

Tessa stroked Valerie's smooth head. The little dog cuddled in tight.

"I thought, Mr. Carter, you didn't have much

patience with mechanicals?"

"Ah, but Mrs. Carter, my thinking on that score has undergone a rather profound change."

"Would that be due to a certain hybrid automaton by name of Patrick Kelly?"

"He's a good man, Tessa. A very good man."

"Not half as good as my husband," Tessa said just before their lips met again. "Because, Mitch Carter, you might think you're the King of Prospect. Truth is you're the king of my heart."

"That's all I ever wanted," Mitch whispered. And all he ever would.

A word about the author...

Born in Buffalo and raised on the Niagara Frontier, Laura Strickland has been an avid reader and writer since childhood. To her the spunky, tenacious, undefeatable ethnic mix that is Buffalo spells the perfect setting for a little Steampunk, so she created her own Victorian world there.

She knows the people of Buffalo are stronger, tougher and smarter than those who haven't survived the muggy summers and blizzard blasts found on the shores of the mighty Niagara. Tough enough to survive a squad of automatons? Well, just maybe.